They Whisper About Us

Joy Vee

BROAD PLACE
publishing

First published in Great Britain in 2022

Broad Place Publishing
83 Nettleham Road,
Lincoln,
LN2 1RU

British Library Cataloguing-in-Publication Data.
A catalogue record for this book is available from the British Library.

Print Book: ISBN 978-1-915034-20-5
E-Book: ISBN 978-1-915034-21-2

Omnibus Hardback – They Whisper About Us and The Letters She Never Wrote – ISBN: 978-1-915034-22-9

The author can be contacted via her website:
www.joyvee.org

SPECIAL NOTE: The Theatre in Lincoln I have referred to in this
story is fictional, not to be confused with the amazing New
Theatre Royal. Many thanks to the New Theatre Royal for your
great work in the city.

Books by Joy Vee

The Sienna Series
The Treasure Man
Love From Sienna
The 'Love from Sienna' Journal

The Kai Series
Kai – Born to be Super
Kai – Making it Count

The Petrov Family Series
They Whisper About Us
The Letters She Never Sent

For more information, visit joyvee.org

Dedication

To Anna,
You inspire me in so many ways!
I love you!

Dear Reader,
If you want some context to the story or help with
pronunciation of words – skip ahead to the Author's Note
at the end. (I promise there are no spoilers).
Joy Vee

Prologue

Leningrad, September 1963

The young teenager looked at his father, tears in his eyes.

'My son.' His father choked on his words. 'Take this.' He thrust a small tin box, the kind that had once held tea, into the boy's hands.

'Why? What is it?'

'This tin holds life. Never lose it. Value it above anything else. Your sister also has one like it. Try to find her...' The whistle of the train drowned out his words. 'Quick, get on board.'

The young man jumped onto the train as the door slammed shut. Looking back through the open window, his eyes asked the question that burned in his heart. *Will I ever see you again?*

With a jolt, the train started, and leaning out as far as he could, he watched his papa disappear out of sight.

Chapter 1

Lincoln, England, present day.

The musty cupboard smelt like it hadn't been opened in years and its only visitors had four legs. Fay sighed, wondering who would keep so much rubbish for so long. Two guys from the theatre summer programme looked over her shoulder.

'Do you think she'll find any buried treasure?' Blake asked.

'More likely a few unburied bodies if the rumours are true.'

Fay shivered but forced a smile as she turned to her new friends.

'When do you want it cleared out by?' she asked.

'We'll need it by the Thursday,' Blake answered. 'The management is annoyed with our props lying around in the dressing rooms. They want everything cleared out before the group come in for the weekend performances.'

Fay looked back at the cupboard. It was stacked floor-to-ceiling with boxes, old props, bits of costumes. She couldn't even see how far back it went.

'Where should I put all of this?'

'Old programmes and stuff like that needs to be kept and put on one side. A volunteer will be in to collect them on Friday. Give any jewellery or costume bits to Kate and chuck the rest.'

Fay looked back at the cupboard. 'Chuck it where?'

'The tip. Get your folks to give you a lift.'

Fay bit her lip. Considering the ongoing tension between her and her parents, she doubted they'd be willing to make multiple trips to the local dump. Any spare time they had this summer would be taken up with Tom or Grandad. Her brother was back from his first year at university, and their grandfather wasn't well.

She took a deep breath and pulled at the first box. If she worked hard, she might get it cleared on time. Hopefully, if the group could see how eager she was to help, they'd accept her.

She'd been so excited when the Theatre announced their summer programme for July and August. Dozens of people had been interested, and she'd been one of the few selected. However, it hadn't quite gone to plan. They were only a week in, and so far, there was no sign of Sabrina, the person leading the programme. Apparently, she was sick. In her absence, those who were invited on the course still attended the theatre, although they seemed to have split into 'Blake's friends' and 'the outsiders.' Blake's parents were patrons of the theatre, and their generous donations, as well as his place at Sheffield Hallam studying drama, gave him influence in the group. The manager had given them a list of jobs that needed doing around the theatre, and these had been divided up among the outsiders which included Fay and Kate, a quiet girl who Fay hadn't really spoken to. The others hung out, went for lunch, and talked about theatre stuff, which Fay didn't quite understand. She'd imagined this summer would equip her with the skills she'd need for her future, but cleaning cupboards wasn't high on that list.

She picked up another box. Opening it, she found a tatty pair of ballet shoes, and a small tin box, rusted over and almost impossible to make out. She threw them on the growing pile of things to send to the tip and wondered what her dad would say if she phoned and asked for a lift.

Leningrad, Soviet Union, September 1962.

A gentle hand shook Vera awake. It was still dark, but she could just make out the familiar figure of a man, crouching by her bed.

'Papa?' she whispered, slowly sitting up, careful not to disturb the younger girls lying next to her. As her eyes got used to the dark, she was surprised at how thin her father's face looked under his bushy beard. She wasn't sure if he'd just got home from work or was heading back out after only a couple of hours rest, but it had been days since she'd last seen him. Her father reached up and held his finger to his lips, and she nodded, noticing that the rest of the family were still deep asleep. As her eyes skimmed the room, she counted six heads. Her two baby sisters beside her, her two younger brothers sharing the small bed across the room, and her mother in the bed she rarely left. Her father smelt of soap, but was wearing his work clothes, so Vera guessed he was on his way out to work.

He lifted a box and placed it on her lap, nodding at her to open it. She glanced down at the nondescript cardboard box, but something about the size and shape was familiar. She gasped, feeling her eyes fill with tears. She looked back at her father, seeing her own tears and joy reflected in his eyes. He nodded again, glancing at the box.

Carefully, reverently, Vera opened it. Inside was a pair of new ballet shoes. The pink silk of the shoes and satin of the ribbon seemed to glisten in the shadowy darkness. Vera lovingly ran her hands over them, tracing the outline of the shoes and ribbons. Her heart ached as she thought of the extra hours her father would have worked to buy them for her. She dared not even imagine how much they cost. She looked up at her father, speechless. There were so many words to say. Too many. Her father cupped her face in his hand, wiping her tears with his large, calloused thumb. For a long moment, they gazed at each other, sharing their hearts openly in the silence.

Vera wanted to thank him, wanted to promise to make him proud, wanted to tell him that one day she'd repay his sacrifice, but words were inadequate and unnecessary. Her father leaned over, kissed her forehead, then he silently rose and left the room. It always amazed Vera at how the huge man could move so silently, slipping in and out of the room while his family slept. The scent he carried with him from long hours at the quarry and the small, carefully wrapped packages of food on the table were the only evidence of his nightly presence. She sat, staring at the packages on the table for a moment, before glancing over to the empty space in the bed next to her mother. Had it all been a dream? She looked down at the box, cradled on her knees. No, it was real. She took out one of the shoes and held it to her face, where her father's hand had been.

Chapter 2

Leningrad

Vera stepped off the trolleybus and waited to cross the street. She looked at the imposing building and clutched her bag to her side. This was the day she'd dreamed of her whole life. This was what she'd worked for, trained for, auditioned for. Those hours of exercises, the practises, the blisters, the sores; they all led here. She had no words to describe her excitement. She loved to dance, to lose herself in the music, and finally, aged fifteen, this was her first day in the chorus of the world-famous Kirov Ballet. Leningrad had several ballets, but the Kirov Ballet was the most prestigious of all.

Quickly crossing the road, she looked up at the main entrance, remembering the first time she'd seen those doors. She'd been five years old, holding hands with Mama. Baby Artyom was at home, being looked after by Baba Rosa, their friendly neighbour, and Baby Vlad was still growing in Mama's tummy. It was Christmas, and they were going to see *The Nutcracker*. Vera had been attending ballet school since she could remember, and already knew small sections of the dance. She hummed a melody and her feet moved like magic as they got off the trolleybus and looked across the road. Mama leaned down and whispered in her ear, 'One day, you'll dance here. Your papa and I will be so proud.'

The memory filled Vera with warmth as she looked at the imposing doors. She'd finally achieved it. She'd worked hard for this moment. The start of her performing life. Could she ever reach the illustrious title of People's Artist – the pinnacle of success in the Soviet cultural world? She so wanted to make her parents proud.

A car door slammed across the street, and reality fractured. Vera was once again a five-year-old child, standing with her mother outside the theatre, but the jovial atmosphere was shattered as two large black cars rolled up in front of the building. Vera felt the tension in the street before she could see what was wrong. Despite the large number of theatre-goers, gathering in all their finery, and including many children, there to witness their first ballet, the crowd fell into a tense silence.

Men dressed in dark uniforms got out of the car and walked boldly into the theatre. Mama stood up straight and moved Vera behind her, so she was hidden behind her long coat. For several minutes, no one moved. The street was frozen, as though in a picture. Vera felt the cold nip through her boots. She wanted to dance the cold away, but looking around, she could see that no one else was moving, and didn't want to draw attention to herself.

Next to her stood a lady in a long fur coat. Vera looked up at her face. She was looking toward the theatre, frozen like marble, as everyone else was, but Vera noticed a tear trickle down her cheek. Vera felt sad for the woman and wondered if she should hold her hand to make her feel better. But Mama was always saying that other people weren't safe. Even the walls had ears. Vera's compassion, however, was stronger than her mother's fear. Vera pulled her hand out of her pocket. She decided it wouldn't hurt to hold the lady's hand. It might even stop her feeling sad, but just as she was about to touch the woman, the crowd gave a gasp. Vera's hand shot back into her pocket. Had they seen her reaching for the lady? Is that why they gasped? She looked up at the lady. She was now holding a handkerchief in front of her face and gazing at the door of the theatre.

Vera looked around her mother's coat, trying to see what was happening. The men in uniform were now coming out of the theatre, but they were dragging a young woman. She was still in her dressing gown and had been halfway through putting her make-up on.

'It's Anna Igorevna,' whispered the woman next to her. 'Surely they've made a mistake?'

Vera looked at the woman being pushed into the back seat of one of the cars. Anna Igorevna was one of the Kirov Ballet's prima ballerinas. She was the star of that evening's performance, and Vera had been so looking forward to seeing her dance. It was said that she moved with such grace that no one could match her.

The young woman looked out at the crowd, her eyes flitted across the people as though looking for someone, anyone, to help. But the crowd remained frozen.

As the door slammed behind her, a whisper swept through the street. 'Enemy of the People. She's an Enemy of the People.'

Vera looked at the pale face of the young woman in the back of the car. Her eyes were wide, and her lips were moving, although Vera couldn't make out what she was saying. She was still scouring the crowd, as though looking for a final friendly face or a last-minute salvation, but the cars swept her away into the darkness as quickly as they had arrived.

The crowd began to move forward towards the theatre. Conversations that had paused at the appearance of the vehicles, resumed as though nothing had happened. No one mentioned the extraordinary sight they had all just witnessed. Vera heard laughter behind her, and someone else whistling a section of music. She glanced up at the lady in the fur coat. She'd wiped away her tears and was talking with the man beside her. Noticing Vera's attention, she smiled at her.

'I remember my first *Nutcracker*,' she said. 'You'll love it.' She looked up and nodded at Mama before moving away. Vera gazed after her, wondering how someone's mouth could smile when their eyes looked so sad.

Looking back at the large doors, Vera felt a shiver run down her spine. Although her programme from that first ballet still had 'Anna Igorevna', no one spoke of her after that. Whenever Vera tried to ask her mother what had happened to her, Mama couldn't meet her eyes, and she told Vera not to ask such questions. She was an Enemy of the People. Mama couldn't tell Vera why or what she'd done, but she made it very clear that Vera should never mention her name again or ask anyone else about her. Vera didn't, although sometimes she longed to. And she never heard that name mentioned again in Leningrad.

Shaking away the memory, Vera quickly moved away from the main entrance to the stage door in the side street. Today was the first day of the rest of her life, and she wanted to make her parents proud, and not do whatever made Anna Igorevna an Enemy of the People.

Lincoln

Fay felt her face turn red as her father's old green Citroen pulled up next to the stage door.

'Thanks for coming, Dad.' She forced a smile and held the door open for him.

'So, this is where you are spending all your time now?' Fay couldn't read Dad's reaction as he glanced down the empty corridors. 'Will I get to meet any of your friends?'

Fay shrugged. 'I think they are busy practising. The stuff is this way.'

'Wow, I wasn't expecting that much.' Fay's dad put his hands on his hips and looked at the boxes piled up in the corridor outside the cupboard. 'You sorted all this yourself? That's a lot of work.'

Fay grinned. She'd worked hard and was grateful to hear the pride in her father's voice.

'Your friends must be really pleased,' he continued. His kind words brought back memories of their harsh comments. They'd obviously expected the cupboard clearing to only take a couple of hours, not the couple of days it had taken so far. Blake had clearly expressed the group's disappointment in the slow progress she was making.

'Let's get this stuff in the car.' Fay sighed. 'I've still got loads to do.'

She felt her dad's hand on her shoulder and shook it off. She picked up a box and quickly marched back to the stage door. She hoped they could get the car loaded and away before the others saw it. Blake and his friends would mock her dad's old car. Not that she could blame them. Conversations about her dad always provoked a reaction.

Fay had grown to dread the question 'So, what do your parents do?'

'My mum's a nurse.' The first part of the answer was always the easiest. 'And my dad helps people with advice and counselling, that kinda stuff.' Fay had learned this was the easiest answer to give. Usually people just nodded, and she didn't have a repeat of the bullying she'd received at school when people found out she was the local pastor's kid. 'Bible-basher!' That was the one she'd heard most often, although she'd never quoted a line from the Bible and made sure she never even mentioned church to her friends. She'd tried to show them she was normal and not some kind of 'Jesus freak.'

'I'll take this load to the tip, then come back for more. OK?' Her dad's voice interrupted her memories.

Fay nodded, not able to meet his eyes. In the last thirty minutes, they'd worked together to clear as many of the boxes as possible. They'd always worked well together, ever since Fay could remember. Whether it was painting someone's house, or doing someone's gardening, they worked as a team, without having to say much. For a moment, she'd forgotten the arguments they'd been having. Even though her parents had assured her that they respected her decisions, she still felt on edge around them.

Just as they were taking the last box out, the group of Blake's friends finished whatever they were doing and, in a noisy swarm, headed out of the stage door, discussing what they could have for lunch at the new café down the road. Fay was sure the lack of invitation was an oversight, or maybe they thought she'd have plans with her dad, but the silence after their departure stung. Dad stood next to her as she watched them leave. He didn't say a word, just reached up and squeezed her shoulder again, before driving off, the Citroen full of boxes.

Chapter 3

Lincoln

'Dinner's nearly ready. Can you set the table?'

Fay sat up with a start. She must've fallen asleep on the sofa. Rubbing her eyes, she wandered through to the dining room. On the table were an old pair of ballet slippers and a tin box. Fay tilted her head on one side, squinting as she looked at them.

'Weren't these from the cupboard in the theatre?' She looked up as her dad came into the room carrying a hot dish with a pair of oven gloves.

'Yes. They were in the last lot of boxes. But when I was sorting out the recycling from the trash, I just couldn't bring myself to throw them away.' He put the dish down and picked up the tin, slowly turning it over and examining the pictures showing through the rust.

'What's for dinner?' Fay's older brother asked. Tom had never walked quietly into a room, he always seemed to walk in talking. 'I'm working at seven, so can't stay and do the washing up. Sorry.' He went through to the kitchen, and Fay heard him gathering the plates and cutlery, while complimenting Mum on how good everything smelt.

Dad put the tin down on the sideboard, shaking his head slightly.

'Dad?' Her quiet question caused him to look back at her. She tilted her head to one side.

'It just reminds me of your grandad. He had a similar tin – a tea tin – when I was younger.'

Fay swallowed the lump that had formed in her throat and looked at the tin box. It was small, like the old-fashioned kind that used to hold Granny Wendy's tea. There were traces of words and pictures, but they were impossible to make out.

'Come on. Let's eat!' Dad said, and Fay realised the rest of the family were already at the table waiting for her.

Over dinner, she and Dad told Mum and Tom about some of the stranger things they'd found in the cupboard. They laughed as Dad told them a story from the tip. A gust of wind that had chosen the wrong time to blow, wrapping a gaudy pink feather boa around his face, just as one of the old women from the church drove past. There would be discussions before Sunday about the inappropriate attire of Pastor Peterson.

After dinner, Tom sat back.

'Mum, that was amazing. You don't get food like that at uni. Sorry to leave you with all the washing up.' He winked at Fay.

'You're not sorry really, are you?' Fay asked.

Tom shrugged. 'Not really!'

'Get off with you and leave your sister alone. We'll see you in the morning. I'm on an early shift, so please don't wake up the house when you come in.' Mum batted Tom away from the table. Leaning over, she picked up the ballet shoes.

'These are beautifully made, Mike. I'm glad you didn't throw them away. I know they look battered and ruined now, but they were obviously very expensive once upon a time.'

'So why would someone leave them in the cupboard?' Fay asked.

Mum shrugged, screwing up her nose a little. 'They smell like they've been in there for years.'

Fay gathered the plates and cleared the table, quickly stacking the dishwasher as she listened to her parents discussing whether they should open the tin.

As she came back into the dining room, Dad was working on it. It seemed to have rusted shut, but after a minute of trying, it popped open. Fay held her breath as she leaned forward.

On top was an old programme from the Theatre. It was a folded piece of A4, printed in back and white. It was a for a One-Night-Only performance by the Kirov Ballet from Leningrad in Lincoln on 21 September 1963. Fay didn't recognise the event, despite finding hundreds of programmes in the cupboard.

'Do you remember this, Lisa?' Dad asked, passing the programme to Mum.

'It's from 1963. I wasn't even born then!' Mum whacked his arm and then turned to look at the programme.

'No, I mean, did you ever hear about this? Surely it would've been a big thing in the dance world? A Soviet ballet troupe, coming and performing in our city?'

'I think you are overexaggerating my abilities. Having dance lessons until I was eleven is hardly being the centre of the dance world. But my ballet teacher was a great lover of Russian ballet and was always talking about when she'd been to see the Moscow State Ballet perform in London. I'm surprised she never mentioned this.'

'There were loads of programmes in the cupboard.' Fay took it and looked at it carefully. 'I had to put them on one side for a volunteer who is compiling a history of the theatre. But I haven't seen one for this event.' On the front was a black-and-white photo of dancers on a stage, and inside was a list of names. Passing it to her dad, Fay checked if there was anything else in the tin.

There were quite a few pieces of folded paper written on both sides with a pencil. Time had diminished the writing to a few loops and curves, but Fay could see that it wasn't written in English. At the bottom of each piece of paper, she could just make out the same word. Could it be a name? 'Вера'.

She passed the papers to her parents and took back the programme from her dad. Running her finger down the list of names, she couldn't see anything that looked like Bepa.

Looking up, she saw her dad examining one of the pieces of paper.

'It looks like it's written in Russian,' he said.

Mum nodded. 'That makes sense if the tin belonged to someone connected with the Kirov Ballet.'

'And you said Grandad had a tin like this?' Fay asked.

Dad sighed. 'Yes, he did. It's one of those things we never talked about. There were lots of things we never talked about, and recently I've been wondering if that wasn't unhealthy. I wonder if your grandad wouldn't be so lost in his own mind if he'd been able to talk about the things that were really important to him.'

Mum reached for Dad's hand and looked up at Fay. 'There's always been some mystery with your grandad. You know, he never spoke of his family or his past, but since his dementia has got worse, he's begun saying some quite frightening things. We've been praying for some insight into what's going on with him, and maybe this tin is some kind of connection.'

Fay tried not to roll her eyes at Mum's mention of prayer.

Dad gave a slight cough.

'When I was growing up, your grandad had a tin similar to this one. I was never allowed to touch it. It lived on the

25

top shelf of the kitchen cupboard, and once, when I got up very early, I saw him holding it. He was looking at it and his lips were moving, but no sound came out. He didn't know I'd seen him, and I always wondered what was inside. I'd never found another like it until today.'

Fay looked at the tin, and back at her parents. What mysteries did it hold, and why did Grandad have a similar one?

Leningrad

The *dejournaiya*, the old caretaker, let Vera in the stage door and explained where she should go. She thanked the old lady, wincing as she noticed her gnarled fingers and painful hobble. How strange it must be to spend the final years of your life holding the door open for young people who could open it themselves. But that was part of her service to the people, and she did it without complaint.

Following the directions the elderly lady had given her, she found herself in a practice room, with several other girls looking equally uncertain. Vera smiled nervously but knew better than to approach and make small talk with strangers. The awkwardness lasted until a woman in her mid-twenties entered the room and confidently introduced herself.

'My name is Novikova, Nadezhda Vladimirovna. I will train you new ones for the chorus.' She stood up tall, with a grace that Vera envied. Vera found herself standing taller and pushing back her shoulders. Nadezhda Vladimirovna nodded slightly as she looked her way.

'There should be more of you. Who are we missing? Where is Ivanova, Irina Andreevna?'

The younger girls looked at each other with wide eyes.

'Never mind,' the instructor said, shaking her head. 'I will show you where you can get changed, then you can start warming up.' She led the way through a maze of corridors that made Vera's head spin. She pointed to a door leading to a spacious changing room. 'Get changed here and meet me back in the hall in five minutes. Please, get to know each other.'

After a few moments of silence, the girls began introducing themselves in small groups. Vera took a deep breath and introduced herself to the two girls nearest her.

'I am Petrova, Vera Mikhailovna.'

The other girls introduced themselves with their full names, Ekaterina and Maria, but quickly requested she use the shorter forms, Katya and Masha. As Vera looked around at her smiling new friends, she felt confident she would enjoy dancing with them. Vera wasn't wearing her new shoes. Today was only the first day, so she pulled on her old shoes, noticing the other girls also wore older ballet shoes, and together they tried to remember how to get back to the practice hall. Fortunately, Masha had a great sense of direction, and they were back within the five minutes Nadezhda Vladimirovna had ordered.

When they returned to the hall, another girl was standing in the centre of the room, already dressed for practise. Vera couldn't help but notice her new ballet shoes; they were almost as beautiful as the ones Papa gave her last night.

'Hi, you must be Ira,' Katya smiled as they stood in position near her.

'Irina Andreevna,' the girl replied, with a frown and a stiff nod. She lifted her head and turned to face the front of the class, holding herself as though she were on stage.

Vera and Masha exchanged a look. Obviously, Irina Andreevna saw herself as much more important than them. Katya rolled her eyes behind Irina's back, and all the girls stood to attention as Nadezhda Vladimirovna re-entered the room.

Chapter 4

Leningrad

Although Vera had been dancing all her life and had trained hard for her place in the Kirov Ballet, as she climbed the stairs to her *kommunalka* that evening, she was sure she'd never felt so tired.

Like most people in Leningrad, Vera lived with her family in a communal flat, known as a *kommunalka*. Each family was allocated one room for living and sleeping and shared a bathroom and kitchen with several other households.

When she entered their room, she saw the twins playing quietly in a corner. She could tell from the way their hair was unbrushed that they hadn't been outside the flat all day. Four-year-old Nadia and Luba looked up and ran to her. Nadia full of the joys of the day, telling her of the little games they had played, as Vera quickly changed from her outdoor clothes, into her housecoat. Luba was more affected by the depression that seemed to emanate from the bed where her mother spent most of the time and held back as her sister talked cheerfully.

Nine-year-old Vlad sat at the table, leaning over his homework. His brows scrunched together, and his lips settled into a frown. Vera sat next to him and looked at the papers. He raised his sad eyes to look at her. Vlad had always hated school. It didn't come as easily to him as it had to her or Artyom. She helped him read the passage he was struggling with, asking him questions, and drawing out his answers, as she brushed the girls' hair.

'Why can't I leave school and go out to work with Artyom? I'd be so much better at work than trying to do this.' He pushed the paper across the table and folded his arms.

Vera smiled and leaned her head against his. 'I'm sure Artyom would love your help. But you need to wait a couple more years.'

At thirteen-years-old, Artyom was already working during the day, and trying to keep up with his studies in the evening. The little of money he brought into the household helped supplement the miniscule wages her father made working fourteen hours a day. Vera had often wondered why her family was worse off than most, but she knew better than to ask.

Having sorted out the girls, she glanced over at her mother, who hadn't moved since she came in. Vera remembered when her mother used to play with her and Artyom, but the depression that had settled on her at

Vlad's birth had slowly got worse after the twins were born. Now she barely moved from her bed or spoke to her family. Vera lifted her weary body out of the chair and headed into the kitchen, sighing as she saw the pile of dirty pots left on the side. She'd been told that every *kommunalka* had a dirty family: a family who never cleaned up after themselves, stole other people's hot water and food, and left crumbs on the worktops, further encouraging the city's already-confident rats. They made life impossible for the other members of the flat, who would raise a petition and file all the paperwork to get them kicked out. After several years, they'd be moved on and the entire process would begin in another communal flat. This family had turned up four years previously, and from the first day, Baba Rosa said they'd be trouble. Baba Rosa was usually right, and this time was no different.

As Vera cooked the vegetables left by their father, the kitchen door opened, and Vera's heart lifted as Artyom's cheery face appeared round the door.

'How is my favourite big sister?' he asked, filling a pan with water, and setting it to heat on the stove.

'Tired,' Vera confessed. Usually she'd smile and say 'fine', but with Artyom she knew she could be completely honest. 'You don't have to do that,' she said as he scraped the food from the dirty plates into the scraps bucket.

'I know, but I hate the thought of you having to cook in this mess.' He winked at her.

Although he was two years younger, Vera relied heavily on her brother, and today she was grateful for his quiet companionship as they worked together.

When they took the food to their room, jar of fresh *smetana* sat on the table. The twins eyed it eagerly as they sat at the table, longing to dip their fingers in the thick soured cream. Mama got out of bed and sat with them for a few minutes, managing a couple of small bites, before returning to her bed, worn out by the effort of interacting with her children.

Vera took a small plate of food and left the room. She stepped across the hall and knocked on the opposite door. A few seconds after her quiet knock, Baba Rosa opened the door and smiled. She took the small plate of food and disappeared into her room. As Vera was about to turn away, the door opened wider, and Baba Rosa handed her a covered bowl. Lifting the tea towel, she saw it contained a handful of cherries. Quickly she pushed it back towards the old woman, shaking her head. It was too generous a gift. Rosa refused to take the bowl, pointing to her mouth, and giving a toothless smile. She couldn't manage the cherries with no teeth. Vera smiled. 'For the babies,' she whispered. Baba Rosa nodded and closed the door before Vera had the chance to thank her. The entire exchange had taken place in silence. Although strange to an on-looker, this was the only way Vera knew to behave.

Mother used to tell stories from her own childhood of the camaraderie in the flats. Each *kommunalka* was like a large family, sharing what little they had through the long hard years of the Siege, grieving together, supporting new life, raising children together. They were tough years, but Mama remembered her living space fondly. The inhabitants of the flat, standing together to face whatever the world threw at them. The 'Them and Us' stance had been internalised during the harsh Stalinist years. Instead of facing the world together, the inhabitants of the flats began to view each other with suspicion. When she went to play with the other children, Mama found the door slammed in her face. Conversations in the kitchen silenced when she entered. Smiles became sneers. Instead of feeling like a large family, each room became the safe space, and venturing out to the kitchen or the bathroom was like walking into no-man's land.

This wasn't helped when Mama married Papa. He was from the village. An outsider. Together they were viewed with even more suspicion. There were rumours of how his family survived the Siege, none of them containing an iota of truth. Despite Mother and Father doing their best to raise a good Soviet family, the award for a large family did not come with the respect of the neighbours. It was met with disapproving tuts and rolls of the eyes, every time Mama's belly began to protrude. There were angry knocks on the door in the night, calling for silence, rather than offers of help and willing hands to relieve a tired mother.

Their room, although generously sized if its only function was a sitting room or bedroom, struggled to be both for a growing family, and finally the bitterness of the neighbours seemed to settle in Mother's soul. She dreaded leaving the room, even if it was just for the bathroom or to prepare a meal in the kitchen. Vera found that more of the work required to keep five children in food and clothes fell on her and her younger brother.

After dinner, Artyom went to heat more water while Vlad helped the twins clear the table.

'Daughter,' Mama patted the edge of her bed. 'Come and tell me about your day.'

'What do you want to know?' Vera asked, surprised her mother was even asking.

'Everything, tell me about the theatre and the people. What about the dances? What moves did you practise? What music did you use? I want to imagine every moment.'

Vera pulled out one of Artyom's shirts that needed mending, and sewed as she recalled every position, every move, every sequence they had run through that day. Mama lay back and closed her eyes, as though picturing every moment, a faint smile on her face.

Lincoln

'So, why aren't you at church today?' Tom came into the kitchen, still dressed in his pyjamas, and opened the fridge.

'We've agreed I don't have to go every week.' Fay bit into her toast, knowing what was coming next.

'That's not fair. I never got to use the "Get Out of Jail Free" card when I lived at home.'

'Well, maybe they've recognised my maturity and are allowing me to make my own decisions,' Fay smirked.

'Or maybe you drove them crazy with your complaining and they gave in for a quiet life,'

She knew Tom was watching her closely. She felt the heat rise in her neck.

'So that's what the tension is in the house? Little sis is backsliding. And what's all this about the theatre? You were never really into that before.'

'I don't know. I enjoy talking and having people listen to me. I love debate class. I enjoy that sense of performance and being able to use my words to inspire and educate. I wanted to learn more presentation skills, how to have a stage presence, that sort of thing. I hoped to learn it during this summer programme, but it's not quite working out like that. This week I have learned how to clean out a cupboard.'

Tom screwed up his face as he sat down next to her. 'Not exactly life-changing, eh?'

'Nope.'

They ate for a few minutes in a friendly silence, like they used to as kids. Fay was still getting used to the half-kid, half-adult that had returned from university. When he wasn't annoying her, she quite enjoyed his company.

'Have you thought about going into politics, rather than theatre? You'd certainly get to use your voice there, although the audience may never bring you flowers.'

'It's something I'd thought about, amongst other things. I can't believe I need to start applying for universities in September, and I still don't know what I want to do.'

'What did Mum and Dad say?'

Fay grimaced. 'They told me to pray about it!'

'Might not be a bad idea.' Tom took a swig of juice.

'Not you too? Why aren't you at church with them today, then?'

'I was working late last night and wanted to have breakfast with my little sister.' He winked at her, and she shoved him gently with her shoulder.

'Are you coming with us to see Grandad this afternoon?'

'No, I'm back at work at three. How is he?'

Fay took a sip of coffee, wondering how to answer the question.

'He has good days and bad days. Sometimes he'll be the old grandad we used to know, full of life and mischief. Other days he can't even recognise us. Even on the good days, he'll talk about Granny Wendy like she's in the next room.'

'I don't blame him. I can't believe she's been gone for two years already. Even coming home, I was thinking about her chocolate cake, and had to remind myself that she's not here.' Tom gave a little cough. 'I can't believe he's had to go into a care home. Sixty-nine is too young to be in one of those places.'

Fay blinked away the tears that were building up in her eyes. 'It is, isn't it? But his dementia got so much worse after Granny Wendy died. I wonder how much she'd been covering how ill he really was. Without her, he just couldn't live on his own, and it was too difficult for all of us having him here. I was heartbroken when he went to the care home, but he seems to have settled, and has more good days now.'

'I'm sorry I wasn't here to help,' Tom said quietly. 'I'll pop up to see him later this week when I get a day off.'

'Please do, I know it'll mean a lot to him,' she nudged his arm, 'even though I'm his favourite.'

Chapter 5

Lincoln

'Good afternoon, Pastor Peterson. Are you going to conduct a short service for us this afternoon?' Fay rolled her eyes at the manager of the care home where her grandfather lived.

'Well, I'm here to see Dad, but I don't mind leading a service after that, if any of the residents would like to join us?'

Fay wondered if her dad knew this would happen. Was this some back-door way to get her to go to church? As though he could read her thoughts, he leaned over as they walked along the corridor.

'You don't need to come to the service. You could go to the car or sit in the garden. It's nice and quiet out there.'

Fay nodded her thanks. Maybe she had been too harsh on her parents. After months of fighting with them about church, it seemed they'd finally accepted her decision not to attend and were trying not to make it an issue. At least now they were free to enjoy being a normal family, without the hassle of bringing religion into everything.

'Hey Dad, how are you today?' Dad knocked lightly on the open door of Grandad's room.

'Mike, is that you, son?' Grandad looked towards the door and smiled. 'Lisa and my baby girl. Come and give your grandad a hug. It's been a long time, little lady.'

Fay stepped forward and accepted the hug. Pulling away, she looked into Grandad's eyes and was relieved to see they were clear and alert. Less of the lost, confused stares that had accompanied her previous visits. Her grandad held on to her hand and squeezed it.

'So, what are you up to? It's been such a long time.'

'I've been busy at the theatre. I got into a performing skills course for summer, remember?'

Grandad furrowed his brow as though searching for that memory. Fay's shoulders tensed. Had her simple question thrown her grandad back into his confused thoughts. She glanced at her parents.

Her dad caught her eye and gave her a slight nod. Moving round the room so he was standing directly in front of Grandad, he spoke brightly.

'She's doing a great job, Dad. You would've been proud to see how hard she worked clearing out a cupboard. She was filthy when she came home.'

Her grandad smiled proudly at her. 'A bit of hard-earned muck hurt no one,' he said, patting her hand, as he sat back down in his chair. Fay pulled up the footstool and sat next to him, while her mum and dad perched on the bed.

'Actually, Dad, she found something really interesting in the cupboard.'

Grandad kept hold of Fay's hand but turned his attention to her dad.

'Mike?' Mum's voice seemed to hold a warning, but Dad paid no attention and kept talking, keeping his voice light.

'She found a small tea tin. It reminded me of that one you had when I was a boy. Do you remember?'

Fay felt butterflies in her stomach. What was Dad thinking? The silence stretched across a few seconds.

'I remember, son.' Grandad returned Dad's steady gaze. 'My father gave it to me when I left home. It once had Georgian tea in it, but it held more than tea when he gave it to me.' Grandad turned to Fay and winked.

Looking back at Dad, Grandad's voice softened a little as he continued. 'He was a good man. My papa. I named you after him. Did you know that? A good man.' Grandad's eyes seem to fog over with memories. Mum and Dad exchanged a worried glance as they waited to see if he had more to say.

After a moment, Fay leaned against him. 'What was inside the tin, Grandad?' Her question seemed to clear the fog, and Grandad shook his head slightly before turning to Fay.

'Inside was life,' he half-whispered. His face broke into a smile. 'It was the most precious gift a father could give his child. One I gave your father, and I know he gave you.' Grandad looked over at Dad.

'Life? How can life be kept in a tea tin?' Fay screwed up her face, wondering if her grandad was thinking clearly.

'But that's the thing. It can't. Life can't be kept in a tea tin, can it? Can't be contained, not by anything. Took me a while to figure that out, to see the truth. But I did in the end. Sometimes it takes a little faith.' He kissed the top of Fay's head.

Fay wondered if she'd ever fully understand her grandad, but the openness of his heart touched her, even though she couldn't understand his words.

Conversation drifted around to Tom and his work at a local pub over summer. Grandad tutted, expressing his disapproval of his choices.

'Will you be doing a service today, son? I feel like it would do us all some good. I like to sing the old songs. Would you play for us, daughter?' Grandad asked Fay's mum.

'Of course,' Lisa replied. 'Do you have any requests?'

'*How Great Thou Art.* That's a favourite of mine.' Grandad turned to Fay. 'Will you sit with me?'

'I'm not sure Fay wants...'

Fay shook her head slightly, offering her mum a weak smile of thanks.

'I'd love to sit with you, Grandad.'

Leningrad

Vera worked hard all week at the exercises and new routines. Their first performance in the chorus would be in two weeks, and they practised many hours to be ready. Although the days were long, leaving Vera's joints aching, she was happier than she could remember. To spend all day dancing, not having to stop for other schoolwork, was something she'd only ever dreamed of, and the friendships freely offered by Katya and Masha were a breath of fresh air. They would share part of the journey home with Vera, and despite their exhaustion, they still found the energy to giggle, even though it attracted the disapproving stares of their fellow passengers on the trolleybus.

The first run-through on the stage of the theatre took her breath away. She looked out over the red velvet seats and imagined them full. She could almost hear the applause and wondered how she'd get through the night without letting her nerves take over.

'Don't get used to it.'

Vera stopped and watched Irina walk away, stretching and practising moves. Had she really just whispered that as she walked past? Irina had been unfriendly since the first day. Initially, it had been directly to all three girls, but as their instructor increasingly chose Vera to show a move or demonstrate a technique, Irina's comments had become even more barbed towards her.

Their instructor seemed oblivious to the growing tension between the group, and increasingly heaped praise on Vera's natural ability and poise. She was chosen to be the second lead in the chorus. She'd be the one leading half of the dancers onto the stage and setting the pace for them. Irina seemed livid when it was announced.

Vera wished she had someone to discuss the growing tension with, maybe someone who could advise her on the best way to handle this tricky situation. However, by the time she got home from the ballet, she needed to finish getting tea ready and help Vlad with his schoolwork. Mother was usually asleep after a long day caring for the twins, and Vera didn't want to burden Artyom. When he came home, he was exhausted and helped her with the housework, even though he still had to study. She wondered if she could discuss the situation with Baba Rosa, but she'd never once been invited into her room, and this wasn't the kind of thing that could be discussed on the doorstep. The walls have ears.

Vera longed to see her father, tell him about the upcoming performance, although none of their family could afford tickets to see her. She didn't want to worry him about the conflict brewing backstage but knew he would have words of wisdom for her. So, after Irina's whispered threat that afternoon, Vera decided that tonight she'd stay up and talk to her father. Maybe she didn't have to mention the theatre, and she certainly wouldn't mention Irina by name, but perhaps she could ask for his advice, without being specific.

She lay down next to the twins, and instead of snuggling down into a deep sleep, she rested and waited for her father to come home.

Chapter 6

Leningrad

Vera wasn't sure what time it was, but something had woken her. She sat up and waited for her eyes to adjust to the darkness. Finally, she made out the shape of her father, sitting at the table and eating the food they had left for him. She got out of bed, wrapping a blanket around her, and went and sat with him.

'Daughter, are you not sleeping? You need all the rest you can get. With the ballet and all you do here to help your mother, you need your sleep.' His voice came in a quiet whisper, which couldn't hide his own exhaustion.

'I'm all right, Papa. I don't do all the work here. Artyom helps me, and even Vlad does so much before I come home. You sound tired. Are you well?' Her hand found his in the dark, and for a moment, they sat in silence, enjoying being together.

'So, what's on your mind, little one? You didn't wait up just to see me eat my dinner.'

Vera could hear the smile in her father's tired voice.

'I'm wondering what to do when someone doesn't like you,' Vera said, glad she'd found a concise way of framing her question.

'Have you done something to deserve their disdain?'

'Not intentionally. It's more like they don't like who I am.'

'Ahh.' Her father nodded and took a sip of tea.

'That, precious one, is something you may always have to contend with. Do you know what I do? I go out of my way to be kind – beyond what I think I can. I heap kindness on them by the bucket-load.'

'Does it work?'

'That depends. It always produces a reaction if that's what you mean. Sometimes it wins them over, and they see the good in you. But some people can't be won over, and for them, every act of kindness is like burning coals being heaped on their head. But there's nothing they can do about it. They can't accuse you of anything except niceness. And that isn't illegal.'

'I'll try it, Papa.'

'You do that and let me know how it goes. Good night, little one.'

Vera leaned over and kissed her father's cheek. He left the room to wash up his bowl, and Vera fell asleep so quickly, she never heard him come back into the room.

Lincoln

'Pastor Peterson, before you leave, could I have a word?' The manager of the care home caught up with Fay and her family as they were leaving after the service. Fay didn't want to tell her parents, but she hadn't minded the old hymns and short Bible readings. She saw that her grandad and the other residents had enjoyed it.

'I'm sorry to disturb you on a Sunday. I could call you tomorrow.'

'No, not at all. What's wrong?'

'You know how your father's mind has been wandering recently. Well, he's started mumbling. I thought nothing of it, but one of the staff, a lady from Latvia, said that he was speaking Russian. We checked his records and there is nothing there about Russian being a preferred language?' The manager's voice raised in a question.

'Could your staff member make out what he was saying?' Dad asked.

'That's the disturbing part. He was telling other residents that the walls have ears. Thankfully, none of them could understand him.'

Dad shifted uncomfortably. 'I'm sorry. I really don't know what to say. Certainly, I've never heard my dad speak it, so I didn't think to put it on the form. Did the member of staff speak to him in Russian?'

'She tried to, but apparently his response was quite foul for such an upstanding Christian man. I've advised her not to engage with him in Russian again.'

Dad nodded. 'Yes, that seems to be a good idea. I am grateful for your wisdom in this situation.' He glanced at his watch. 'I'm sorry, we really must be going.'

'Of course, thank you for the service today. It certainly cheers up the residents.'

'What was that about Grandad speaking Russian? Is that what you meant when you said Grandad's been saying worrying things?' Fay waited for an answer, watching her parents exchange a worried glance. 'Is something going on?' She raised her voice slightly. It was one thing to not go to church, but that didn't mean she wasn't part of the family.

Dad flicked the indicator and drove into a local park.

'Let's walk and talk,' he said, pulling into a parking space. They all got out of the car and walked towards the pond at the centre of the park. There were several families around, mostly with little children and a few older couples, but not many people. After a few minutes, Mum began to talk.

'We don't know all the details, and much of it is still a mystery, but your grandad was originally from Russia.'

Fay nodded. This wasn't really a surprise.

'He never spoke about his childhood,' Dad continued. 'By the time I was born, he already had British Citizenship.

Of course, he had an accent when I was growing up, but that was just Dad. I was told not to ask questions, so I didn't.'

'So, how did he end up here?'

'We don't know. In fact, he told us more about his family today than he ever has. I never knew he'd named me after his father. He's never mentioned his family at all.'

'So, can you speak Russian?' Fay looked up at her dad.

'Yes, I learned it at university. I felt an affinity to the language and wondered if I could ever go there and try to track down Dad's family. I also studied some of the history, although I've forgotten most of the details now.'

'So, the pieces of paper inside the tin. Can you read them?'

'I'd need to have a proper look, but, yes, I can read parts of them.'

'What did they say?'

'What I saw didn't quite make sense. I'd like to look at them again.'

'Let's go home and look, then.' Fay walked faster. They were on the wrong side of the large pond, and the car park was quite a distance.

'Let's just slow down a little.' Mum's voice broke into Fay's thoughts. 'I'm not so sure we want to be digging too deeply. If Grandad's life had been all wonderful in Russia, surely, he would have told us about it? There must be a reason he has never mentioned his family or his father, and why he totally hid that part of his life. From what the manager said today, "The walls have ears", it sounds as though Grandad's association with the Russian language is quite negative. Whatever his reason for leaving Russia, he has had a good life here. He was happy with Granny Wendy and raised you well, Mike. He adores you, Fay. In fact, he was the one who named you too. Did you know that?'

Fay shook her head. Her name was still a sore point in their relationship. All her life, she'd hated the name her parents had given her. It shackled her to their old, out-dated religion, and meant that everyone judged her without ever getting to know her. She'd chosen the nickname 'Fay' and had educated everyone to use it. Even her parents now called her by her new chosen name, but to know that her grandfather had given her the birth name she so detested shamed her a little. She felt her face go red, and stared at the ground, blinking away the tears that had appeared in her eyes.

'Sorry, I didn't mean to upset you.' Her mum gave her a squeeze, and, for a moment, they walked in silence. 'All I'm saying, Mike, is that your dad has had a good life. Please, let's not go digging into the past and maybe bring up things he doesn't want or need to remember.'

Dad sighed heavily. 'I understand what you are saying, Lisa. But I don't think it's a coincidence that Fay found a tin exactly like Dad's in the theatre. I think there might be a connection, and I wonder if it isn't providential that we can still discover these things now, before the dementia takes him from us totally.'

Mum shook her head. 'I'm just not sure. We need to pray and tread carefully.'

Chapter 7

Leningrad

'Today is all about precision. We will block the dances and look at your positionings.' Nadezhda Vladimirovna led the group of girls onto the main stage again. Vera always got a sense of excitement there, but today, she couldn't shake off a feeling of trepidation.

'On the floor, you will see a series of black dots,' the instructor continued. 'These will be your base points. The dots are only there for you to practise today. You must learn your correct positioning for when the dots are removed.'

They spent the rest of the morning practising moving to and from the dots, learning where the other dancers were and looking at various ways of moving off and onto the stage.

'Good, after lunch we will look at the pointe work needed for this piece.'

Vera loved pointe work; dancing on tiptoe always looked so elegant, even though it hurt. Vera loved dancing in her new shoes. She felt as though she could dance better in them when she remembered the love in her father's eyes as he'd given her them.

As usual, Irina didn't have lunch with them, and no one was surprised to see her on the stage when they returned. She glared at Vera, her top lip turned up in a sneer.

Nadezhda Vladimirovna made them practise coming on and off stage to their black dot, walking on their pointes, with their heads lifted high. Every time she tried, Vera couldn't seem to land on her dot. She was always just a touch behind it. But looking around, she was sure she was in the correct position. Catching Irina watching her carefully whenever she was near her dot, the thought suddenly struck her; what if Irina had tampered with her dot and adjusted it to get her into trouble?

Vera felt her heart beat faster. From the side of the stage, she looked at the line of dots, and could see that hers was indeed out of place. Before she could mention it, Nadezhda Vladimirovna was explaining the next move she wanted them to perform. This would be at the end of the piece, as part of the finale. The girls were to enter the stage and instead of dancing to their spots, they had to jump, doing the splits in the air, and land on the dots on their pointes.

Nadezhda Vladimirovna asked Vera to go first. The instructor stood behind the dot, to judge how precise

Vera's landing was. Vera knew she could do this. It was something she had often practised in the park. Choosing a spot on the ground, then leaping and landing on it.

As she started the move, she saw Nadezhda Vladimirovna frown as she looked at her dot. She looked down the row of dots, and Vera wondered if she'd noticed that hers was out of place.

Vera launched herself into the air, her arms and legs strong, her feet pointed. She slightly adjusted her body in mid-air, to aim and land perfectly on the dot. But as her foot made contact with the small black circle, Vera knew that something was very wrong. She felt her toes continue to move at speed, despite hitting the dot precisely. Her ankle twisted painfully as the rest of her body tried to land where it should, with her foot moving further and further away. Vera couldn't understand why she had no control over her landing foot, but before she could think about it, a searing pain took her breath away. She crumpled to the floor.

The other girls came running. Nadezhda Vladimirovna shouted to one of the stagehands to get some ice and call for help. Although the pain was intense, Vera looked around accusingly at the little dot, hoping it could give away the secrets of why her foot hadn't stopped. Sure enough, she saw a tiny tell-tale trail of light leading from the black circle. Masha followed her stare and her eyes widened as she saw the evidence of sabotage. Masha reached over and touched the thin trail, rubbing the liquid between her figures.

'Oil,' she whispered. 'Sunflower oil,' sniffing her fingers lightly. Vera stared at Irina, who was looking at her ankle with wide eyes. She waited until the girl met her eyes. The look of embarrassment and fear that shot across her face was all the confirmation she needed. Irina had deliberately set out to remove Vera from the ballet, and the pain in her ankle told her she had succeeded.

Lincoln

Back home, Fay and her parents sat at the table, staring at the small tea tin. Anyone looking through the window would have wondered why it held their attention for so long. They sat silently for about five minutes.

Fay wrestled with her parents' words. The idea that Dad understood Russian and could read the slips of paper excited her. But her mum's warning rang loudly in her mind. What if they were opening a can of worms that could ruin her grandfather's last few years on this earth? How were they supposed to know what was right?

Looking at her parents, Fay could see that they were praying. To anyone else, it looked like they were just looking at the tin. But Fay knew the tell-tale signs. The slight movement of the lips, the occasional closing of the eyes, the patient waiting, as though God was going to answer. Fay didn't know whether to pity them for praying to a god who wasn't real or envy them for having someone bigger than themselves to rely on.

Waiting for her parents to finish, she picked up the ballet shoes and examined them more closely. They looked unusually long to Fay, as though the person who wore them had extra-long, thin feet. Putting her hand inside, she felt to the end of the toes, and found that the last three or four centimetres of the shoe comprised a wooden block.

'That's so they can stand on their pointes – on tip-toes,' Mum said, watching Fay feel the outline of the wooden block. Fay hadn't inherited her mother's love or interest in ballet. She'd always been relieved when her grandad moaned about her ballet classes. She took his side so often, eventually Mum had relented and let her drop the classes after a year. Mum pulled the programme out of the tin and pointed to the ballerinas on the cover. One woman was folded over in the foreground, as though she was in a deep, elegant bow, and behind her, were dancers on their tiptoes providing a moving backdrop.

'Is that painful?' Fay looked up.

'I didn't do too much pointe work. It wasn't really encouraged, as it could leave you with crippled toes. But the Russians specialised in it. They were constantly up on their pointes, and apparently many of the ballerinas suffered for it, with arthritis and rheumatism in later life.'

'They look so elegant, don't they?' Fay passed the shoes to Mum.

'I was just thinking the same thing.' Mum took one shoe and examined it carefully. 'Although it's been battered and worn, you can see it was beautifully made. But look, can you see this tiny smudge, right on the tip of the toe here? It looks like oil.'

Chapter 8

Leningrad

'Your father's here to take you home.'

Vera opened her eyes and smiled at the nurse. It was a relief to everyone that her ankle wasn't broken. They had assured her that the sprain would heal if she could stay off it totally for a few weeks. Vera bit her lip, wondering how that would be possible in the *kommunalka* with the girls to look after and the family to cook for.

As soon as her father walked in the room, she could tell something was wrong. He thanked the nurses for their care, picked up Vera's small bag and then reached down and scooped up Vera, without looking in her eyes.

'Papa?' That one word held a hundred questions, but her father silenced her with the tiniest shake of his head.

Outside the hospital, he walked to a different trolleybus stop, not the one that took them home, and Vera couldn't explain why her eyes filled with tears. As they waited for the trolleybus, he leaned forward and whispered in her ear.

'I've spoken with your mother and brother. We've all agreed that the most important thing is for you to get well, and you'll never get the rest you need in the flat.'

'But, Papa...'

'No, daughter, it's been decided. Don't argue with me. You are going to stay with my family in the village. They can help you heal faster than we can. You will get strong and come back to us better than before. You need fresh air, peace, fresh vegetables and milk. You can have all that in the village.'

For the first time that day, her father looked her in the eyes. She could see the pain and knew that this separation was more costly to him than all the expenses of the hospital stay. He seemed to have aged in the last couple of days, even more than in the previous few months.

'And at home?' Vera asked quietly.

Her father's face broke into a smile. 'Artyom has everything under control. He even had the girls pulling their weight and doing chores.' He leaned forward, glancing around, as though worried about being overheard. 'Although his cooking is not a patch on yours!'

Vera laughed despite the immense sadness in her heart. The thought of being sent away, to stay with relatives she didn't know, without having the chance to say goodbye to her mother, brothers and sisters, was more than she could physically bear. She wanted to beg her father to take her home for one last goodbye, but she knew he was already losing several hours' pay by picking her up from hospital, and then there was the cost of the train ticket. She couldn't inconvenience him any further, no matter how her heart ached.

At the train station, her father settled her on a bench in the large ticket hall and went to join the long queues. He left her with her small bag from the hospital, and a larger rucksack he'd been carrying on his back. Looking inside, she saw her clothes, and tried not to cry again as she imagined her mother packing her things.

'Don't cry' whispered a familiar voice, and before she realised what was happening, four little arms were reaching around her neck.

'Mind her ankle, girls.'

Vera grabbed her little sisters and held on to them so long and so tight that they fidgeted and asked to get down. When she finally released them, their faces all wet with tears, she looked up at her brothers, standing awkwardly in front of the bench. She knew she couldn't hug them in the same way as the babies, but she hoped that her love showed through her smile.

'Thank you for coming,' she whispered through a throat that could hardly open.

'Of course. We couldn't let you go without saying goodbye.'

'I asked Papa if I could go too, to help you,' Vlad grinned. 'But he said Artyom needed me more than you did, so I have to stay.' He pulled a face that made Vera laugh.

'We have jobs to do at home,' Nadia said, stroking Vera's face to get her full attention.

'I have to fold the clothes. Even Vlad's underpants.' Luba pulled a face, and Nadia and Vera giggled together. She pulled them into another hug, whispering how proud she was of them.

'Time to go. Girls, say goodbye now. We don't all need to go to the platform.' Vera's father returned to the bench. 'Thank you for bringing them, son.' He rested his hand on Artyom's shoulder. 'I'll head back to work after this and be home late today.'

Artyom nodded and leaned over to kiss Vera's cheek.

'Be good and rest,' he whispered in her ear. She smiled as he took the girls from her arms. He looked so much older than his thirteen years. People often mistook them for twins. She held his gaze for a moment. She wanted to apologise for leaving him with all the work and thank him for everything he was doing. But she didn't have the words. He winked at her, and took the girls' hands, one on each side. Saying goodbye to Artyom, Vera felt like she was leaving a part of herself behind.

Vlad also leaned over to kiss her cheek, resting his head against hers for a moment.

'Get well,' he whispered. 'Don't worry about us. We all just want you to get better.'

Vera nodded, her throat too full of tears to speak. As Vlad stepped back, her father hoisted her and the bags into his arms. As he walked through the crowds to the train, carefully making sure her ankle wasn't knocked, he gave her directions for the journey.

She'd be travelling alone, but he'd pay the conductor extra to lift her out of the train at the right station. His mother – her babushka - had promised someone would be waiting for her and had assured Papa that she would be brought home safely without having to put weight on her ankle.

'Write to us every week, and when your babushka tells us you are well enough, I'll send you the money for the return ticket.' Vera nodded. She wanted to bury her head in her father's shoulder and beg him not to leave her, but she knew she had to be strong.

'Thank you, Papa. For everything.' She was pleased that she said it without tears, and her father's smile was genuine.

He jumped up onto the train with surprising grace and lowered Vera into a seat.

'I love you, daughter. And I hope you find more than just health out in that village.'

Vera tilted her head on one side. 'What do you mean?'

Her father winked at her before being swallowed up by the crowd of passengers. She briefly saw him talking to the conductor and pointing her out, as other people climbed on to the train, weighed down with bags that were sometimes bigger than them. She strained to catch a last glance but was distracted by a knock on the window. Looking out, she saw her father standing on the platform. For a few moments, until the train moved, they stared at each other, communicating freely without words, as they had done for as long as Vera could remember.

Finally, the train shook. Her father stepped back, and Vera raised her hand to wave as the train pulled away from the station.

Lincoln

Almost a week had passed since their visit to Grandad. Mum and Dad had agreed that for now they would pack the tea tin away. They wouldn't attempt to understand any more about its mysteries unless Grandad said something about his past.

Fay had worked late at the theatre every evening. Despite buying storage units and clearly labelling everything, she often found things thrown into the cupboard, and after asking people to be more vigilant and pack their things away, she'd been given the unenviable title of 'Keeper of the Cupboard'. Now, whenever anything needed packing away, it would be shoved into her arms, or left for her to deal with. Often, Fay and Kate, who had been given the title 'Keeper of the Wardrobe', were left with costumes and props to sort out after everyone else had gone home.

Fay tried not to resent it, but this wasn't what she'd had in mind when she signed up for the summer programme. There was still no word on whether Sabrina would come back. Already some of the other participants had left, but Fay was determined to give it her best shot and hope for the best.

She let herself out of the stage door later than she would have liked. Blake and his friends had been workshopping, looking at different ways of moving and using props. Although this looked interesting and Fay would have loved to have taken part, she was 'Keeper of the Cupboard', and had to constantly fetch or pack away the various pieces the group required. At the end of the workshop, they'd stood round in a circle, applauding one another loudly, before dropping their props on the floor and leaving the stage. At first, Fay thought it was a joke; that they'd deliberately tried to fool her. She picked up a couple of props and headed to the cupboard, expecting them all to burst back in, offering to help and apologising for tricking her into thinking they'd leave her with all the work. But after the third visit to the cupboard, she realised they had actually left her. She was the last one in the theatre, and she still had six or seven more trips to the cupboard before she could leave.

Fay drew her coat around her, and reached into her pocket for her house keys, carefully threading the keys through her fingers as she'd been taught in self-defence class. The city centre was busier than she was comfortable with. She wondered about ringing her parents and asking for a lift, but usually Mum and Dad had a meal and shared a bottle of wine on a Saturday night, so they wouldn't be able to help her. As she stepped out of the shadows of the theatre, she heard a voice shout her name. For a moment the blood rushed into her ears. Everything in her told her to run, but she was frozen to the spot. She was aware of someone shouting again but couldn't make out who it was or what they were saying. Forcing herself to breathe, the noise in her ears died down as she heard her name called again, this time recognising it as her father's voice. She turned to where the sound came from and saw her dad's familiar green Citroen. She'd never been so relieved to see the disgusting-coloured car.

She hurried over and let herself in the passenger door. Taking a moment to catch her breath, she turned and smiled.

'Thanks, Dad. I really appreciate it. But what are you doing here?'

Her dad was quiet for a moment as he negotiated turning into the traffic.

'It's funny. Mum and I were sitting down to our dinner. I'd just opened the wine, and I had the thought, "Go and pick up Fay tonight." I know you hate us coming down here, so I ignored it. I poured myself a glass of wine, but just as I was about to drink, your mum said, "I think you need to go pick up Fay tonight. Let's have the wine another night." So here I am.'

Fay found it hard to swallow around the lump in her throat.

'Don't worry,' Dad added, mistaking her silence for disapproval. 'Your friends didn't see me when they left.'

'Thanks, Dad,' Fay croaked, leaning back in the seat and realising just how exhausted she was.

Dad glanced over.

'How about resting tomorrow and not going to the theatre? You can have a lie in while we go to church, then we'll go see Grandad again. What do you think?'

Fay closed her eyes and smiled. 'That sounds good.'

Chapter 9

Lincoln

The house was quiet when Fay got up the next day. Padding through to the kitchen in her dressing gown and slippers, she saw her mum had left her and Tom a couple of Danish pastries for breakfast. She turned the kettle on and wandered into the dining room. Picking the ballet shoes off the sideboard, she wondered about the person who'd owned them.

'You didn't eat all the pastries, did you? Mum said she'd left enough for both of us.' Tom walked into the room, rubbing the sleep out of his eyes.

'No, they're still there. Another late shift? Grandad's not too happy about you working in a pub. And if he knew you were missing church...'

'Grandad was the one who always taught us we can follow God anywhere,' Tom countered. 'It's not about going to church; it's about living every day for Him. But what about you? Have you told him you're not going anymore?'

'Oh, the kettle's boiling. Can you make me a coffee?' Fay ignored her brother's question.

'What did your last slave die of? Are you taking up ballet again?'

'No, I found them in a cupboard in the Theatre. Look, can you see? That looks like letters.'

Fay pointed to some tiny stitches on the inside of the shoe, near where the ribbon was sewn on.

Tom took the shoe and held it up to the light. 'It seems to be a square, without the bottom line – like a Pi sign - then a B and an M.'

Forgetting about breakfast, Fay opened the tea tin and carefully pulled out the programme.

'Maybe we can find someone with those initials in here,' she said, running her fingers down the list of names, looking for a B and an M. 'The names are really strange. Each one seems to be made of three different parts. The middle bit seemed to be girls' names, but the last bit seemed to be male names. I don't get it.'

'But if they are Russian names, doesn't Russian use a different alphabet? So you probably won't find those initials anyway,' Tom said, glancing over her shoulder. 'Come on, let's get breakfast.'

Fay packed away the programme, and shaking her head slightly, followed her brother to the kitchen in time to see him grab the largest pastry.

Pulling into the drive of the care home, Mum voiced the thought in everyone's mind.

'I wonder how Grandad is going to be today.'

'Apparently he hasn't had a good week,' Dad sighed.

'Maybe having another Sunday service would help?' Fay was surprised she was suggesting it. 'It seemed to help him last Sunday.'

'Yes, it did,' Mum agreed. 'I popped in on Wednesday afternoon and played a few of the old hymns. That seemed to settle him, and he had a better day on Thursday.'

'Sorry I've been so busy at the theatre. I could've come and helped you.' Fay thought back to Wednesday afternoon. She'd been sorting out the cupboard again. A visit to Grandad would've been a welcome break.

'Oh no,' Mum turned in her seat to face Fay. 'We want you to live your life fully. None of us, least of all Grandad, wants to hold you back from your dreams. It's an amazing opportunity you have this summer to learn about performance and speech and engaging a crowd. You keep doing what you love. Grandad is our responsibility, not yours.'

Fay felt her face go red. She hadn't told her parents of her new title amongst the group, or that her days were spent in a small cupboard, with only a tiny window near the ceiling to tell her if it was day or night. Maybe she'd slightly exaggerated how good her summer was. Mum's last statement grated slightly.

'Grandad's not a responsibility, Mum. He's Grandad. It's important to me that he's OK.'

'Of course. I didn't mean it like that. We don't resent having to take the extra time to reassure Grandad at the moment, but it is a worry, and we want to protect you from that as much as we can.'

Fay nodded and gave her mum a weak smile.

'Well, let's go see how he is today.'

Outside Leningrad

As the train moved away from the station, Vera tried to get comfy on the wooden seat. Without full use of both legs, she struggled to stay in one place, sliding up and down the bench with every turn the train took.

An older woman sat on the opposite bench, observing her. Vera felt uncomfortable but schooled her features to seem nonchalant. She could feel her head getting heavier and heavier, but the increasing pain in her ankle kept her from falling asleep.

'Where are you going?' the woman called, leaning forward. She had one tooth in the middle of her bottom gum and her breath smelt sickly sweet in a way that made Vera's nose crinkle.

Vera just shrugged and looked out of the window. She knew better than to talk to strangers.

'You don't look too good. 'What happened to your leg?'

Vera continued to stare out of the window, her fingers tightening on her bags.

The older woman leaned closer, and Vera could smell her sickly-sweet breath. Vera glanced at her.

'I've got something that'll help with the pain,' The older woman opened her coat slightly, and showed a small glass bottle. Vera's eyes opened wide. Whatever was in that bottle was not legal and was not what she wanted to share.

'Now then, madam. Leave the poor girl alone. She'll not be telling you anything.' Vera was relieved to see the conductor approach.

'I'm just being friendly,' the woman shrugged at him.

'You wouldn't be if you knew where she was going,' the conductor said with a sneer.

'Why? Where's she going?' The woman turned to Vera. 'Where are you going?'

Vera ignored the question and turned back to the window.

'Let's just say,' the conductor whispered, leaning towards to woman. 'I've been told to get her off the train at...' He lowered his voice to a whisper. Vera didn't hear the name of the village but saw the reaction in the woman's face reflected in the window and knew that she'd heard.

'And she looked down at me like she's a princess. Dirty little traitor,' the woman spluttered. She gathered her coat tighter around her and glared at Vera, her lip curled. She drew herself as far away as the wooden seating would allow. She didn't say another word to Vera, although she occasionally glanced in her direction and muttered something unintelligible to herself.

The almost-toothless woman got off the train at the next station, and Vera relaxed a little when the bench opposite her remained empty. She dozed lightly, despite the discomfort in her leg, and woke in the late afternoon, hungry and uncomfortable. Just as she was wondering how much further she'd have to travel, the conductor approached and told her he would help her off at the next stop. He continued through the carriage, calling out the name of the next station, and Vera quickly pulled her bags closer and checked her hair was still neat.

As the train slowed, the conductor came back. He put Vera's rucksack on his back, and picked her up, straining in a way her father hadn't. He wasn't as attentive, either, and Vera winced as her bandaged foot hit the back of a seat and then the edge of the door. When they finally reached the platform, Vera thanked the conductor and looked around. She didn't really know who she was looking for. She had met her babushka once when Papa had taken her to visit, but that was years ago, when Artyom was only a baby. Vera could barely remember it.

The conductor had disappeared back onto the train, and Vera stood on her good leg, with her rucksack at her feet and her small bag in her hand. She noticed an older boy, maybe about seventeen or eighteen years old, leaning against the station wall. His dark hair flopped over his face, so different from the short hair boys preferred in the city. She wondered whether he'd have to cut his hair when he entered the army for his mandatory two years of service. It suited him long.

He turned and noticed her looking at him. Vera felt her face turn red and glanced away. As she watched out of the corner of her eye, he pushed himself off the wall and slowly ambled towards her. As he got closer, Vera felt trembly. He was even better looking close up.

'Vera Mikhailovna? I'm Slavic. Your babushka sent me to get you. Can I help you with your things?'

Vera looked up at him. His face was kind and open, with a smile hiding at the corner of his mouth. Had her grandmother really sent him? Could she trust him? Did she have any choice? She stared at him for a few moments.

'OK. She said you might be wary.' The young man stepped back slightly. 'She gave me this for you.' Slavic reached into his pocket and pulled out a piece of paper which seemed to contain a shopping list. Instantly, Vera recognised her grandmother's handwriting. Her monthly letters used to be read out by Papa every Sunday afternoon, but since he was now working so much, the responsibility for reading and responding to the letters had fallen to Vera and Artyom. The handwriting on the list was more familiar to Vera than her own.

She handed the paper back to Slavic and nodded. He looked at her, then the rucksack, then her ankle, as though considering what to do.

'Can you lean on me?' he asked, swinging her rucksack on to his back.

'I'm not supposed to put any weight on my ankle.' Vera bit her bottom lip. She leaned on the arm he held out to her but had to put her weight on her foot to move forward.

Stepping as lightly and quickly as she could on the bandaged ankle, shooting pains exploded through her leg. She cried out and stumbled.

'This isn't working. It is OK if I carry you?' Slavic asked. His neck and cheeks growing red.

Vera nodded, not caring about the tears that ran down her face.

Slavic wasn't as strong as Papa, but he was certainly stronger than the conductor. He carried her easily through the simple ticket office, carefully making sure her ankle didn't hit anything. Before Vera could fully register where they were, he placed her down on a rough wooden surface.

Looking around, she could see she was in a small wooden cart, looking at the back end of a horse.

'That's Nelly,' Slavic nodded at the horse, although Vera wasn't sure she'd be able to recognise it from the front. 'Your grandmother only lives a couple of miles from here. We'll be there before you know it.' He looked at her for a moment, before breaking into a smile which seemed to light up his entire face. Before Vera could respond, he turned away, swung himself up onto the front of the cart, and with a gentle word to the horse, they were off.

The journey would have been pleasant if Vera hadn't been in so much pain, so tired and so hungry. The autumn colours were unlike any that she'd seen in Leningrad. A blazing display of reds, yellows and oranges almost made Vera forget how much colder it was without the closeness of the buildings and people she'd grown up surrounded by.

She must have dozed off again, because the next thing she noticed, the cart had stopped in front of a small hut, and Slavic was getting down. He quickly picked Vera up without even looking at her.

As he walked towards the hut, the door opened, and a face that Vera vaguely remembered greeted them. Slavic was careful to turn his body so that Vera's ankle didn't hit the narrow door frame and carried her to an old couch that filled one end of the tiny kitchen. After placing her down, he accepted her thanks with a nod and grunted a farewell to her grandmother, who pushed a small package into his hands before he left.

'Right, let's get you comfortable, fed and find something to stop the throbbing in that ankle, yes?'

Vera smiled and leaned back on the sofa. For the first time since the accident, she felt herself relax.

Chapter 10

Lincoln

'Arthur, your family are here to see you.' The carer gently shook Grandad's arm. His eyes shot open, and he flinched. Mum and Fay exchanged a glance. It would not be an easy visit.

'No, they aren't my family. Where's my Wendy? And our baby, Mishka? Why haven't they come to see me?'

The carer tried to soothe Grandad, but Fay's heart broke for him. How awful to feel so lost in the world. Dad quickly intervened.

'Hello, my friend. I am Pastor Peterson. Would you care to join us for Sunday service?'

Upon hearing those words, the look of anxiety seemed to lift off Grandad, although he still seemed confused. He glanced from one person to the next, but when his eyes alighted on Fay, his face broke into a huge smile.

'Ah yes, now that sounds like a good idea.' He allowed himself to be led to the lounge, although he was careful to choose a chair far away from the other residents, viewing them through narrowed eyes. He beckoned Fay to sit next to him and helped her pull her chair close to his. He held her hand, patting it occasionally, while shooting daggers at his fellow residents if they even dared to look his way.

As the music played, Grandad's shoulders dropped, his face fell into a smile, and he closed his eyes, swaying gently to the music.

After the hymns, Dad read a short psalm, and led them in a simple prayer before Mum played one final hymn.

The service ended, and Dad spent a few moments chatting with each of the residents. Fay stayed close to Grandad, whose eyes were still shut, and he hummed slightly, although Fay couldn't make out the melody. As Dad approached, Grandad opened his eyes.

'Ahh, Pastor. Lovely service. Thank you for coming. Will you be coming again? I could do with this more often.'

Dad shook hands with Grandad and smiled warmly, although Fay could only imagine how hard it must be to have your own father not recognise you.

'My Wendy would've loved that service. I'm not sure where she is.' Grandad leaned forward and began to look around the room. 'She's off somewhere. I'm sure she'll be back in a minute.'

'So, Arthur,' Dad's voice caught on his father's name. 'Is there anything we can pray about for you this week? Anything you're worried about?'

'We all carry worries, don't we?' Grandad nodded slowly, his eyes looking off into the distance. 'I have to leave them at the cross. That's what I've learned. But no, no particular worries for you to pray about, Pastor. Today has been a good day. I've had a visitor,' Grandad leaned forward, and Dad moved closer. In a loud stage whisper, which Fay knew she was meant to hear, he said, 'She's one of my favourite people in the world.'

Dad glanced up and smiled at Fay. She felt bad that Grandad remembered her but didn't seem to recognise his own son.

'It's been a breath of fresh air seeing her again.' Grandad reached for Fay's hand and held it. 'I don't think she knows how much I love her.' He looked at her, his eyes turning red with tears.

'Do you remember me, Grandad? Do you remember my name?'

Grandad laughed loudly, leaning back in his chair.

'Remember your name? What a question! As though I could forget the most precious name ever, except for my dear Wendy. You need to meet her; I don't know where she is.' Again, Grandad looked around.

'So, who's your friend here, Arthur?' Dad winked at Fay. Grandad looked back at Dad.

'I'm sorry, Pastor, I've forgotten my manners. This is my Vera.'

A village outside Leningrad

Dear Papa, Mama, Artyom, Vlad, Nadia and Luba!

It's hard to believe I arrived here a week ago. My new friend, Slavic, has promised to post this letter to you and check at the station to see if your letter has arrived. Please write to me with all the family news. I miss you all so very, very much.

Babushka tells me that when I am stronger, she will show me the places where Papa played when he was growing up. It is a small hut with two rooms. I sleep in the main room, next to the chimney to stay warm, and they sleep in the other room. Babushka lives with Baba Tonya. Baba Tonya is ancient. She isn't related to Babushka; they are just close friends.

Everyone comes to see Baba Tonya for help when they have coughs and fevers. She knows all about herbs and how to mix them into medicines. She made a compress for my ankle, and it took the pain away immediately. Babushka said that some people in the village think she has magic, but she doesn't. She is just very old and very wise.

I told her about mother, and she said that she knows some herbs that will help. When I come home, she will give me a tea to make up for you, Mama, that will make you feel stronger.

I don't have anything else to write. Until my ankle is healed, I can't go far or do much, although Babushka makes sure I sit out in the garden every day to enjoy the fresh air.

Please write to me with your news.

I hug and kiss you all,

Vera.

Dear Vera!

Papa asked me to write to you, as he is working very hard at the moment. He sends his love. Thank you for your last letter, but I'm afraid not everyone was glad about what you wrote. Mama was very unhappy when Papa read out about Baba Tonya. (Mama called her a witch!) She is angry at Papa for sending you there, and she certainly doesn't want you to bring back any tea or herbs. Mama wanted to write to Babushka, telling her to make Baba Tonya leave while you are there, but Papa said no. He said that she wasn't a witch, if anything she was the opposite.

What do you think that means, dearest sister? What is the opposite of a witch? I've been thinking about it all week. On Saturday, when I go to the quarry and work with Papa, I will try to ask him.

Vlad is doing better with his schoolwork, and the girls are getting good at their chores. Mama got up twice last week and cooked for us. I think my cooking must taste terrible if Mama is finding it easier to go into the kitchen herself and cook, than eat my food. I try my best, but no one's cooking is as good as yours.

Yesterday, your friends Masha and Katya came to the flat. They didn't know you'd gone to the village and were sad they couldn't speak to you. They said Irina didn't get into trouble for what she did to you. It turns out her dad is high up in the Party, so there was nothing the Ballet could do to punish her. That is dreadfully unfair, isn't it? She is trying to be nice to them now, but they avoid her. Your instructor, Nadezhda Vladimirovna, told them you are welcome back at the ballet as soon as your ankle is healed. She said you have natural talent, and as long as you rest enough for it to get strong, she thinks you will dance with the Kirov Ballet for many years. That's such good news. Mama was so happy when I told her, she actually cried.

We all miss you very much, but I am glad you are getting the fresh air you need. Maybe in the summer you could take the younger ones to visit Babushka. It would do them so much good to be in the fresh air. But I wonder if Mama would let them go. She's still suspicious of life in the village. She doesn't like Babushka and she can't stand Baba Tonya. Please don't mention Baba Tonya in future letters and only say good things about Babushka. That might help.

I'd better go. I need to wake the others soon. We love you and miss you,

Your dear brother,

Artyom.

Dear Papa, Mama, Artyom, Vlad, Nadia and Luba!

Thank you for the letter, Artyom. I'm so pleased that the Ballet still wants me to come back. You'd all be so proud of my progress. My ankle is healing well. Babushka is making sure I get the best food I can, and the fresh air is strengthening me.

Slavic took me for a drive the other evening. We rode on his cart, and he showed me the village. We sat by a lake and watched the sunset. We saw a fox. I never realised there were so many birds, animals and insects here in Russia. It's like the village is a whole new world to me. I wish I could share it with you all...

Vera chewed on the end of the pencil. What else could she write, without mentioning Baba Tonya and other things, which would upset her mother. She pulled out another piece of paper. This one had a shopping list on one side. It was scrap paper waiting to be reused. She began to write everything that she couldn't say in her proper letter.

Every morning, Babushka builds up the fire in the kitchen and puts the water on to heat. While we are waiting, instead of doing chores or getting dressed, we sit together, and Babushka reads a song or a few words from a Book of Wisdom. I've never seen the book, but she keeps passages written in an old schoolbook. Sometimes she'll read a story or a poem, but they aren't like the poems we study at school, where every line has the same rhythm and rhyme. This is like someone dancing wild in a field, not following the rules, just following their heart.

Today's words were really beautiful, I tried to learn them:

When I consider your heavens,
the work of your fingers,
the moon and the stars,
which you have set in place,
What is mankind that you are mindful of them?
human beings that you care for them?

Yesterday when I watched the sunset with Slavic, it took my breath away. I couldn't help thinking 'Who made all of this?' In Leningrad, everything is made by people. Every building had an architect and a builder. But out here, nothing is built by men, but it is all so beautifully designed. In the city, it's easy to believe there is no God. But here in the village, to think that feels like foolishness.

The only way I can understand it is to imagine myself as two different people – Leningrad Vera and Village Vera. Leningrad Vera works hard for her family; she's a good Pioneer, dances in the ballet, maybe one day she'll even become the People's Artist. Village Vera is like a new baby, unable to walk, reliant on everyone else, learning new ways of thinking, and discovering a whole new world.

Babushka is teaching me about what food is good for the body, and Baba Tonya is showing me the herbs and how each one can help the body in a different way. I don't know how Village Vera will ever be able to return to the city and play the part of Leningrad Vera.

These are the things I can never tell you, and having these secrets makes me feel so far away from you. I wish I could share them with you all.

Vera.

Chapter 11

Lincoln

'Who's Vera?' Fay asked as she got into the car.

'I don't know. I've never heard my dad use that name before. Unless...' Dad fell silent.

'You responded really well, Fay. I appreciate you not arguing with him,' Mum said.

'I think I was too shocked to speak. But aren't we lying to him, not telling him who we really are?'

Mum glanced at Fay in the back seat. 'I honestly don't have an answer for you. Are we lying to him, or are we just meeting him where he is, and loving him in that place, without forcing him to come into our reality?'

'When he expected to see Granny Wendy and you as a baby, it broke my heart.' Fay noticed both her parents nod and Dad sniffed. 'Imagine finding out that Granny Wendy has gone, over and over again, every day. It's so painful. I can understand why his reality, where his wife is just off making a coffee, is a much more inviting place for him.'

Everyone was silent. After a few moments, Dad started the car.

'But who's Vera?' Fay repeated. 'She's obviously someone special to Grandad. And I must remind him of her.'

Dad turned the engine off and twisted around so he could see Fay.

'I've never heard him mention that name before. It must be someone from his past. Someone who, for whatever reason, Grandad never felt he could share with us.' Dad rubbed his hand over his face. 'When I was growing up, Mum would often talk about her family. We'd go visit them at Christmas. There were cousins and things. But whenever I asked Dad about his family, he'd just say, "Some things are not to be talked of."

'When I was a teenager, I asked a lot of questions. I wanted to know where Dad came from, why he left. Was there any family or cousins on his side that I could get to know? Initially he got angry with me, told me it was none of my business and who was I to question him. But after a while, the questions made him sad. If I pushed him for answers, he'd disappear into himself. He'd be depressed for days on end, so I stopped asking. Mum explained that whatever had happened was so bad that he left behind his country, any family he had, and even his own name, to create a new life here. It wasn't fair of us to drag that information from him, if he felt he was protecting us by not telling us.'

'That makes sense. Granny Wendy was so good at understanding people. So, he never even told her?'

'I don't think so. She never pushed or asked questions. She just loved him for who he was, without needing to know about his past. She seemed to create a safe place where he could be accepted, even in his depression.' Dad took a deep breath and started the engine.

'I always loved your mother,' Mum said, smiling at Dad. 'Do you remember the first time I visited them? She just wrapped me in a hug and loved me. You'd told her I liked chocolate eclairs, and she'd made a batch specially for me. She was always in the kitchen, making food or cups of tea. I'm not surprised that's where your dad thinks she is now.'

Mum looked out of the window for a minute. 'You know what?' she asked, turning back to Dad, 'She never asked me questions about my past either. She only ever wanted to know about now – who I was, what would encourage me, my hopes and dreams... It's like she saw people for who they were. She didn't need to hear their past story and let that affect or colour her impression of someone. She just loved and wanted to build people up.'

'I miss her so much,' Fay whispered, not ashamed of the tears that were falling down her face. She felt her mum's hand reach over and hold hers. No one said anything else for the rest of the journey home.

A village outside Leningrad

'You've been here for three weeks now, another three weeks, and we'll need to think about you going home.'

Vera looked up in surprise, drawn away from her plans with Slavic that evening. 'Home? To Leningrad?'

Babushka laughed, her eyes twinkling, 'Of course, where else would you go? It'll be a busy time in the Ballet, and if you are careful, maybe there'll be some part you can play during the New Year celebrations. Although I don't recommend pointe-work for another couple of months.'

Vera's thoughts went back to the ballet. This would've been her first New Year season. She should have been dancing *The Nutcracker* in front of audiences of eager children, dreaming of one day being on stage. As though reading her mind, Babushka pulled up a stool and joined Vera at the table.

'I remember my first *Nutcracker*,' she smiled.

'You went to see the *Nutcracker*? In the city?' Vera's eyes opened wide.

'Of course! It was before the Revolution. It used to be called the Mariinsky Ballet then, but it was the same building. It took my breath away. I don't think I'll ever forget it. I must say, I felt very proud when your papa wrote and told me you'd be dancing there.'

Vera's mind was racing. She tilted her head and looked at her grandmother.

'But Babushka, before the Revolution, only the richest people in the country went to the ballet. The Revolution meant that the ballet and the opera weren't just the right of the bourgeoisie. If you went to see the Mariinsky Ballet...' Vera struggled to find the right words to say.

'You're not wrong, Granddaughter. My family had money when I was younger. Money, influence and a large house with servants. But unfortunately, like many, my father was on the wrong side of the Revolution. He was sent to Siberia, and Mother and I escaped here.'

'That must've been awful. To go from having everything, to having nothing.' Vera looked at her grandmother, trying to imagine her as a small child, leaving a beautiful big house in the city, and ending up in this small hut, smaller than their room in the *kommunalka*.

'It was harder for my mother than for me. I was too young to remember much about life before. I remember missing my father. My mother had sewn some jewels into my winter coat, and she sold them for this house and piece of land. For a long time, the rest of the village ignored us, until Baba Tonya reached out.'

'How did she do that?'

'Mama got sick. I was only seven years old. We'd been in the village for about two years, and during that time, no one had spoken a kind word to us. They'd thrown rocks and stones, shouted abuse at us. When Mama got sick, I didn't know what to do. I felt so alone.'

Vera reached out and held her grandmother's hand. She knew the helplessness of watching a mother grow sicker and sicker.

'One night, Mama's fever was so high, she called out in pain when I tried to put a cool cloth on her head. I didn't know what to do. I'd never felt so lost. Suddenly, there was a knock at the window. It was Baba Tonya. I'd seen her in the village. She'd never spoken to us, but she had reprimanded the boys who threw stones, so I felt it was safe to let her in. To be honest, I was so frightened for my mother, I'd have let anyone in!'

'And was she able to help?'

'Mother was too sick. She never got better, but thanks to Baba Tonya, her last few days were pain-free and lucid. Baba Tonya promised her she'd look after me and make sure no one took the house from me. And that's what she did. She raised me as her own, teaching me how to look after myself, cook, raise a garden, care for chickens and goats. And slowly the village came round. I owe my life to Baba Tonya, in so many ways.'

Chapter 12

A village outside Leningrad

'Your Babushka tells me I've got three weeks to get you strong enough to dance again. So, let me have a look at that ankle.' Baba Tonya hobbled over to where Vera was sitting. Vera lifted her leg on to the couch, and Baba Tonya felt the ankle, twisting the foot, prodding and asking where it hurt.

'That's healing nicely.' Baba Tonya reached towards the kitchen table and grabbed a small pot she had been stirring. She applied the mixture to Vera's ankle. It felt strange, but Vera had learned over the last month not to complain. As the old lady worked, applying the ointment then bandaging up the foot, she muttered softly under her breath.

Vera waited till she'd finished, then asked the question that'd been burning in her mind since the first day.

'Baba Tonya, what is it you're saying as you work on my ankle?'

The old lady smiled. Clearly, this wasn't the first time she'd been asked.

'Ah, my "spells"? Because everyone knows that's what makes the potions work. Not the herbs, but my magic words.' She lowered herself down onto a stool and slowly rubbed her own leg, wincing slightly. 'No, daughter, it's not spells. But it is powerful words. And although I don't listen to village gossips, they are right when they say the words have more strength than the herbs.' Baba Tonya sat back slightly, looking around the room. 'The truth is, little one, what I am really doing is praying.'

'Praying? To God?' Vera lifted her head and looked at her. She knew that Baba Tonya's words were the foolish old thoughts of an uneducated woman, but they still left her feeling cold. 'Like the priests?' Vera had always wondered about the priests in their flowing garments who worked in Leningrad's beautiful cathedrals. What did they do? Why did the Party leaders go to them for blessing, while telling the rest of the people they were just old fools?

'Yes and no.' Baba gave a small smile. 'Yes, to God, but not at all like the priests.'

'How does it work?'

'We see God all around us, don't we? In the design of nature, the gentleness of dew on a spiderweb, the earth-shaking rumble of thunder, the way food comes up from the little seeds we plant in the ground, and the rivers that give us fish that are good for us and keep us strong. The more time we spend surrounded by nature, the more we have to acknowledge the hand of God.'

Vera nodded slowly, recognising her own change in perspective in the old lady's words.

'Well, the Book of Wisdom teaches us that God made everything, and He designed it so perfectly for us because He loved us so much.'

Vera remembered the words she'd written in the letter she never sent, the one that was stuffed under her mattress.

'When I consider your heavens... what is mankind that you are mindful of them?' she recited.

'Exactly.' Baba Tonya smiled. 'It's good you've been listening. These words are life. A better life than you'll find anywhere else. Nature around us, and the Book of Wisdom, show us a God who cares. When I apply my lotions, I just ask Him to show that same care to the person I am helping.'

'How do you do that? What do you actually say?' Vera leaned forward, her head racing with all these new ideas.

'Ah, sweet one, that is for another day. But what about you? As you think on His care for you, what words come out of your heart in response?'

Vera didn't quite understand what Baba Tonya meant, but before she could answer, the old lady clicked her tongue and signalled to Vera's ankle.

'I've wrapped that up strong enough for you to walk on. You need to take this,' she lifted a small basket from the floor, 'to Slavic's grandmother's neighbour – the one with the tree in front of the house – and tell her Baba Tonya sent it for her daughter. Tell her I'll come tomorrow to check on her, but she needs to drink a mouthful of this tea every fifteen minutes.'

'I need to write this down, Baba Tonya.' Vera looked around for a pencil and paper.

'No, you need to remember. Never write my instructions. You must learn them. Now, repeat the instructions for Olya.'

After repeating the instructions several times, Vera got up slowly and gingerly put weight on her ankle. she was surprised to find that the only discomfort was caused by the tight bandage.

'Try to walk straight, head up,' Baba Tonya called after her as she left the small hut.

It was the first time Vera had walked through the village on her own. Slavic had driven her around, and she was familiar with the layout and where certain people lived. But walking gave her a different perspective. She remembered her grandmother's story of coming to the village as a small child. She tried to imagine what that would feel like to walk those dirty unpaved roadways made of packed mud, after the pavements of St Petersburg (as it had been before it was renamed Leningrad after the Revolution). Had her grandmother found it difficult or frightening? How did she and her mother cope with the poverty and hard work of the village, after the luxury of their previous lives?

Vera didn't have to imagine the hostile glances from the villagers. She was receiving them herself. Babushka had warned her that new people were viewed suspiciously. Apparently, it was different before, much friendlier. But when the village had been overrun in the Nazi invasion, anyone who didn't host the German army was forcibly removed. That's when Baba Tonya had moved in with Babushka and Papa. Because the village was so close to Leningrad, it was watched carefully. The Nazis suspected that the villagers smuggled food into the city but they could never prove it. No one would ever know the sacrifices these simple folk made to get essentials into the city right under the noses of the German army. Babushka told Vera that she'd never meet braver, more courageous people than the ones in that village. But the heroism had come at the cost of their innocence. From then on, everyone new was greeted with a frown and glare. What the Stalinist years had done in the *kommunalki* had been done here in the war years. Vera wondered if there was anywhere in the Soviet Union where strangers were greeted with a genuine smile.

The village was quite spread out. Each house had its own patch of land, and Vera walked for a mile before reaching Slavic's grandmother's house. Leaning on the gatepost for a moment, catching her breath and stretching out her ankle, she noted the house with the tree outside.

Hesitantly, she approached the fence, calling out a greeting before reaching for the gate.

The front door opened, and a lady stepped outside, shutting it behind her. She folded her arms and glared at Vera.

'What do you want?'

'I have some tea for your daughter.'

The woman's eyes narrowed into slits and her knuckles whitened.

'It's from Baba Tonya,' Vera called, wondering what she should do if the woman refused to take it. Hearing Baba Tonya's name, the woman's fists loosened slightly, and she raised her chin.

'Oh, yes? So, who are you?'

'I'm Petrova, Vera Mikhailovna. I am staying with my grandmother...'

Before she could get any further, the woman rushed off the steps, opening her arms wide. Vera stepped back in surprise.

'Mishka's girl? I should've guessed! You're the copy of him. I heard Slavic had been sent to get you from the station, but with such a bad sprain I wasn't expecting to see you walking up my path anytime soon, but then, I shouldn't be surprised if you have your babushka and Baba Tonya looking after you. You'll be back on that stage before you know it. Who'd believe, a daughter of our Mishka's dancing at the Mariinsky? Sorry, the Kirov. I forget sometimes.'

During this unexpectedly long speech, the woman had opened the gate, ushered Vera down the path into her small hut. It was very similar to Babushka's, although the walls were covered in old photographs of people Vera assumed were family members. She wondered why Babushka didn't have any photos in her house.

'I would've loved to have danced, but I reckon that pulling potatoes ruined my posture before I was old enough for classes. But Baba Tonya will fix you up good and proper. Hard to think of Mishka married with such a grown-up daughter. We were in school together. Did he ever mention Olya? Of course not. But then, my own daughter isn't much younger than you, I suppose. How old are you now, sixteen?'

'I'm fifteen, and talking of your daughter, I have some tea from Baba Tonya,' Vera prised the words into the conversation as quickly and politely as she could. She'd never met anyone who spoke as much, or as fast, as this woman.

'Fifteen, yes. My daughter, God have mercy on her, is only fourteen. But she's not a well child. She struggles with so many things, and even as we speak, she's ailing again.'

'Baba Tonya sent this.' Vera pulled the package out of the basket and pressed it into Olya's hands. 'She said she needs to drink a mouthful every fifteen minutes. Baba will come and check on her tomorrow.'

Olya clasped the tea to her chest and lifted her eyes to the ceiling. 'Lord, thank You for Your mercy, for this tea, for

Baba Tonya and for Mishka's daughter here who brought it.'

Vera tilted her head on one side. Something about the simple words was more real than the thankful tidings traditionally uttered by older people upon receiving an unexpected gift. She'd spoken as though talking to a friend.

'Will you stay for some tea?' Olya asked, getting up and moving a kettle from the table to the stove and stoking the fire.

'No, I need to get back or Babushka will be worried. It's the first time I've been out alone, and I wouldn't want them to think I got lost.'

'Here, take this with you,' Olya disappeared for a moment and came back with a small jar of jam. 'The blackcurrants have only just come in, and I know the ladies love my jam. You take that back with my thanks, and when you see your father again, remember Olya to him.'

Vera put the jam into the basket and covered it with the cloth. She thanked Olya and hurried out the door and down the path before the woman could start talking again.

Lincoln

Fay examined the programme, hoping it might give her some clues.

'Dad, how do these names work? It looks like there are three names. The second ones are mostly girls' names, the third ones look like boys' names, and the first ones I haven't figured out yet.'

Dad sat next to her. He pointed at the programme.

'The first one is the surname. You can spot the female dancers because their names end in an "a". The male ones don't.'

'So, this last one, "Voloshina", is a girl and this one, "Kiril", is a boy?'

'Yes, that's right. The second one is their forename or what we would call their first name.'

Fay followed the names across.

'So Voloshina's first name is Elena – a girl, and Kiril's first name is Alexei – a boy. So, what about the third name?'

'That's the patronymic. We don't have that in English, but it's a male or female form of your father's name. The male form usually has "ovich" on the end, and the female form has "ovna".'

'So, I would be Peterson, Fay Michaelovna,' Fay giggled.

'Yes, and I would be Peterson, Michael Arthurovich,' Dad grinned.

'But isn't there a Russian version of Michael?' Fay asked, glancing back at the list.

'Mikhail. So, correctly speaking, you would be Fay Mikhailovna.'

'That's so strange.' Fay looked at the list of names. There were quite a few ending in Mikhailovna. 'Is Mikhail quite popular in Russia?'

'I think so. The nickname is Mishka, and that's quite popular too.'

'Mishka,' Fay grinned. 'That's what Grandad calls you sometimes.'

'Yes, that's what he called me as a boy.'

Fay pointed to one of the names. 'Grandad called me "Vera". There is a Vera here. Do you think that's just a coincidence?'

Chapter 13

Lincoln

'What's with all the serious faces?' Tom walked into the room, taking off his coat.

'You're finished early,' Mum said, glancing at the clock.

'I was in earlier today to cover Sunday lunch. So, I have the evening free. What's going on with these shoes and this tin? Every time I walk in the room, one of you is looking at them.'

'That's what we are trying to figure out.' Dad pulled out a chair. 'Come and join us. We think they might have something to do with Grandad, but we're not sure.'

'With Grandad?' Tom sat down, pulling an apple from the fruit bowl. 'How?'

'That's what we are trying to figure out,' Mum said. 'Let's see what we know already.'

'We know my dad was born in Russia but moved to England at some point. We assume he changed his name to Arthur Peterson, since that isn't a very Russian name,'

Dad said. 'But we don't know why he left or anything about his life or family back there.'

'Except that his father's name was Mikhail – because he named you after him,' Fay added. 'And he knew someone called Vera, who was special to him.'

'Fay found these shoes and this tea tin together in the theatre, so we are assuming they're connected in some way. The fact that there was an old programme from the Kirov Ballet also ties the ballet shoes to the tin.' Mum moved the shoes a little nearer, as though hoping for further inspiration.

'I remember Dad having a similar tin when I was a boy, although no one knows where it is now,' Dad added.

'He said his dad gave it to him, and what it contained was life,' Fay added, remembering her grandad's words.

'But we don't know what exactly. He was always so secretive.' Dad leaned back and blew air out of his mouth.

'So, what's in this one? Apart from the programme?' Tom asked.

Fay opened it and took out the pieces of paper. 'Can you read any of them, Dad?' She pushed them across the table towards him. He picked up one piece, looking at it carefully.

'This one just looks like a shopping list. Flour, salt, sugar.'

'What's on the back? And what does this mean at the bottom?' Fay turned the paper over and pointed to the word clearly written in the bottom corner. 'Bepa. What's Bepa? It's written on all of them.'

Dad looked carefully, slowly picking up other pieces of paper and looking at the bottom. Finally, he looked at Mum, then Fay.

'They seem to be letters, written and signed by the same person.' He pointed to the name on the bottom of each paper.

'So, they were written by Bepa. Do we know who they were to?' Tom tapped his fingers on the table.

'But this is the thing. In English we use the Latin script, ABC and so on. But Russian is written in Cyrillic script. The letters sometimes make different sounds to what they make in our language.'

'That's what I thought when we were looking at the ballet shoe, remember?' Tom asked Fay.

Dad laid one piece of paper in the middle of the table and pointed to the name at the bottom.

'The B here isn't an English B. It actually sounds like our V. And the P letter here makes an R sound. So, the letters weren't written by Bepa...'

Fay's mouth dropped open as Mum finished Dad's sentence.

'They were written by Vera.'

A village outside Leningrad

What happened to Babushka's father? The question buzzed around Vera's head until she finally plucked up the courage to ask Babushka. The older lady was quiet for a very long time.

'Come on, I want to show you something,' she finally said.

They walked into the woods surrounding the village. Although Vera was familiar with the immediate area, she soon became disorientated as they walked deeper through the forest. After about half an hour, Babushka stopped next to a large dead tree, which was hollow inside. She slowly walked round it, dragging her hands across the uneven bark. Finally, she looked at Vera.

'This is where Mama and I slept for the first three nights after our escape from St Petersburg.'

'Inside this tree?' Vera asked, looking inside. An adult and a child could squeeze together in it, but they would have had to sleep standing up.

'But why?'

'We needed to make sure no one had seen us get off the train and followed us here. And we needed to arrive in the village on a different date, so if they were ever asked, we didn't arrive at the same time that father's family disappeared.'

'I don't understand,' Vera said.

Babushka nodded. 'I didn't understand at the time either and I was never able to ask Mother about it. From what I can piece together and remember, Mama and Papa had heard rumours of revolution. There had already been several uprisings in the city, and when Papa heard that Lenin was coming back to Russia, he knew it was time to act. But because of his job, he had to stay in the city. He made plans to smuggle Mama and me out. I remember being woken up in the dark and dressed in horrid scratchy clothes and a big heavy coat that smelled funny. I had to wear old shoes that weren't mine, and that was the bit I was most angry about. I'd always loved my nice shoes. Now I had to wear ugly peasant shoes.'

Vera couldn't help thinking of the twins, and how particular they were about their shoes.

'We were taken to the train station,' Babushka continued. 'Papa paid a man to let us travel in the back with all the cargo. Usually, I enjoyed travelling by train. I loved the little rooms in the carriage, with their soft red seats and the tiny curtains at the window. My favourite part was drinking the hot tea from the special glasses they had on the train. But we didn't get any tea this time, and we weren't in a carriage. We were in a wagon with lots of boxes.'

'Were you and your mother alone there?' Vera asked.

'No, there was another family, some friends of Papa's, I think. But Mama wouldn't let me talk to them, and they never spoke to us. I must have slept on the train because suddenly Mama was shaking me. It was still dark, but a man helped us both off the train, and we ran into the woods. We didn't have a torch, but Mama seemed to know where she was going. We kept walking, and it was very muddy. I remember thinking how glad I was that I wasn't wearing my nice shoes. At least they would be waiting for me when we got home.'

Babushka stopped for a moment. She took a deep breath before continuing. 'We seemed to walk for hours. My feet were hurting in the unfamiliar shoes, but whenever I cried, Mama told me to be quiet. Finally, she told me we were going to get some sleep. I remember looking around and not seeing a house or anything.

'"Where, Mama?" I asked, and mother stepped inside the tree, pulling me in after her. She told me it was a special adventure, and wouldn't we have a lot to tell Papa when he joined us in a few days? We'd come and show him our sleeping tree, and he'd be so amazed we had such a splendid adventure.'

Vera tried to imagine Nadia or Luba trying to sleep inside the tree. A tear fell down her face.

'I remember that first night. I'd never been so afraid. Maybe because I'd dozed on the train, or maybe because my feet hurt so much, I barely slept at all. I heard Mama's deep breathing and knew she was asleep. Her legs relaxed a little and squashed me into the edge of the tree. Then I began to hear the noises of the night. There were lots of them. Noises I'd never heard before. Of course, as a grownup, I now know about nocturnal animals and recognise a badger from a fox or a bear. But imagine a five-year-old child for whom the wildest sound she'd ever heard was the clatter of horseshoes on a cobbled pavement. All my life I'd been told fairy tales of witches that lived in the wood. I honestly thought they were going to get me. I'd never been so terrified.'

Babushka sat down on a small rock and looked around at the trees, as though seeing them through the eyes of a child again. For Vera, this was the first time she'd been so deep in the forest, and she found it easy to identify with her grandmother's words.

After a few minutes, Vera's next question bubbled up inside her and she couldn't keep it in.

'Did you have family or friends in the village? Did your mother tell you where you were going?'

'No, not at all. Mother and father had deliberately chosen a village they had no links to, somewhere they had never been. They didn't want us to be tracked down. Mama told me later that she didn't know how many houses were in the village or whether they'd even be welcome. But they had to leave the city. It turns out, the reason my coat was so heavy was because mother had hidden jewels and money in the lining. She figured that even if they got caught, no one would imagine a little child's thick winter coat would hide anything of value.'

Babushka looked around again.

'We stayed here for three days, living off food that we'd brought with us, drinking rainwater that collected in small hollows, eating any berries that we could find. Finally, Mama decided it was time for us to go to the village.' Babushka held her hand out to Vera, and they slowly walked back together.

'We must've looked a sight when we got there, like real peasants, but as soon as Mother spoke, they knew the truth. They guessed who we were and where we were escaping from, but they never told on us. Although they weren't friendly towards us, not for years, they never betrayed us. And I am forever grateful for that.' Babushka squeezed Vera's hand, and they kept walking.

'And your papa?'

A shadow flickered over Babushka's face.

'Papa never came, although I know he would've tried with every fibre of his being. For a long time, we waited for him, and after Mama passed away, I waited for him. I kept a spare set of men's clothes ready and refused to sell the medal that the Tsar had given him, in case he ever came back. But he never did.'

'A medal?' Vera's voice was breathless. 'From the Tsar himself? Do you still have it?'

Babushka snorted. 'Oh no. Any trinket like that was sold in exchange for food at the time of the Siege. Anything precious we had from before was given up so we could smuggle as much food into the city as we could. We lost a lot of our young men, but we also know we saved many lives.'

Vera's curiosity was peaked. The word 'Siege' hung over the city of Leningrad like a shroud, but there never seemed to be any information for young, curious minds.

'Tell me about the Siege, Babushka?'

'Oh no, my daughter. Such things are too terrible to talk of, too awful to describe, and yet too painful to forget. I never want you to live through such a time. Our hope for you is a better future. We will not burden you with our past.'

Vera nodded and continued to walk. It was the answer she'd always received when asking about the past. She pushed down all her questions and continued walking next to Babushka.

Chapter 14

A village outside Leningrad

'Did you ever find out about *Pra-dedushka*?' Vera asked, using the unfamiliar word meaning great-grandad, as the village came into sight.

Babushka shrugged. 'As much as we'll ever find out. Your papa went to work in the city when he was seventeen. He searched and asked questions, as discreetly as he could. He told me he couldn't find any of the people who had been friends with my father but had found his name on a list of people sent to Siberia. After dedicating his life to Russia and her betterment, I can only assume that he died in a labour camp as an "Enemy of the People".'

Vera gasped and her hand flew to her mouth. No wonder her father mentioned nothing about his family. Imagine the shame if people knew his grandfather was an Enemy of the People. That probably explained why Papa had to work so hard and didn't enjoy the perks of those further up the Party.

Babushka noted Vera's response and shook her head slightly. 'You are your mother's daughter. You share the same fear of that title as she does.'

Vera felt heat rush through her body. 'And you don't?'

Babushka grunted, 'Not at all. Most of the people in this village could be tarred with that brush, and many were under Stalin.'

Vera drew in a breath sharply. Now as she looked around the village, she wondered what treachery lay in the hearts of the people living behind the doors.

'But aren't you afraid?'

Babushka looked her in the eye. 'I think I should ask you - why are you afraid?'

Under her grandmother's kind gaze, Vera found herself transported back to her childhood. Once again, she was a five-year-old, standing on the street outside the Kirov Ballet. She felt again the tremor of fear that had passed through the crowd as the black cars pulled up.

'Anna Igorevna... She was an Enemy of the People.' Vera spoke quietly, but even the noises of the forest seemed to stop upon hearing her words.

'Ah, yes. I remember that,' Babushka said. 'Your Papa wrote and told me how upset you were. I'm not surprised. You were very little, and it sounded awful.' Babushka stroked Vera's hair. 'Were you very afraid?'

'I didn't really understand what was happening.' Vera said, choking on her words. 'I just remember thinking she must have done something so bad to be called an Enemy of the People. Imagine preparing to dance on the stage, and then, suddenly, you're taken away in a black car. Everyone is watching you, but for all the wrong reasons. I can't think of anything worse. I don't even know what she did.'

Babushka took a deep breath. 'Sometimes news reaches us, even here in the village. We heard about Anna Igorevna. So sad. We spent a long time praying for her, after hearing about her arrest. Apparently, she was released two years later, after the death of Stalin. I don't know if you remember, but most of the gulags were closed, and many people were released. She was one of them. From what I heard, she moved to Moscow and is still involved in ballet, although now she mainly teaches.'

'But what did she do?' Vera asked. 'What could a ballerina do that was so bad it made her an Enemy of the People?'

The old lady sighed, glancing at Vera. 'She was a believer, although she tried to keep her faith a secret. But even the esteemed Kirov Ballet could not save her from the paranoia of Stalin's rule.'

'A believer? What's that?' Vera tilted her head on one side.

'Someone who believes in God.'

'But there is no God.' The words Vera had memorised since childhood slipped out. Babushka smiled and raised an eyebrow.

'Can you truthfully say that, little one? Are you really able to look at the nature surrounding us and say that you don't see the hand of a Master Creator?'

'Well, er, I suppose,' Vera glanced around, as though expecting a rational response to hit her out of the blue. 'But I've always been taught that there is no God.'

'Yes,' Babushka's eyes sparkled. 'I've always wondered, if there *really* wasn't a God, why do children have to spend so much time and energy repeating it. You don't spend the same energy declaring that fairies in the woods aren't real, do you?'

Vera giggled a little. 'No.'

'You don't spend time every day in class, proclaiming that there are no talking animals, do you?'

Vera laughed out loud.

'So, why spend so much time trying to convince yourselves there is no God?' Babushka said. 'It reminds me of a little child trying to convince themselves and their parents that they aren't tired, when everyone can see that they are.'

Vera smiled, knowing how much the twins complained about not being tired when they were exhausted. 'I'd never thought of it like that.'

Babushka nodded, watching Vera out of the corner of her eye. 'I'd say, before you arrived here, you'd never really thought about God at all.'

Vera frowned, hearing her grandmother's words, but as they slowly return home, she realised she was speaking the truth.

Lincoln

Fay, Tom and Mum sat silently at the table, while Dad slowly read.

My dear family!
There's so much I desire to tell you. I'm just back home from a walk with Slavic. He is so wise and understanding. He reminds me of you, Papa. He doesn't talk much to other people, but when we are alone together, we talk for hours and hours. I am learning so much about nature and life here in the village. I've also been learning about our family.

It turns out our family has not always been poor. Babushka told me about her parents. Her father was very important – he even had a medal from the Tsar. They had a lot of money and a very big house – but that was before the Revolution. I don't know how to feel about it. On one side I feel proud, but on the other hand, Great-grandfather was sent off to Siberia as an Enemy of the People and that is an embarrassment to our family. Papa, is that why you've never mentioned it? Mama, did you know about this? Is this why you've never wanted us to go out to the village?

I'd love to see the house where they used to live. Can you imagine? But Babushka was only five when she left and says she can't remember where it is. I told her that Nadia and Luba both know where we live; they can find their way home from the market. But Babushka said that nothing could be gained by me seeing the house. It would only make me ungrateful for the home we have. Babushka said she had more happiness in this little hut than she ever had in that huge house. But it makes me curious. What other secrets are our family hiding? What did my great-grandfather do wrong? I wonder if I'll ever find out.

I miss you, but you'll never receive this letter.
Vera.

For a few minutes, there was silence. The family stared at the letter, trying to understand the implication of the words.

'What's an Enemy of the People, and what is Siberia?' Fay finally asked.

'Siberia's not a what, it's a where,' Dad explained. 'Russia is an immense country that spans Europe and Asia. Siberia is in the Asian part, quite far north. It's a vast expanse of land and ice, and during the first half of the twentieth century, the government had concentration camps – called gulags – there, and that's where they sent anyone who disagreed with them.'

'But wouldn't that be really cold?' Fay grimaced at the thought.

'It was, and many died. People lived in fear of their neighbours telling on them or lying about them. When Stalin ruled the Soviet Union from 1922 to 1952, it was known as "the reign of terror". It wasn't just criminals and troublemakers who were sent to the gulags, it was teachers, professors, intellectuals, even religious people. Anyone could be accused of being an Enemy of the People or a traitor to the Motherland. Everyone lived in fear of the "Knock" at the door and a loved one being taken away.'

Fay felt her body go cold. 'So, you, as a pastor, would've been sent away.'

'Yes, and you, as my family, would've been viewed with suspicion by the neighbours.'

'Could that have been what your father meant when he said, "the walls had ears"?' Mum asked.

Dad scratched his chin for a minute, squinting his eyes as though thinking very hard.

'Dad was born in 1949, which was just before Stalin died. So, although he wouldn't have remembered that necessarily, the terror would've permeated every part of his younger life. That would explain why speaking Russian upsets him so much. It would remind him of such overwhelming fear.'

Fay felt a shiver run down her spine.

Chapter 15

A village outside Leningrad

'Do you *really* believe in God?' Vera asked as she and Slavic walked towards the lake. Their sunset walks had become the highlight of Vera's day.

'Of course, don't you?' Slavic flicked his hair off his face. His hand brushed against hers as they walked.

'I don't know. I hadn't really thought about God before coming here.' They walked side by side on the narrow trail through the forest. 'It's different in the city. I suppose I was different, too. When you are here, it's hard *not* to imagine a God who creates things and cares for us. But in the city, life is too busy. There isn't time to think about such things. Even the parks and the open spaces are designed by people. It's as though the city is built to stop us thinking about God.'

Slavic walked next to her without talking. Vera wasn't put off by his silence. In some ways, it reminded her of her father.

A tree had fallen across the path in front of them. Slavic reached out his hand to help her. On the other side, he didn't let go, and Vera felt warm inside as they continued to walk.

They had become close over the previous month, and Vera had often wondered if they could be more than friends. She'd never found anyone she could share her heart with so easily, besides Artyom. She and Slavic had watched so many sunsets over the lake, and despite his quiet ways, Vera found him easy to talk to.

Initially Vera had talked about Leningrad and the Ballet, but the more she appreciated the slower pace of life, the natural beauty all around them, the way the world changed as the season progressed, the more she'd listened, and the more Slavic had spoken. He explained to her how the land would lie dormant over winter, often covered with several feet of snow. He described the first awakenings of spring, from the quiet drip of the melting icicles on the roofs of the houses, to the slightly warmer winds that thawed the ice. He talked about how the birds' songs changed and the tracks of smaller animals in the melting snow showed that the long hibernation was ending.

'What are your plans for the future?'

Vera jumped slightly as his words disturbed her musing. 'What do you mean? I plan to go back to the Ballet and dance.'

'But after that? Maybe in a couple of years?' Slavic looked at her carefully, and Vera realised they had stopped walking.

'I don't know. I honestly hadn't thought about it. I suppose I'd always imagined I'd have a similar life to my mother's. Taking my children to their first *Nutcracker*, walking down Nevsky Prospect in the Midnight Sun. I don't think I ever considered anything different.' Vera stumbled on her words as Slavic let go of her hand. She looked up at him, her stomach churning, as she watched him scan the horizon.

'And is that still what you want? Even now?'

'I'm not sure.' Vera closed her eyes and took a deep breath. 'It's not like I have much choice or say in the matter. Mother and Father married each other because they were advised it would be good for the Motherland. I suppose I was waiting for someone else to make those decisions for me. I haven't allowed myself to have any dreams. I dance at the Ballet because my mother wanted me to. I am here because my father arranged it. I don't have a choice over those things.'

'So, you would just allow others to control your life? Like a good Pioneer? A good little Communist?' Slavic spat out the word.

'What else am I supposed to do?' Vera looked at Slavic with wide eyes. A muscle twitched in his jaw.

'Live the life you were destined to live, Vera.' Slavic turned to face her, taking both her hands in his. 'Have

119

faith! Dare to believe that God has a better plan for your life, a greater adventure, beyond what you could ever imagine.'

Vera felt tears well up and struggled to catch her breath.

'I don't know how,' she whispered. She stared into his deep brown eyes. Could she believe like he did? Was she able to let go of the familiarity of her plans and chase a God she was only just beginning to believe in?

'I'm scared of adventures. I don't have the same faith you do. I'm sorry,' she muttered.

Vera watched Slavic's shoulders drop. He let her go, dragging his hands through his hair as he straightened up and looked around.

'We need to hurry back,' he said. 'It looks like there's a storm brewing.'

Vera looked around in surprise. Nothing in the sky or the air around them felt like a storm. Slavic turned and began to walk back to the village, pushing his hands deep into his pockets, his shoulders hunched. Vera struggled to catch up with him, tripping over small twigs in the path.

'Please, wait,' she gasped as she reached the log that blocked the track.

Slavic slowed down and turned. Seeing her struggle, he returned and held her elbow as she climbed over the obstacle. He stayed at her side as they continued to walk, although he maintained a gap of a few centimetres. That small space was enough to allow cold air between them.

And that cold air seemed to wrap around Vera's heart. She tried to catch his eye, but he seemed intent on something up ahead, although she couldn't see anything worth looking at.

The distance between them remained as they walked back to the village. Their friendly closeness seemed to have disappeared, replaced by an uncomfortable silence.

'Will I see you tomorrow?' Vera asked when they reached Babushka's gate.

'No, I don't think so.' Slavic avoided her gaze, looking anywhere except at her. With her stomach in knots, Vera reached out and rested her hand on his, on top of the gate. He looked at her then, his brown eyes filled with a sadness that took her breath away. Without saying a word, he turned and left. She watched him walk down the road. He never once looked back.

Lincoln

'Can you read another letter, Dad?' Tom asked, picking a piece of paper out of the tin.

Dad took the paper and started reading.

My dearest family!
Another letter I'll never send to you, but I had a nightmare last night. I was waiting to perform at the Kirov. It was my first performance as a prima ballerina, and the whole family had come to watch. Just as I was putting my make-

up on, men in dark coats burst into my room and grabbed me. They took me out of the ballet and pushed me into a car. Everyone in the street began shouting, 'Enemy of the People, Enemy of the People.' I saw you all in the crowd, and you were shouting too. You were all shouting about me – an Enemy of the People.

I woke up sweating. I am filled with fear that somehow, when I return to Leningrad, Village Vera might pop out and I'll be exposed as an Enemy of the People, just for having been in a house with someone who believes in God and prays. I don't know what to do. I understand why Babushka and Baba Tonya believe what they do, but it's all still so new to me. Can I be an Enemy of the People just for staying with them?

Vera.

'So, Vera's family were believers. Do you think Grandad's were too?' Fay asked.

'It's possible,' Mum shook her head, 'But that doesn't necessarily mean there is a connection.'

'Your mum's right,' Dad chipped in. 'Vera and Mikhail were both popular names in the Soviet Union.'

'But don't forget the tin. You said your dad had one just like it,' Fay pointed out.

'Yes, but maybe that was common too, like the tins we used to get sweets in as a kid. Maybe every home had these tea tins,' Dad suggested.

122

Fay picked up the tin and examined it, carefully removing all the pieces of paper until only the metal bottom remained.

'Grandad said his tin contained life. What could that mean?' she wondered out loud. 'What do you think would happen if we took this with us when we went to see Grandad? Would he recognise it and tell us about his?' Fay looked up at her parents.

'I'm not sure,' Mum said. 'What if seeing it upsets him again, or confuses him further? I just don't think it's worth it.'

'I don't honestly know,' Dad said. 'It may be our only chance to find out if this tin and this Vera are in any way connected to Dad's tin and Dad's Vera. He may take one look at it and say it isn't anything like his.' He paused for a moment, drumming his fingers on the table. 'Why don't we take it in next time we go to see him, but maybe keep it in a bag and only bring it out if we feel he'll be able to handle it?'

Fay nodded. 'That sounds like a plan. I can't wait till next Sunday!'

Chapter 16

Lincoln

'Grab your coat, we're off out!' Tom's head popped into the room.

'I've only just got in. Where are we going?' Fay dragged herself off the sofa, weary after a long day of running back and forth to the cupboard.

'I start work in an hour. Thought you could walk me up the hill. You look like you need the fresh air.'

Knowing it was pointless arguing with her brother, she pulled on her coat and followed him out of the door. It was a pleasant evening and would still be light until around eight o'clock.

'I went to see Grandad this week.' Tom started talking as soon as she caught up with him.

'Did he recognise you?'

'Kind of. But it was like he remembered me several years ago. Remember how he and Granny Wendy prayed for me when I was doing my GCSE's? It seemed like

Grandad was stuck back then. He was asking how the exams had gone and was I happy with what I'd chosen to take next year? I mentioned I was at uni, but he looked confused for a moment, then shook his head, and kept talking about the exams. I hadn't realised he was so muddled.'

'To be honest, that sounds like a good visit. When we went last Sunday, we didn't know any of us. He thought Dad was the pastor, and he called me "Vera", it was really sad.'

They walked in silence for a few minutes. Once they were over the steepest part of the hill, Fay resumed the conversation.

'I guess Grandad didn't remember that you are working in a pub. You managed to get away with that.'

Tom shrugged. 'It's no big deal. If I'm being honest, I feel more aware of God now, working in a pub, than I ever did when I lived at home and went to church every Sunday.'

'What do you mean?'

'When I went to uni, it was difficult at first. I had to discover my faith for myself. I couldn't just go along with our parents and their views. I had to ask myself, is God real, and if He is, what does that mean for me?'

Fay had never heard Tom speak so openly about his own faith.

'Until then, I think I was just doing the church thing because that's what our family did,' he continued. It didn't offend me, but neither did I own it. Being away from home made me question what I really believed for myself. I looked into it more, studied what Jesus actually said, and what it meant to the people who heard him.'

'And what did you decide? Did you have a revelation moment?'

'Not a revelation, no. Just a deepening realisation that this made sense, and life without God somehow didn't.'

Fay nodded and started walking again. 'I guess I'm happy you've found some sense of reason or purpose in it. But for me, it still feels distant, like Mum and Dad have been invited to a party and I didn't get an invitation. I'm just there because there was no other option. I don't see what it has to do with me. Does that make sense?'

Tom dug his hands in his pockets. 'Would you be offended if I said I was praying for you?'

'I guess that if you believe it, and want to pray for me, if nothing else, it's a sign that you care for me. I can accept that without getting upset about it. But it doesn't stop me thinking maybe you're a little deluded. Anyway, tell me about uni? Is it really everything you'd hoped it to be?'

'I'm enjoying being away from home, and lectures aren't that stressful. It's certainly easier than the last two years of school. Are you thinking of going? You've never said much about it.'

'Still trying to decide. But I do know that I don't want to end up spending my summers working in a pub!' Fay grinned as Tom's workplace came into view.

A village outside Leningrad

Vera didn't sleep well. She got up early, eager to rebuild the friendship with Slavic. After breakfast, she asked her grandmother if she could make a cake to take to him.

Babushka stared at her for a moment.

'But he's gone already,' she said, when her voice returned.

'Gone? Gone where?' Vera asked, her heart drumming in her chest.

'He's gone to the army. Like all young men do. He was given special leave to stay and help his grandmother through the harvest, but now he's starting his two-year conscription. Didn't he tell you?'

Vera shook her head slowly. 'But why didn't he say anything? Why wasn't there a party or a big send off?'

'We wanted one,' Babushka came and sat next to Vera. 'But he said he just wanted a quiet evening with you by the lake. Didn't he ask you something important? Something about the future?'

Vera shook her head slightly. 'He asked about my plans, but I... I didn't know...'

Babushka patted her hand and waited until she continued.

'We argued. He asked me to believe in God, in His plans for us, but I couldn't promise. I don't believe like he does.' The words came tumbling out. Vera found her eyes filling up with tears and her throat closing as though she'd eaten cotton. 'He was really quiet and refused to talk to me after that. I didn't know he was going away.' Vera stared at the table through her tears.

'Would your answer have been different if you'd known?' Babushka pulled her into a hug.

'I don't know, but I wouldn't have let him leave thinking I don't care. He didn't even say goodbye.' Vera's body shook, and her grandmother held her as she grieved for the closest friendship she'd ever had.

Chapter 17

A village outside Leningrad

Vera's ankle was getting stronger, although every day in the village seemed to drag without her evening walks to look forward to. Every morning, after listening to Babushka read from the Book of Wisdom, Baba Tonya would instruct her in exercises to help strengthen her ankle. Despite the nasty sprain, Baba Tonya was sure that the ankle would eventually be stronger than before.

'Does that mean I'll get my place back in the Ballet? I was the second head of the chorus. It was my job to lead everyone on stage and make sure we all reached the right positions.' Vera noticed the two ladies exchange a glance.

'And who's doing that now? While you're away?' Babushka asked.

'Irina Andreevna.'

'Is that the girl who put the oil on the stage for you to fall on?'

Vera nodded.

'And she was never punished, but given your place instead?' Babushka continued.

'Masha and Katya said that her father was quite high up in the Party.'

Babushka shrugged. 'Then, no, I don't think you'll get your place back.'

'But Nadezhda Vladimirovna said that I have natural talent.' Vera's voice wobbled.

'But sweet one, even natural talent is no weapon when you're fighting against the Communist Party. Remember Anna Igorevna?'

Vera's head snapped back as though her grandmother had slapped her.

'But I'm not an Enemy of the People!'

'That title isn't used so much anymore. But you've been staying with us for the last month or so, and certainly our village is not good at toeing the Party line. We have always been viewed with suspicion by those in the city.'

'So, I'm never going to be anything in the Ballet? I'll never get to dance solo or even have my chance to perform as a prima ballerina?'

'I didn't say that,' Babushka spoke gently. 'Your instructor says you have talent. You have shown us you have determination and strength. You could be everything you dreamed of, but you won't get back the position that Irina has taken from you. Your path will be different from the one you planned.'

'Why don't you take a walk to the station and see if there is any mail for us?' Baba Tonya asked, pushing herself up from the stool. 'We must be due a letter from that brother of yours soon.'

Vera smiled. A letter from Artyom was exactly what she needed right now.

'I've come for the post,' Vera said to the stationmaster, pushing the door shut against the wind that was picking up outside.

'Of course you have,' the old man's eyes twinkled, 'and you'll be glad you did. There's one here for your grandmother from your father.'

Vera frowned, wondering what had prevented Artyom from writing.

'And there's one for you from your young man. That'll wipe that frown off your face.'

'My young man?' Vera repeated, her voice wobbling slightly.

The stationmaster handed her a small bundle of letters. On top was one to her, on regulation paper, with Slavic's name and a return address clearly written in the top left-hand corner. She clasped the letter to her chest, hoping it contained an invitation to pick up their friendship where they'd left it in the forest ten days before.

'Well, I can see that has warmed you through, but you'll need to hurry back. That storm won't wait for you to be home.'

She quickly flicked through the other letters, making a mental note of the route she'd need to take home in order to deliver the rest of the mail to the villagers. Tucking the letters into the inside pocket of her coat, Vera thanked the stationmaster and headed back out into the gathering gloom.

The rain started the moment Vera stepped out of the station. Fortunately, the wind was now behind her, and although the rain whipped her skirt around her legs, it wasn't blowing into her face. The letters for her and Babushka seemed to burn a hole in her pocket as she walked. She was convinced one was good news, but the other, she worried, wasn't.

She carefully avoided thinking about Slavic's letter. The fact he'd written to her and now she could write back was enough for her heart to jump. Their friendship could continue, and she could arrange a time to see him again when he had breaks. She refused to entertain the fear that skipped around the edges of her mind. The Soviet Army conscripted all young men to serve for a minimum of two years. They left their families as young boys at ease with themselves and their neighbours, but often returned hardened men, unable to speak of what they had seen and experienced, a silence that quickly found comfort in a bottle of home-made brew. But that wouldn't happen to Slavic. It obviously hadn't happened to her own father. So, she needn't worry. Maybe Papa could write to Slavic and encourage him during his conscription.

At the thought of her father writing, she almost stumbled. Why had he written to them? Why hadn't Artyom? Maybe it was nothing. Maybe Papa had slightly more time. She knew he'd been working double shifts to cover all the extra expenses caused by her accident and trip here. Maybe things had calmed down, they had paid everything back, and he now had time to write again. Maybe that was all it was. Even so, she couldn't fight the feeling that something was wrong.

Desperate to get home, Vera stood on her tiptoes, testing out her ankle. It was much quicker dancing home than walking. She tried a few strides, and small jumps and spins and a few more long strides. Hearing the music strike up in her head, she tentatively joined the dance.

Lincoln

Sundays had fallen into a comfortable rhythm. Fay usually slept in while her parents went to church. She'd get up when she heard Tom moving about, and they'd have breakfast together before he headed off to work.

By the time her parents came back, Fay had a light lunch ready for them and after that, they went to visit Grandad. There was always an unspoken anticipation buzzing around the car. How would Grandad be today? Would he remember them? Would he remember anything? Fay knew her mum and dad were praying on that car journey, and for once, she understood why.

'Do you have the tea tin?' Mum asked as they pulled into the car park.

'It's here.' Fay patted the tote bag on her knee.

'What's the plan?' Dad asked, glancing at Fay in the rear-view mirror. Fay shrugged and looked at Mum, who always seemed to have everything planned out.

'I think we'll see how he is, and then, maybe while he is distracted, why not put the tin down on a table or the sideboard? Not so it's obvious, but just there, maybe even a bit away from Grandad. He may just ignore it, or he may not. But let's not ask him outright. Just have it on the side. That way, hopefully it won't upset or challenge him.'

Fay found her heart was hammering in her chest as they walked in. The manager smiled as she saw them approach.

'Ah, Pastor Peterson. I'm glad you are here. Several of the residents have been asking if you'd be coming today. They are waiting for you in the lounge. I know you want to spend time with your father, but it really lifts their week when you do a short service. Maybe we can talk about making it a regular thing; maybe having it in the diary officially?'

'I'd be happy to. We'll pop and see Dad, and then start the service in half an hour. I'll make an appointment to see you later this week.'

'Excellent. I'll make sure everyone is gathered. I think your dad is in his room.'

'Afternoon, Arthur!' Mum walked in with a smile and kissed Grandad on the cheek. He sat in his chair, looking down at his knees, but hearing her greeting, he lifted his head and smiled.

'Lisa, looking lovely as ever,' he said, pushing himself to his feet and greeting Dad with an outstretched hand.

'Michael, you're a lucky man, my son!'

Fay beamed at the familiar greeting that had become part of their family folklore. The familiar phrases she'd heard repeated every week in her childhood were a balm to her soul and, looking at the genuine smiles on her parents' faces, she knew they felt the same way.

'Beautiful Faith! The delight of her grandad's life. How are you, my dearest one?'

The smiles fell from Mum and Dad's faces, and Mum flinched.

'Arthur, do you remember? She prefers to be called Fay now.' Mum leaned forward and touched Grandad's arm.

Fay shook her head, trying to communicate with Mum that it wasn't worth upsetting Grandad over this. Before Grandad's mind had become confused, they'd had angry arguments about her birth name. Fay blushed, feeling shame at her previous selfishness.

'But why?' Grandad looked up at Fay, who was a couple of inches taller than him. 'Why would you change your beautiful name?' His eyes filled with tears, and he reached backwards for the chair, lowering himself into it, and settling his gaze on his knees again.

Fay looked at her parents. Mum shrugged.

'Mum said you gave me my name,' Fay squatted down in front of her grandad, determined to bring him back from the sad place he'd retreated to in his mind. 'Why did you call me "Faith"? It's not a popular name.'

Grandad choked on a bitter laugh. 'Who said that popular is always good? Haven't you heard the phrase "Fools bandy together"? No, I suggested it because it was the name of the sweetest person I knew.' Fay was aware of her dad's sharp intake of breath, but she ignored him, concentrating on her grandfather's words. 'And because it is a name that speaks truth, even when everyone around is speaking lies. Just because something is popular doesn't make it right. It doesn't make it good for us. I wanted you to know who you were, no matter what box the world tried to force you into. Faith. It's not just a name, it's the promise of your destiny. Never lose that, my girl. Don't let the words of others steal that away from you.'

Fay could feel her face getting redder and her skin prickled. She needed to process everything Grandad was saying but felt stifled by the number of people in the small room.

'It's a lovely day, Arthur.' Mum said, looking out the window. 'Would you mind showing us the garden before the Sunday service?'

Grandad smiled at Fay, patting her hand, before looking up at Mum. 'That sounds like a good idea. Can you pass me my coat?'

Dad reached for the coat on the back of the door. Fay noticed his face was pale.

Fay tilted her head on one side and raised her eyebrows. Her dad gave the tiniest shake of his head, and Fay knew that whatever it was could wait. He quickly glanced at the tote bag under her arm and shook his head again, slightly more fervently this time. For whatever reason, her dad felt that today wasn't the right day to show Grandad the tin.

Chapter 18

Lincoln

'Thank you for another lovely service, Pastor. I look forward to talking more later in the week.'

'Yes,' Dad smiled at the manager. 'I'll give you a call. I know these services are helping my dad, and if they are beneficial for others, we should get something in the diary.'

'Arthur is doing better. Even the bad weeks are slightly better than before. He is still confused but doesn't seem as frightened.'

'Can I ask a quick question?' Dad beckoned Fay over and quickly pointed to her bag. 'Have you or your staff ever seen a tin like this in Dad's room?' Fay held up the tea tin.

The manager looked at it carefully before shaking her head with a frown.

'Not that I remember. Certainly, it isn't out in his room, and we are not in the habit of snooping through our residents' things, Pastor Peterson.'

Fay raised her eyebrows at the slight reprimand in the manager's voice. She turned away quickly, hiding a grin as she climbed into the car.

'I think Dad is getting a telling off,' Fay whispered to Mum, as they both watched Dad say goodbye to the manager and jog over to the car.

Dad opened the car door, climbed into the seat, and leaned over, resting his head on the steering wheel.

'Was it that bad, Dad? Did she really have a go at you?'

Dad took a few deep breaths before looking up at Fay.

'Who? Sorry, what?' he asked.

'The manager. She didn't seem too impressed.'

Dad looked back across the empty car park. 'I wasn't really listening to her.'

'Then what's wrong?' Fay asked, concerned that her dad's face was still quite pale.

Mum reached over and gently rubbed his shoulders. 'You didn't seem yourself in the service.'

Dad turned to her. 'Was it that obvious?' He gave a deep sigh.

'Only to me,' Mum said. 'Let's swap places. You aren't fit to drive right now.'

Fay watched her parents get out of the car. As they passed each other, Mum pulled Dad into a hug.

'Dad, what's wrong?' Fay asked as they got back into the car. She ignored the annoyed look her mum shot her. But Dad hadn't heard her question.

'If only I knew more. If only there was a way to find out what really happened. I feel so helpless.' Dad ran his hand through his hair, and Mum gently squeezed his knee before starting the car.

Instead of driving home, Mum drove out of the city. Fay didn't ask where they were going as they drove along the familiar roads. After a few miles, they pulled into a village and stopped outside an old council house.

Fay had been here every week in her childhood. Even now, she could practically taste Granny Wendy's cooking, and hear the familiar whistle of the kettle on the stove. Mum and Dad had brought her an electric kettle, but it took her years to get round to using it. She said the whistle always kept her singing in tune.

For a while, no one in the car spoke, each lost in their own thoughts.

'I just don't know why I didn't put the two together earlier.' Dad shook his head. 'If only I'd noticed when he first said it – I could've asked, and it wouldn't have frightened him.'

'But we did ask, don't you remember?' Mum spoke softly. 'He just told us to trust him and some things we didn't need to know.'

'Know what? Ask what? What are you two talking about? You're scaring me now.'

Mum and Dad looked at each other for a long moment. Fay thought back through the day, trying to remember where it all went wrong.

'Is this something about my name?' Fay watched her dad swallow. 'What did Grandad say? That I was named after someone he knew – someone sweet. Did he know someone called Faith, Dad?' Fay ran through all the possibilities in her head and then one sprung to mind.

'Do you think he had an affair with someone called Faith?' Fay shook her head, struggling to believe the words that had just come out of her mouth. 'Poor Granny Wendy.'

'No, Fay. Of all the options open to us, that one we can safely rule out. Your grandad adored his wife.' Mum's voice was firm.

'You know my dad is from Russia?'

Fay tried not to roll her eyes at the question, keeping her response to a curt nod.

'Well, Faith was a popular Russian name, even in the Soviet Union.'

Fay screwed up her nose. 'It doesn't sound very Russian.'

Dad took a deep breath. 'The Russian version is the name "Vera".'

A village outside Leningrad

Vera's hand shook as she held out the letter to Babushka. She could see her own confusion echoed in her grandmother's frown. She looked at the address, and then back at Vera.

'Why is it addressed to me? Not to you?' She looked over at Baba Tonya, who held Babushka's gaze, and gave a slight shrug. Vera wasn't sure what was communicated between the two women, but Babushka sat down heavily, looking at the envelope. 'Oh,' she said, as though someone had just answered her question.

'Do you think something has happened? Maybe to Artyom?'

'Oh no, daughter. Not at all. Your family is safe.' Babushka gave a weak smile.

'How do you know? You haven't even opened it.'

'Old village secrets!'

'I don't understand,' Vera said, glancing between the women.

'Back in the day, we couldn't trust the mail. Our letters were often opened, and parts removed or crossed out. Once the whole letter was removed, and all I got was the envelope. So, we began to use the envelope to give all the important information. If ever we were just shown the envelope, we'd know everything important, even if the long-awaited letter was never opened or read.'

Vera didn't ask who would be so cruel as to remove the letters. Often their own letters arrived opened, and sometimes with a line or name inked out. Babushka studied the envelope.

'Everyone is well,' she announced, pointing to a small selection of dots in the top left-hand corner, that looked

142

like it was part of the address. Two on top, then four underneath. 'But look at the stamp.'

Vera looked but couldn't see anything out of the ordinary.

'It's not straight,' Babushka pointed out.

Vera squinted and looked carefully. She saw that the top of the stamp was slightly further right than the bottom. 'What does that mean?' she asked.

'Rumours,' Babushka sighed.

Baba Tonya clicked her teeth. 'It never stops,' she muttered, resting her hand lightly on Babushka's shoulder, as she got up and hobbled out into the garden.

'Rumours?' Vera was confused. 'Is someone telling lies about us?'

'It isn't lies. It's the truth that has somehow got out.'

'The truth?' Vera echoed.

'Look, the stamp slants to the right. It means the rumours are true. If it'd slanted to the left, it would've meant they were false rumours.'

Vera crossed her arms. 'I don't understand, Babushka. I'm so confused.'

Her grandmother took one last long look at the envelope, then moved the kettle to the stove. She pottered around the kitchen, making a new pot of tea and something to eat. She sliced some bread and put a jar of homemade jam on the table. Vera recognised it as the jar Olya had given her. She'd learned not to interrupt Babushka in the kitchen or offer to help. If she needed help, she'd ask for it. This was Babushka's time to think and process. She would be ready to talk by the time she sat down.

After taking much longer than usual to prepare such a simple meal, Babushka sat down, and raising her eyes, said,

'For these Your generous gifts, we are grateful.'

At first, this blessing over the food had been strange to Vera, but now it was comforting, and she found she was grateful for the simple meal before her. But she wasn't prepared for what her grandmother said next.

'You need to go home.'

'I'm going back in just over a week.'

'No, you will go tomorrow.' Babushka's voice told her there was no room for argument. Finally, she turned and looked at Vera. 'My sweet one,' she said, stroking Vera's hair, as tears welled up in her eyes. 'You know the suspicion that our village has always been under. Those in the city wonder how we survived the Nazi's scorched-earth policy. They accuse us of treason, not knowing that so many from this village gave their lives as part of the essential flow of food smuggled into Leningrad during the Siege. The only way this village could survive was to lie to both sides, and we did such a good job that our own countrymen still view us as the enemy.'

Vera found it hard to imagine. To be accused of collaborating with the enemy, when really you were using those relationships to serve your own people.

'Your mother feels that the only way for you and your brothers and sisters to get ahead in this world is to totally hide your connection with this village.' Babushka shook her head. 'That is why you have never spent summers out here, preferring to stay in the mosquito-infested city rather than run around in the fresh air, choosing the confinement of one room in a *kommunalka* to the freedom of the forests and the lake.

'Obviously, word of where you are staying has got out, not in a good way. Possibly, people have been keeping track of the mail, or maybe the children have spoken carelessly amongst their friends.'

Vera sat up, riled by the accusation.

'I'm not blaming them. It's perfectly understandable. They are children. Of course, they want to talk. All this secrecy is unnatural. *The walls have ears* – it just breeds fear and distrust. It isn't right to live with such fear.'

'So, people are talking, but if my name is connected with this village, could it damage my place in the Ballet?'

'Yes, and Artyom's military conscription. He may not have the easiest time if he has connections with this place.'

Vera pulled out the final envelope.

'Speaking of military conscription, I got a letter from Slavic.'

Her grandmother put down her piece of bread. Wiped her hands on her apron and took the envelope. She examined the front and back carefully, her face broadening into a smile.

'I know we've just sat down to eat, but you need to run and show this to Slavic's grandmother right now. OK? You don't need to share the inside, just the envelope.'

Vera got up, quickly pulled on her damp coat and boots, and putting the envelope safely in her inside pocket, she dashed to Slavic's grandmother's house, wondering how someone as normal as Papa could come from such a peculiar village.

Chapter 19

A village outside Leningrad

After showing Slavic's grandmother the envelope and seeing her face break into a smile, Vera stepped into the garden with the tree, to say goodbye to Olya.

'So, you'll be leaving us soon. When do you go?' Olya's greeting surprised Vera. How did people in the village know her news before she did? Slavic's grandmother had also said a tearful farewell, wishing joy on her and her children.

'Tomorrow,' Vera answered. Olya nodded. For a moment, there was silence. 'How is your daughter?' Vera remembered the tea she'd brought for her before.

'Much better. If you were staying longer, I'm sure she would've enjoyed the chance to visit with you. But you are away, as folks usually are. Remember me to your father. We were good friends. Pity to see you leave, but it's not surprising. I didn't think you'd be here long after Slavic left. But maybe you'll be back.' Olya winked and smiled, making Vera wonder exactly what people in the village thought her relationship was with the young man.

Suddenly remembering that until she opened the letter, *she* didn't know what her relationship was with Slavic, Vera politely excused herself and ran back home.

Back in the warmth of the kitchen, she finished her meal, cleaned the kitchen thoroughly, and finally sat down with her letter.

Dear Vera,
I'm sorry I left without saying goodbye. That was wrong of me. There is so much I want to say to you, but not in a letter. May I see you when I am on leave?
With love,
Slavic.

Vera didn't know if she was delighted with the letter, or disappointed with its brevity. Reading again, she realised that even a longer letter couldn't have expressed Slavic's thoughts any more clearly.

As she was reading, Babushka came in. She'd been outside and carried the cold in with her. Vera hurried to move the kettle onto the stove to make her a drink, while she took off her boots and coat.

'Happy with your letter?' Babushka asked as she settled down with the hot tea Vera had made her.

Vera nodded.

'What did you find so amusing about the envelope? Slavic's grandmother seemed unusually happy with it too.'

Babushka turned the envelope over and pointed to the address. 'He misspelt the village name, but it still got here.'

Vera pointed to the numbers after it. 'Doesn't the post rely on these numbers to get it to the right place?'

'Yes, it does, but those numbers mean nothing to ordinary people. They just recognise names of villages. And ours has a reputation which isn't good. However, there is a similar named village south of Moscow. A village that doesn't have the same reputation as ours. Clearly Slavic has kept his hometown a secret, and this slight slip of the pen lets us know he isn't being mistreated because of his association with us.'

'Wouldn't it be hard to keep up the pretence? He wouldn't be able to mention the Midnight Sun, or the harsh winters. He'd have to be so careful.'

'I wouldn't worry,' Babushka smiled. 'Until you came along, I don't think I'd heard that boy utter two words together his whole life. He's quite a secret soul. That's how we all knew he had such deep feelings for you.'

'But he's only known me for a month. How can he be so sure?'

'Life is too short and unpredictable to let an opportunity pass you by.' Babushka patted her hand. 'But you are still young. You have your whole life ahead of you. Go and live your dreams in the Ballet... but when you find it isn't all you've longed for, he'll be here, waiting for you.'

Lincoln

Something woke Fay in the middle of the night. She lay awake for a while, thoughts streaming through her head.

Why did she so hate the name 'Faith'? Somehow the connection with the church was so strong, she had seen *Faith* as a holy person, someone who always did what was right. The number of times, in school, if she'd said something wrong or been rude to someone, she'd hear the taunt, 'You can't say that – you're a Christian.' *Faith* became an ideal Wonder-Woman that she could never be. Being Fay allowed her to make mistakes, say the odd bad thing, choose not to go to church, without being constantly made to feel a failure. It was as though everyone – teachers, friends, parents of friends – expected a level of perfection from Faith that was never required of Fay. How did names have that power? How could the smallest '*th*' sound at the end of word change someone's expectations?

But obviously, to her grandad, that '*th*' made a lot of difference. He'd always used her birth name, but until now, Fay hadn't realised that someone else shared it. Did it have the same connotations in Russian? Were the same expectations put on you to behave and live uprightly? Or did the name 'Faith' lose its significance in a country where belief in God was illegal.

Fay couldn't stay in bed any longer. She felt drawn to the tin and the programme, wanting the connection with the dancer called Vera. She pulled on her dressing gown and reached for the tote bag she'd left at the end of her bed. The bag was there, but the tin wasn't inside it. Fay felt around on the floor in case it had fallen out but couldn't find anything. She was sure it had been there yesterday. She remembered dropping the tote and hearing the metal clang of the tin. She'd been so concerned it might be damaged, she'd checked and been relieved to see it looked fine. Obviously, it had received worse handling in its long life.

But now, the tin wasn't there. She turned the light on and checked again but couldn't see it. Maybe she'd left it downstairs. She opened her door and was surprised to see a light coming from the dining room. Creeping downstairs as quietly as she could, Fay peered into the room. Her mum sat at the table, leaning over something. She knocked quietly, so as not to frighten her, and entered the room. On the table was the tea tin. Mum was poring over the programme. They must have both had the same thought.

'Sorry, I didn't mean to wake you. I thought I could get the tea tin without disturbing you.'

'That's OK,' Fay waved off her mother's apology. 'I don't think I was sleeping too deeply. I was drawn to the Vera in the programme. Looks like you had the same idea.'

'Yes, I did. You mentioned a volunteer was going to pick up the programmes you found in the cupboard,' Mum said. 'I don't suppose you mentioned this one, did you?'

'No, and I didn't see any more like it. Maybe I can find out when she is coming in again and ask her about this one.'

Fay sat down and Mum pushed the programme towards her so Fay could see it clearly. She ran her finger down the middle column. Near the bottom, she saw the name Vera.

'Petrova, Vera Mikhailovna. Could this be Grandad's Vera?'

'I think it might be. Do you remember Grandad saying that he'd named Dad after his own father? That means that Grandad's patronymic was Mikhailovich, and if he had a sister, hers would be Mikhailovna. And the surname – Petrov. I checked online. It means son of Peter.'

'Peterson!' Fay whispered. 'I always wondered why I couldn't find any more Petersons when we did that unit on the family tree at school. Everyone said our roots must have been Scandinavian, but I didn't think so with this hair colour.' Fay tugged at her mousy brown hair. 'Could it be that when Grandad moved to England from Russia, he took a new first name, Arthur, and adapted his Russian name to an English version - Petrova to Peterson?'

'Nearly,' Mum said. 'As a male, his surname would have been Petrov. Only females in the family would have the added *a* on the end.'

Fay rested her head on her hand. 'So, Grandad came over here, changed his identity, never spoke of his past again, and the only thing he kept to remember his family back home was a tea tin.'

'But he honoured his family in the best way possible. He named your dad after his own father, and his granddaughter after his sister, possibly.' Mum leaned over and nudged Fay's shoulder. 'That's pretty intense, huh?'

Fay nodded. 'I understand now why he never wanted to call me Fay. I wonder what happened to her. Is it strange that I feel a sense of connection to her?' Fay looked back at the programme. 'This programme is from 1963. Where was Grandad living then?'

'I'm not sure. I don't know when he came here from Russia.'

'So, we have a brother and sister,' Fay summarised.

'Maybe,' interjected Mum.

'Maybe,' agreed Fay. 'One danced here in 1963, the other moved here before or after that. Who came first? And what happened to Vera?'

Chapter 20

Leningrad

The letter from Slavic burned a hole in Vera's pocket.

'Babushka, do I have time to write to Slavic before travelling home?'

Babushka shook her head.

'No, not at all. You need to wait until you get back to Leningrad. No letter can ever be sent to Slavic from this village. But come, let me show you how to address the envelope.'

The old lady demonstrated the marks that needed to be made on the envelope to tell Slavic that all was well with herself and his grandmother. Babushka wrote on her father's address on the back of a shopping list, demonstrating which marks on the envelope would show that Slavic's grandmother was well, and how that would change should she get ill or die. Vera felt quite uncomfortable.

'But Babushka, if something happens to his grandmother, wouldn't he rather hear in person?'

'Little one, you know that is impossible in the army. We couldn't send a letter from this village. It would put him in danger, and he wouldn't be able to get time off to visit, anyway. Slavic understands how fragile life is. He knew, when he went away, that he might never see his grandmother again. Every message that he gets that says she is keeping in good health is an additional blessing. And when he gets the last piece of news, he'll rejoice that she has gone to her eternal home, where there are no more tears or pain.'

Vera raised her eyebrows. Babushka laughed.

'Don't tell me you believe all that Soviet propaganda about death being the end? Let me tell you a secret. It's only the beginning!'

Vera had many more questions, dangerous questions. Questions that would get her in trouble if her mother or anyone from the Ballet knew she was asking. But the day was full of packing to return to the city. Babushka announced that she'd be on the train the following afternoon and checked thoroughly that she knew the way from the train station back home. Vera tried not to roll her eyes. She'd been travelling through the city since she was younger than Vlad, but she patiently repeated every step of the process, until her grandmother was convinced that she knew where she was going.

In the afternoon, Vera noticed that the envelope from her father remained unopened on the table. As they sat down for dinner, later that day, it was still there. After the blessing for the food they would eat, Vera pointed to the letter.

'Will we read it after dinner?' she asked, as she scooped a spoonful of *kasha* into her mouth.

'Oh, yes, if you want to. I think you might be disappointed. He isn't the letter writer that your brother is. I've enjoyed listening to his weekly babblings. I'll miss them.'

'He can still write to you, Babushka, and I can, too. I'd love to write and tell you about the Ballet and everything.'

Babushka and Baba Tonya exchanged a look, and Vera blew out her breath and closed her eyes momentarily.

'Let me guess,' she said, putting down her spoon. 'I can't write to you, because anything out of the norm of Papa's monthly messages will raise suspicion.' Suddenly, Vera felt her body go cold. 'Is that what happened? Did someone get suspicious because the family was getting letters from this village? Did someone tell on us? Why would they do that?'

'Vera, you know your mother has always hated this village. Her sentiment is the same as everyone else's. Questions of how we survived the Nazi occupation, then the Siege, have left a feeling of hatred towards us that has lasted all these years. I suspect that maybe an eyebrow has been raised, nothing more. But an eyebrow raised in the wrong place is not a good thing.'

'But Babushka, things are different now. It's not like it was under Stalin. So many of those horrible gulags were closed and people came home.'

'That's true,' Baba Tonya interrupted, 'But the stigma remains, and so does the suspicion. It's best you get home before there are any more questions.'

The return journey was an opportunity for Vera to contemplate her life. These weeks in the village had changed her. Her time surrounded by nature and listening to her grandmother read from the Book of Wisdom had lifted her gaze and made her aware of things she had never considered. The idea that God had created a world perfectly adapted for people to live in, able to sustain and nourish them, was a concept that had not previously entered her mind. The recovery of her ankle was almost miraculous, and Vera couldn't help but put it down to Baba Tonya's prayers. Did God really listen to her? Was he really able to intervene in people's lives?

Vera pondered these things on the train. She felt like she'd learned so much in the last five weeks and wondered how she'd fit back into life again. Thinking of the Ballet, she found her body automatically responded. She sat up straighter, lifted her head, and felt her feet point slightly in her boots. She was eager to get back to practise. Although Baba Tonya's exercises had been thorough, she knew parts of her would ache once she got back into the practice hall.

As the industrial outskirts of Leningrad passed the window, Vera wasn't sure whether the flutter in her chest was excitement or anxiety about the life she was returning to. Certainly, she would miss the peace and restful rhythms she'd discovered in the village.

The train station was busy. Vera hoisted her rucksack and gripped tightly onto the bag Babushka had given her as she left. Jostling through the crowds, she quickly wound her way down to the Metro station.

Getting off at her stop, she made her way above ground, crossed the street, and headed for the trolleybus stop. After buying a coupon with the few kopeks her babushka has pushed in her hand before she waved her off, Vera waited for the trolleybus. Three other people were also waiting. Vera noticed they paid her no attention. One woman looked out at the passing traffic. The gentleman seemed intent on a spot on the pavement, and a young girl not much older than herself was examining her fingernails. As though she felt Vera's attention, the girl looked up, scowled, and returned to the scrutiny of her hands, turning her body slightly away.

Vera had never noticed people at the trolleybus stop before and wondered why she noticed them now. Certainly, Baba Tonya had insisted that she notice every detail in the village. She'd quiz her on the return from her walks as to whose gate was open, whose washing was on the line, were these curtains open or closed? It would appear that this training was now kicking in when it wasn't wanted or appreciated.

Vera was relieved when the trolleybus arrived. She franked her coupon, found an empty seat and looked out the window as the familiar streets shuffled past. Finally, she arrived at the stop near her building. She climbed down from the trolleybus and let herself in through the entrance. Climbing the steps to their *kommunalka*, Vera felt like she was seeing it for the first time. She marvelled at the lack of light coming through the thin, dusty windows on the stairwell. Although the stairs were swept daily by one of the residents who always talked to herself as she worked, it still felt tatty and unloved.

Reaching the third floor, she took out her key and opened the large door. She hurried through the corridor, ducked down to remove her outside boots and quickly used the bathroom to wash her hands and face, before opening the door to the room that had been home for her whole life.

Nadia and Luba were playing in the corner, Mama was resting on her bed. Vlad's school bag was in the corner, although there was no sign of her brother, and she knew Papa and Artyom would still be working. The girls looked up when they heard the door open. Joy was written across their faces as they silently rose and ran into her arms.

'You're home,' whispered Nadia, stroking her face.

'We missed you,' Luba planted kisses on her cheek.

Although the girls barely made a sound, it was enough to wake her mother.

'Hi Mama, I've brought fresh *tvorog* and preserves from the village. How are you feeling?' Vera put the girls down, took off her coat, and crossed the room to her mother.

Her mother stared at her silently for a moment, as though measuring how deeply village life had contaminated her. She gave a slight nod, as though acknowledging that her daughter had returned to her unscathed. 'Welcome home,' she whispered. 'Your brother has tried hard, but no one can cook as well as you can.'

Vera laughed out loud, breaking the spell of silence over the room. The girls returned to their game, this time chattering out loud instead of in whispers.

'I'll unpack, then make a start on tea, shall I?' Vera asked, moving around the room, opening and closing drawers and cupboards.

By eight o'clock, the whole family was sitting round the table. Vera was delighted that Papa had come home early, and she was positive that Artyom had grown while she'd been away. Over dinner, she eagerly told tales from the village, being careful to not mention anything that would upset her mother. After she'd shared, she listened as each member of the family recounted their lives. Vlad was quieter than she'd known him before, and Vera noticed that the nine-year-old had little to contribute to the conversation. He shrugged when she asked about school and got angry when she pushed for details. She made a

160

mental note to find out what was wrong with him. Catching Artyom's eye, she smiled when he offered to help her clean up after dinner. They had so much to catch up, although the kitchen of the *kommunalka* wasn't the right place for a heart to heart.

Lincoln

'Do you remember the volunteer who picked up those old programmes I found? Is there any way I could contact her?'

The theatre manager nodded. 'I can call her. Do you have more stuff for her?'

'A couple more pieces, but mainly I'd just like the chance to talk to her. I have some questions and since she seems to know a lot about the history of the theatre, maybe she can help me.'

'Oh yes, Linda is the best person to talk to about our history. She grew up in the theatre. Her father was the manager for a while, but then there was some sort of scandal.' He shrugged. 'You know how it is.'

Fay nodded politely, trying not to tap her feet or glance at her watch.

'I'll call her. She usually pops in on a Friday. Would that work for you?'

'Yes, that'd be great,' Fay smiled, hiding the disappointment of not being able to see her today.

.

Chapter 21

Lincoln

'Hi, my name's Linda. Darren told me you had some questions about the theatre. How can I help you?'

Fay smiled at the bespeckled woman, who reminded her a little of Granny Wendy. Fay led her through to a small meeting room and pointed to a chair.

'Thank you for coming. Can I get you a tea or coffee?'

'No, thank you. I'm fine.' Linda tucked her bag under her chair.

'I found another programme,' Fay watched Linda carefully, 'and I wondered if you could tell me any more information about it. I haven't found any others like it, and it's become quite personal in some ways.'

Linda leaned forward. 'Oh, this sounds like my kind of story. There aren't many mysteries here that I don't know about. I've been in and out of this theatre for over fifty years. What was the programme for? Do you have it?' She rubbed her hands.

'It's for a performance by the Kirov Ballet from Russia in 1963,' Fay explained, reaching into her bag for the original programme, glad that her dad had taken a photocopy for them to keep at home.

Linda's head snapped up. 'Is this a joke? Is this some kind of cruel prank you young people like to play?'

Fay felt her mouth fall open.

'No, not at all. I'm sorry, I honestly didn't mean to upset you. I just think there might be a connection between myself and one of the dancers.'

Linda scoffed, leaning towards Fay, and pointing into her face. 'Let me guess, you are Vera's long-lost granddaughter? Ha ha. If it was April the first, this might just have worked, but it isn't, and I'm not fooled. Darren will hear of this rudeness.' Linda picked up her bag and started to get up.

Fay felt her own face blanching. She struggled to speak. 'You've heard about Vera? What do you know?'

The older lady stopped and turned to Fay. 'Are you serious? This isn't a wind-up?'

Fay choked and shook her head. She could feel her eyes welling up with tears. She gave a cough and pushed her voice out.

'I'm sorry, this isn't a setup or anything. I don't know if there is some connection between Vera and my grandad. We are trying to find out any information we can. I just want to know what happened. Did she perform here?'

'Did she perform here?' Linda echoed. 'You really don't know?'

Fay shook her head, aware of tears running down her cheeks.

'Where did you find the programme? I thought they'd all been destroyed,' Linda said, handing Fay a tissue from her bag.

'There was a tea tin in the cupboard I was clearing out. I asked Dad to take it to the tip, but he remembered Grandad had a similar tin when he was a child, so he brought it home and we opened it. In it were some letters in Russian, written by Vera, and the programme.'

'And you think they are connected? This tin and your grandfather's?' Linda narrowed her eyes and stared at Fay.

Fay shrugged and blew her nose.

Linda grunted and stood up. 'I can see you're upset, and I didn't mean to make you cry. Honestly, I'm rattled too. I'm not sure I'm ready to talk about everything that happened then.' She walked towards the door.

Fay closed her eyes for a moment. Linda knew something that could be key, but Fay knew she couldn't push her for information.

'I need some time. I might come back next week if I feel able to talk about it. But promise me, no more tears. I can't handle folk crying.'

Fay nodded. 'Thank you,' she croaked as Linda disappeared out the door.

Fay was relieved it was the weekend, but so disappointed that she'd waited so long, and was still none the wiser. Linda had known about Vera, even though her name was so far down the programme. Something must have happened to Vera here in Lincoln, for Linda still to remember her name nearly sixty years later.

Leningrad

Vera finished reading Nadia and Luba a story and kissed their heads. Looking around the room, she saw Vlad laid on his bed, looking out the window, and Artyom was studying at the table. Like many boys his age, he kept up with his schoolwork by studying in the evening after a long day at work. Papa sat next to him, reading a newspaper. Mama was already in bed. The room was dark, except for the light on the table.

'Thank you for the letters, brother,' Vera slid into the chair next to Artyom.

'I enjoyed writing them. But the new family began asking why we were receiving so much mail. Then one of them saw the return address. They began saying something to the other residents, who mostly ignored them, but Papa thought it was best for you to come straight home.'

They both turned and looked at their father. He closed the newspaper, glanced at Vera, then at the door. She gave a slight nod and turned back to her brother.

'Papa and I are going for a walk. There's so much I have to tell you; can we spend time together this weekend?'

Artyom nodded. 'We need to go to the market anyway. We need to get some fabric. The girls have outgrown their winter clothes.'

Vera groaned. She hated sewing.

'Don't worry. Baba Rosa has promised to sew them for us in return for keeping the scraps.'

'Oh, we can't ask her to do that,' Vera whispered.

'I didn't ask. She volunteered. And Papa said we should buy a little extra for her.'

Vera nodded. 'OK, Let's talk more on Saturday.' She squeezed her brother's arm and hurriedly changed into outdoor clothing.

Vera and Papa walked for a long time in silence. The streets were busy and noisy. They walked along the canals, not willing to share their thoughts until they knew they were in a safe place. Past the beautifully domed Church of the Saviour on the Spilled Blood, which made Vera shiver in the evening shadows, they made their way into the park behind it with its hedged rows and winding paths.

'Auntie Olya says hi.' Vera was the first to speak, smiling as she remembered the friendly woman.

Papa chuckled. 'I bet that wasn't all she said!'

'No, she had quite a lot to say.' Vera grinned.

'I suppose she hasn't changed much in the last twenty years.' Papa shook his head.

'Were you two ever close? You know?' Vera nudged his elbow.

'No, I was never sweet on her like Slavic is on you.'

Vera's mouth dropped open. 'How do you know about Slavic?'

'You think you can keep a secret like that from your old papa? I know what a young lady in love looks like.'

Vera felt the smile wash out of her face. 'I don't think I'm in love. I enjoyed my time with him. We could talk about anything. We'd watch the sunsets but stay and talk long after the sun had gone down. I think it was the first time I ever felt truly free to talk about whatever I wanted to. But I wouldn't call that love. We didn't hold hands or kiss or anything like that.'

'What you've described is the sweetest part of love; being together, talking, sharing the very essence of who you are. Here's the important question: Do you think you could live without him in your life?'

Vera thought for a moment. 'I love the city, and I love the Ballet and can't wait to return. But I can't help feeling that without Slavic to talk to about it, it loses its colour and excitement.'

'As though the world isn't as full or beautiful without him to share it with?' Papa asked.

Vera nodded.

'That sounds like love to me. Did he say anything to you?'

'He asked me about the future before he left, but I didn't know he'd been conscripted – he never told me. So, I just told him how I'd always imagined my life before I moved to the village. I'm still trying to understand everything in me that's changed.'

'How did you change in the village?'

Vera looked up at her father's question. Painfully aware that in the city, there was never a totally safe space to talk, she tried to answer her father in a way she hoped he'd understand.

'I began to see things differently. I enjoyed the poems and stories that Babushka read every day.' Vera wondered if she should mention the Book of Wisdom, but the twinkle in her father's eye told her he knew what she was speaking of. 'It made me ask questions I hadn't asked before.'

'And did you discover any answers?' Papa gazed into her eyes. She looked away, uncomfortable with the intensity.

'Not really, not yet. I feel like I am on a journey, as though I have been shown a new place, but am still trying to find my way there.'

'And decide whether you are willing to pay the price.' Her father's words were the missing piece of understanding she'd been looking for since first sitting on the train earlier that day. To follow the path of faith that her grandmother, and maybe even her father, had, it would cost her greatly. Although believers were no longer in danger of the gulags, they were still ostracised and looked down on as fools. She would lose her place in the Ballet if she chose that path.

'Is it worth it?' Vera asked the question that burned the deepest in her heart. Looking into her father's eyes, she understood for the first time the depth of his own faith and the cost to himself and his family; a misunderstanding wife, an undervalued job, lower wages than his contemporaries, last on the list for a larger flat, the withdrawal of the large family medal and the financial help that assured.

'It's worth it,' Papa said, quietly but firmly.

They continued walking through the park in silence. As they passed back along the Griboyedov Canal, Vera nudged her father.

'How did you know about Slavic? Did Babushka tell you?' she asked.

'No, I received a letter from your young man asking for permission to court you.'

'And what did you say?'

'I said that was for you to decide, not me, but if he wanted my blessing, he had it.'

Vera felt her face grow hot and was grateful for the darkness of the evening and the cool breeze that blew in their faces.

Chapter 22

Lincoln

'I'm just so disappointed. I waited all week to talk to her and I still don't have any more information.' Fay collapsed into the chair.

'And you're positive she knew what you were talking about?' Mum sat on the couch and leaned forward.

'Yes, she actually said, "Don't tell me you are Vera's long-lost granddaughter?" She mentioned Vera first. Why would she mention Vera when there were so many ballerinas? And she was furious that I'd mentioned it. She took it personally, like I'd deliberately set out to trick her or fool her.'

'It sounds like there's a story there. Maybe there's some scandal around it.'

'Darren, the theatre manager, mentioned the word scandal,' Fay recalled. 'He said that Linda's father used to manage the theatre until there was some kind of scandal. Maybe that has something to do with it?'

'It may do. I honestly don't know.' Mum tapped her fingers lightly on her knee. Fay could almost see her mother's methodical brain picking out different options and putting them back, trying to decide the next step. 'If there was a scandal, something that made Vera stand out in such a firm way in Linda's mind, do you think there would be anything about it in the *Lincolnshire Echo*?'

'There may have been. Are there online editions?' Fay pulled out her phone.

'I don't think they would go back that far, but I know where we can find out. Have you ever been to the archives in the library?'

'No, do you think we might find something?' Fay felt a glimmer of hope.

'We can try it. We know the date the ballet came, so it won't take us too long to look at the newspaper records for those dates. Are you doing anything tomorrow?'

'Hi, we're looking for copies of the *Echo* from September 1963. Are you able to help us?'

The assistant looked tired, as though she wanted to be anywhere else.

'Can you work the micro-fiche reader?'

Fay shook her head.

'I've used one before,' Mum said. 'But it was a long time ago.'

The assistant sighed and pushed herself up from her chair. She moved to a cupboard and pulled out a small box. Giving it to Fay's mum, she pointed to a couple of machines that looked like computers with very large screens, before wincing and hobbling back to her workspace.

'Come on, I'll teach you how to use it.' Mum said, settling down in front of one of the machines.

Mum opened the box, sifted through the contents, and pulled out a small film. She placed it on a small shelf on the side of the screen. Moving her hand slightly, she stared intently at the screen.

'The fifth of September. Do you want to have a look?'

Fay didn't need to check the programme.

'The performance was on the twenty-first, but maybe there'll be something about it.'

Mum showed Fay how to move the slider so she could see each page.

'You keep looking here, and I'll check the sixth.'

For a few moments, it was silent.

'There's an advert in the back of mine. Here, look,' Mum said, moving slightly so Fay could pull her chair over.

Fay peered into the screen and saw the same picture from the front of the programme. Above it was written: 'One Night Only – The Famous Leningrad Kirov Ballet. Tickets still available.'

Fay shrugged. 'That's what you'd expect to see, I guess. Although I'm surprised there were still seats available. Usually these things are sold out weeks in advance.'

'Yes, but you're forgetting this was before social media. The newspaper was about the only way to let people know about events like this. And the sixties were a bit of a rough time for Lincoln. We were more of a backwater then. No university, nothing like the shops and restaurants we have now. People just didn't have the money for the ballet. I'm actually surprised they came here. Nottingham or Sheffield I could understand, but not sleepy old Lincoln.'

'Can we go straight to the twenty-second and see if anything is there?' Fay asked.

Mum flicked through the box before handing her a small film.

'Try this one.'

Fay put the film on the shelf, and turned to the first page, gasping as the front cover came into view. There was the same photo from the programme, but next to it was the headline "Soviet Ballerina absconds during performance".

'Absconds? She ran away?' Fay asked.

'It seems like it. Can you read the article?'

Fay leaned in and zoomed in on the first paragraph.

Last night's performance of Swan Lake was the first opportunity Lincoln ever had to witness the elegance and poise of a Soviet Ballet troupe. The world-famous Leningrad Kirov Ballet found themselves in Lincoln because of a slight error in translation; a secretary mis-wrote London as Lincoln, being unfamiliar with the Roman script. Although many thought this was a boon for the city, that initial mistake would prove to be an omen of the misfortune surrounding the Ballet's visit to Lincoln, resulting in the disappearance of one of its dancers.

Fay gasped, rereading the last line. 'Do you think that's Vera? It must be!'

'Let's keep reading,' said Mum, her eyes firmly on the screen.

The Soviets unfairly insisted that the catalogue of errors lay firmly at the feet of Lincoln's Theatre's manager, Mr Philip Peel. Had he followed their strict protocols, the escape could never have happened. This reporter understands that instead of all the female dancers sharing a dressing room as requested, Mr Peel had split the chorus into different rooms, saying that the Theatre was not equipped for such a large group. From what is understood at present, this was the first time during the UK tour the dancers were not all under the watchful eye of their minders.

During the performance, one of the chorus dancers, Miss Vera Petrova, returned to her dressing room with her colleagues. She excused herself for personal reasons, but instead, it appears that she let herself into a cupboard and absconded through a small window.

Although her disappearance was noticed immediately, her escape route was not discovered until after the performance, and by then, there was no way to track down the missing ballerina. It was as though she disappeared into thin   air.
The head of the dance troupe said of Vera that she was recently of unstable mind and was only taken on the trip because of her outstanding dancing, and position as understudy. It was also revealed that she had come from a family with a suspicious history and several of the dancers felt it was

unsuitable for her to come along and represent the Soviet Union.

Fay leaned back in her chair. 'I honestly don't know what to say. What does it mean, unstable mind and suspicious history?'

'Here's my question,' Mum asked, looking at the screen. 'If Vera and Grandad are brother and sister, did she leave the ballet looking for him, or did he come here looking for her?'

'And, most importantly,' Fay met her mother's gaze. 'Did they find each other?'

Leningrad

Vera had imagined her first day back at the ballet. It was as physically challenging as she'd expected. She delighted in the laughter of Masha and Katya; she kept her distance from a silent Irina. But there was something she hadn't expected.

Previously, when she danced, it was as though the world made sense. Lost in the music and movement, she no longer cared about the inconvenience of the *kommunalka*, the demands of caring for her siblings, the whispers of neighbours, and the deep shadows that filled more than the streets of Leningrad. When she danced, she was free. It all disappeared.

This time, it was different. She was different. When she danced, the music became birdsong; as she moved, she could feel the breeze beside the lake. Instead of her heart lifting above the dirt and grime of the city, her dancing took her back to the village. The same sense of freedom, of purpose, of belonging that she'd felt there, was released when she danced. She finished the familiar practise piece, and the room around her was silent.

Nadezhda Vladimirovna came over and took her hands. 'I don't know what they did in that hospital, but I have never seen so much heart and passion in such a young dancer.'

Vera felt her cheeks burn. Looking over at her friends, she saw Masha smile, and Katya wipe a tear from her eye. Irina's face remained stony.

'Where did you go to recover?' Irina asked. 'The girls said you weren't home when they visited.'

'I went to stay with family, out of the city,' Vera had been warned to never mention her father's village. Now her grandmother's fears of the tarnishing connection rang in her ears.

'Yes, but where? You must know where you've been for the last month,' Irina pushed, her eyes narrowing.

Vera's palms were sweaty. She couldn't just ignore the question. She tried to think of a response that would satisfy Irina, but no words formed in her mind.

'It isn't important where she's been.' Nadezhda Vladimirovna's voice broke through the circle of girls. 'If it makes her dance like that, I think you should all go and stay for a month. Come on! I have new pieces to teach you.'

Vera focused on the new steps Nadezhda Vladimirovna taught, constantly aware of Irina's hateful stares.

Chapter 23

Leningrad

Vera sensed the tension when she opened the door. She scanned the room. The twins were sitting on the couch they slept on, their arms wrapped around each other, traces of tears on their faces. Vlad slouched in a chair at the table, glaring angrily at the little girls, and their mother sat on the edge of her bed, her eyes darting between her children.

'Oh good. You're home,' Mama acknowledged Vera's presence. 'You sort him out. I'm sick and tired of his attitude.' She nodded towards Vlad and moved to comfort the girls.

Vera quickly took off her coat and outdoor clothes, changing into her housecoat. Pulling some parcels of food out of the cupboard, she turned to her brother, who was still staring at his sisters.

'Come and help me in the kitchen, Vlad,' she said gently.

He sullenly raised himself out of the chair and followed her out of the door.

Vera's heart fell as she walked into the kitchen. It obviously hadn't been cleaned all day. Although Vera knew it wasn't her responsibility to clean up after the others, she wasn't willing to make food for her family surrounded by such a mess. She quickly filled their large pan with water and put it on the stove to heat. While she was waiting for it to warm, she turned to her brother in time to see him wipe a sleeve across his face.

'Why did you have to go out to that village?' Vlad hissed at her. 'It's made a whole load of trouble for me at school.'

'What do you mean?' Vera asked, noticing harsh purple bruises on her brother's arm as the shirt sleeve rose up. She reached over, but he withdrew his arm quickly.

'The boy from the new family,' Vlad pointed to the mess around them. 'He saw the letter from you and knew you had been *there*. He told the others at school and now they say that we are traitors.'

Vera felt her heart jump to her throat. She struggled to take in a breath and suddenly the room seemed very small.

'Does Papa know?' she asked.

'I'm not a snitch,' Vlad snapped back. 'Of course he doesn't know, neither does Artyom. And they don't need to.'

'But, Vlad...'

'Did you tell, Vera? Did you snitch on the girl who sprained your ankle? It could've been broken. She could have ruined your whole life. But you didn't tell anyone. Why would you expect less of me? I can handle it.'

'So, what just happened in the room?' Vera asked, softening her gaze as she looked at her brother.

'Nadia jumped on my arm, and it hurt. Without thinking, I shook her off, but she fell backwards and knocked Luba over.'

Vera blew out her breath, knowing how her mother would have reacted to what she'd seen.

'OK, I'll talk to Mama. Let her know you didn't mean to hurt the girls. Vlad, is it really that bad?'

Vlad looked at her, tears filling his eyes. He didn't need to give an answer.

When her father got home that evening, Artyom and Vera were waiting for him on the pavement outside the *kommunalka*. When he saw his eldest children, he nodded, accepted the package of food that Vera held out, and led them through the streets of Leningrad. It was quieter than the previous night, and soon they found a park where there were very few people around.

'It's Vlad,' whispered Vera when they were finally sure they were alone.

'The new boy?' asked Artyom, watching her carefully and reading her mind as only he could. Vera nodded, biting her lip.

'I can buy us some time.' Papa wiped the back of his hand across his mouth. Artyom met his eye and nodded. Vera got the distinct impression she was being left out of something.

'I have some information his father may want to keep quiet. I think I can speak to him about an arrangement,' Papa smiled. 'Tell your brother it is sorted.'

They walked silently back to the building, entered the big front door, and noiselessly climbed the three flights, nodding to an older resident who was sweeping the stairs and muttering to herself. Inside their *kommunalka*, Papa stopped Vera at the door of their room.

'Here.' He gave her a blank, stamped envelope. 'I think a certain young man is waiting for a letter.'

'Oh Papa, I was going to write at the weekend. Thank you so much!' She hugged him and then watched as he walked further down the corridor. As he quietly knocked at the door of the new family, Vera slipped into their room to write an important letter.

Lincoln

'So, you don't have any idea when Grandad arrived in the UK? Did he ever talk about watching England win the World Cup in 1966?'

Dad grinned at Fay through the rear-view mirror. 'Someone's been looking up their history. I can't say he ever mentioned it – but he was never really into football.'

'What about the Beatles? Did he like their music?'

Mum laughed, 'Everyone liked the Beatles, even after they split up! They were popular for decades, on and off.'

'All I know for sure is that Mum and Dad got married in 1970, and they hadn't known each other a year. Certainly, if Vera ran away from the ballet in 1963, he would have been about fourteen years old. Too young to be crossing international borders, even for someone as plucky and bold as he is. If he arrived when he was eighteen or nineteen, he'd probably have settled here in Lincoln trying to find her, or at least wanting to be close to the last place she'd been.'

'And was Granny Wendy from Lincoln originally?'

'No, she came from Sheffield. Apparently, they met at a prayer meeting for the persecuted Church. Your grandfather was a bit of a celebrity on that stage, and Mum was bowled over by his faith and charm.'

Fay smiled. She could easily imagine a younger Arthur, meeting Wendy, taking her hands, and kissing them, the way he had greeted her and Mum for as long as she could remember. That would be quite overwhelming.

'I've got the tea tin again. Shall we play it by ear?'

'Yes, I've been praying for the right time, so let's see what happens.'

'Does anyone have a final hymn they'd like to sing?'

Fay knew Grandad would request *How Great Thou Art*, since they hadn't sung it for a couple of weeks, and it was one of his favourites.

'Could we sing *How Great Thou Art*?' Grandad asked, and Fay smiled.

Grandad looked over at her and patted her hand, causing her to drop the leaflet Mum had printed out with the words of some of the most popular songs. Grandad leaned over to get it. It had fallen into her tote bag, and as he pulled it out, he saw the tin underneath. Immediately, his face went pale, then red. He muttered something under his breath that Fay couldn't catch and looked up, his eyes darting around the room.

'I'll be right back,' Grandad whispered to Fay. 'Nothing to worry about.'

Moving faster than Fay had seen in a long time, he scooped up the tin from her bag, pushing it under his pullover, and raced out of the room.

He still wasn't back by the time the song ended. Fay quickly got Dad's attention before he went round to say goodbye to everyone, and updated him and Mum. They excused themselves and hurried down the long corridors until they reached Grandad's room.

Grandad was sitting on his bed, looking at two similar tins laid on his pillow. He glanced up, confusion across his face, then back at the tin.

'I thought you had my tin, so I brought it back to its hiding place. But mine was already there. Whose tin is this?'

For a moment, no one knew what to say.

'Whose tin is it?' His voice was stronger but wobbled with emotion.

'We think it's Vera's,' Dad whispered.

Grandad nodded, gently picking up the tea tin and holding it tenderly to his face.

'My dearest Vera. My beautiful sister.'

Fay felt dizzy. They had been right.

'So sad,' Grandad continued. 'It's so sad. I asked about her things. They said they didn't have anything. Why, oh Vera, why? But you are safe now, my little one. Safe in the arms of Jesus.'

Mum quickly moved across the room and squatted down at Grandad's feet, tugging his hand until he looked at her.

'Where is Vera? Is she dead?'

Fay heard herself gasp at the words. Somehow, deep inside her, she refused to believe it was true.

'They said she is. I would never have named you after her if she was still alive,' Grandad said, glancing over at Fay. 'But sometimes I still don't believe it. I went back to the ballet, even though Papa told me not to. I waited outside for them to come out. They'd just got back the week before. I knew I had to be careful, but I couldn't stay away. Katya – she was a kind girl – said Vera had gone missing in Lincoln. Another girl, a nasty piece of work, said that she'd...' Grandad broke off, bringing his hand to his mouth. A slight moan escaped. 'I never believed it. It never sat right with me. She had so much to live for. She'd never end her own life – that wasn't part of our plan.'

'What do you mean, Grandad?' Fay joined her mother. 'What plan?'

Chapter 24

Leningrad

Finally, the days were getting lighter. The winter months had passed in a flurry of practices and performances, punctuated by letters from Slavic. He was doing well in the army, popular with the other young men and earning the trust of his supervisors. He'd been granted leave to return to the village for the harvesting, starting in July, since he was his grandmother's only remaining family, and he'd asked if Vera could join him there. Although it was not the wisest idea, Vera found herself desperate for the peace of the village and determined to find a way to get there.

Papa had insisted that she keep a small amount of the money she earned from her performances. Although she gave most of it to her mother, she had saved enough to take Vlad and the twins to the village for the summer. The new family had finally moved out, and the tension at Vlad's school had disappeared when they did. Vera had agreed with her father that if they went, they would not write letters home, to not raise suspicions. Mother wasn't happy at the idea but had found that the girls were more difficult to control as they got older and agreed that Vera could take them for a month.

Vlad refused to go. This year he was ten years old, and he had planned to work with his brother over the summer break. Vera reluctantly agreed but felt grieved that neither of her brothers would have the chance to spend time with Babushka and benefit from her wisdom.

One morning, as she hurried to the Ballet, welcoming the lighter mornings and the lifting of the long gloom of winter, Vera had a feeling of destiny. She looked up to the sky far above the buildings that towered over her. Babushka's poem came back to her mind, as it had so many times before.

When I consider the heavens... What is man that you are mindful of him?

'Thank you,' she breathed out, finding her feet dancing and a sense of rightness with the world.

'I have something very exciting to announce to you all today.' Nadezhda Vladimirovna clapped her hands, a smile slipping out the sides of her usually sober expression. 'The Kirov Ballet is going on tour in September. We will dance *Swan Lake* in several large cities throughout Europe.'

Vera felt her cheeks flush and heat run through her body. She wasn't sure if it was excitement or fear. This was something she'd never imagined would happen to her. She still wondered if the secrets that Babushka had told her about her great-grandfather would adversely affect her paperwork for going abroad.

'Are we all going?' Masha asked the very question in Vera's mind.

'The Alpha team will go, and your chorus has been selected to go with them. The Beta team will stay here and prepare for winter with the new chorus.'

'What about all the paperwork? It might be tricky for some of us to get everything in place.' Irina looked pointedly at Vera.

'The whole troupe is being given a group passport and visas, so you don't need to worry about that.'

Vera released a sigh she hadn't realised she was holding in.

Summer in the village, then autumn in Europe. This year was so different from anything she could have imagined - as though it had all been designed for her. That day she danced with such joy and emotion, her heart full of gratitude. She was surprised when her instructor called her back as she was about to leave with everyone else at the end of the day.

'Vera, I wanted to talk to you about something. I'd like you to understudy for the role of Odette. It means you staying late most evenings to learn the dances, but I know you can do it.'

'Thank you, Nadezhda Vladimirovna. It is such an honour. I will talk it over with my parents. Can I give you my answer tomorrow?'

'It isn't a request, Vera. You can come tomorrow prepared to work two hours longer than usual.'

However tired Vera used to feel, it was nothing compared to the exhaustion of the next two months. She hobbled home at the end of hours of dancing, collapsed into bed, usually without eating, and was often woken by Artyom bringing her a cup of tea the following day. Slavic's letters continued to arrive regularly, and Vera made sure that she replied every weekend. Babushka's letters arrived once a month, and whenever she had new information about his grandmother's health, she would add the tiny dot above the e in her name, to show that all was well. Only the countdown to the summer holidays, when everyone left Leningrad and the mosquitoes took over, kept Vera going through those physically exhausting weeks.

Lincoln

'Did we do the right thing, taking the tin to him?' Dad switched off the phone and turned to Mum. 'The manager says he still won't come out of his room. He just sits with the tins on his knee, muttering.'

190

'Could he be praying?' Fay asked. Her parents looked at her and she shrugged. 'Maybe the manager's never seen anyone pray like that before.'

Dad raised his shoulder in an unconscious mimic. 'Maybe. I think I need to go and see him.'

'Can I come too?'

'Not this time. I'll go tomorrow, you're at the theatre on Wednesdays, aren't you?'

Fay examined her fingernails and spoke slowly. 'The thing is... I honestly don't know if I'm doing the right thing.' She didn't look up, but she felt her parents' full attention. 'I just wonder if I'm wasting my time there.'

'What do you mean?' asked Mum.

'I don't know,' Fay continued. 'I knew it wouldn't be like school, but I thought there'd be some adult supervision or at least structure.'

'But wasn't the official programme cancelled, because the person leading it got sick at the last minute?'

'Yes, but we were told we could still come along if we wanted to. One of the drama students who was home from uni stepped in, but some of the stuff Blake does is just weird. I feel uncomfortable sometimes, and other times the group seems to split along friendship lines, leaving a few of us on the outside, and it can get unkind. They say it's joking, but it can be cruel.'

'So, what did you want to achieve over summer?' Dad asked.

'I'd wanted to learn performance skills and body language – how to add emotion and passion to what I'm saying, how to connect with an audience, that sort of thing,' Fay explained.

'How would you use those skills?'

'I guess I always liked the idea of bringing comfort and joy to people through my words. You know how you feel when you've watched an amazing performance, or heard a beautiful song performed well? I want to give people that feeling. But I also want to inspire people, to empower them.'

'I can see why the summer programme would've been so good for you, but there are still ways you could work on those skills outside of the theatre,' Mum said. 'Would you be willing to come into the hospital with me sometime? We have patients there who don't have visitors. They sit alone all day and the only interaction they get is with us nurses when we're caring for their needs. Would you consider coming in and reading to them?'

'Is that allowed?' Fay looked up.

'Yes, we often have volunteers in, but not all of them are blessed with your ability to make a text come alive.'

'Can I think about it?'

'Sure,' Mum smiled.

'Would it help if we prayed with you?' Dad said, earning himself a glare from Mum. 'That God shows you the right path to take?'

Fay shrugged. 'If you want to!'

Dad sat next to her on the arm of the sofa, and Mum reached over to hold her hand.

'Father,' Dad prayed, 'Thank You for Fay. Please show her the best way to spend the rest of the summer and help her make great choices.'

'Please may she be a friend to anyone who needs a friend tomorrow and continue to lead her into her destiny,' Mum chimed in.

'And I pray for Grandad too.' Fay was surprised when her own voice joined those of her parents. 'Please can he find peace, and please can he find Vera? Amen.'

Fay looked up to catch a strange glance pass between her parents.

'What?' she asked.

'You think Vera could be found?' Dad raised his eyebrows.

'I never thought of it before.' Fay narrowed her eyes, trying to figure out what she'd just said. 'I just suddenly had an impression of Grandad and an old lady meeting, and I really wanted that to happen.'

Dad nodded and shrugged lightly.

Fay was surprised to find the door of her cupboard slightly ajar. As she opened it, the person inside jumped and spun around.

'Kate? Are you looking for something? Can I help you?'

Fay and Kate had increasingly sought refuge in the cupboard when Blake and his friends were in a difficult mood. Looking carefully, she saw Kate's eyes were rimmed with red, and her face was quite pale.

'Er, yes, everything looks fine here, and I, er, was just wanting to check…'

Fay had never seen Kate so flustered. Outside of the door, a couple of members of the troupe walked past, laughing and joking. Fay watched Kate visibly shrink back. Remembering the words of her mother's prayer the previous day, she pulled the door shut and pointed to the box containing the jewellery.

'I was actually going to ask for your help. I've put all the jewellery in this box, but really, I need to catalogue it and make sure it's stored properly. Are you free to help me with that today?'

Kate looked at her and gave a weak smile. 'Yes, I can help.'

Fay looked around the cupboard, then had another idea.

'Look, there isn't much room here. How about we go to my house? My parents are at work all day, and we could spread everything out without anyone coming in and disturbing us.'

Kate's shoulders relaxed, and she nodded.

It was only a half-mile walk to Fay's house, and fortunately it wasn't up the hill that Lincoln is famous for. Carrying the box between them caused quite a few giggles, and by the time they got home, Fay and Kate discovered they had more in common than they'd first thought.

They spent the day laying out the jewellery and discussing the best ways to catalogue and store it.

When Mum came back from her shift, she found the two girls looking at storage solutions online.

'Mum, this is Kate, from the theatre. We came here to sort out the jewellery.'

Mum smiled. 'Hi Kate, please call me Lisa. Can I get you guys a cup of tea?'

Fay stood up. 'It's OK, I'll get you one. You must be tired after work.'

When Fay came back with the tea, Mum and Kate were sitting on the sofa, Kate was crying, and Mum was giving her a hug and talking quietly. Fay put down the tea and quickly went back into the kitchen. At least she could start prepping dinner, while Mum and Kate talked.

Chapter 25

Lincoln

'I have a serious question to ask you.' Mum put down her knife and fork. Fay noticed her mum hadn't eaten much dinner. 'You mentioned concerns about the group at the theatre yesterday, and I think we might have dismissed them without properly hearing you out. You mentioned unkindness. Can you tell us more?'

Fay took a sip of water.

'It started with small things. They nicknamed me "Keeper of the Cupboard" and Kate was "Keeper of the Wardrobe". A few others were given names too, some of them were quite cruel. Then they refused to use our real names, just these titles. If we challenged them, they said they were method acting and needed to stay in character.'

'OK, do you feel uncomfortable?' Mum asked.

'Yes, I do.'

'Have we been pushing you to stay with the theatre? Would you have left already if we hadn't been so enthusiastic?'

Dad lifted his eyebrows, hearing Mum's question.

'I don't know. Maybe. I didn't want to disappoint you again. I know you are already disappointed in me not going to church with you. I guess I didn't want to seem like a flake, dropping out of something else.'

'We aren't disappointed in you, Faith.' Dad's voice was forceful. 'You are on a journey, and I know that isn't easy. I'm glad you are examining and questioning. That's how you'll come to your own answers, instead of just living off ours.'

Fay reached over and squeezed her dad's hand.

'And whatever decision you make about the theatre, we'll support you every step of the way.' Mum rested her hand on Fay's. They sat for a moment in silence, before Mum stood to clear the table.

'How was Arthur today?' Mum asked Dad.

'He didn't recognise me, but I don't think I expected him to. I sat with him, and I think Fay was right. I think he is praying.'

'How did you know?' Fay asked.

'I tried to talk to him, but he shushed me. But when I prayed for his family, he let me continue. I prayed for their safety. For whatever is lost to be found, for peace for Grandad, and for answers to his questions. After a while, I left. I'll pop back in tomorrow.'

'Can I come with you? I don't think I'll go back to the theatre.'

Leningrad

'Tell me again, everything about the village!' Nadia jumped up and down in excitement. Mama grunted her disapproval, took her towel and toiletry bag, and left the room. Vera sat with a hairbrush, working her way through the tangles in Luba's hair, enjoying a quiet morning off after a late performance the night before.

'Well, we'll be staying with Babushka and Baba Tonya.'

'Is she really a witch, like Mama said?' Luba asked, clearly not sharing her sister's excitement.

'No, she understands herbs, but she isn't a witch. She doesn't do spells or anything like that!'

'I don't have to sleep in the same room as her, do I?' Luba seemed unconvinced.

'No, we will sleep in the kitchen. They sleep in the bedroom.'

'And what will we do all day?' Nadia pulled Vera's arm.

'We'll have to help Babushka with the harvest. We'll help her pick the fruit and make it into jam, and any other jobs she wants us to do. We'll also have time to go to the lake and maybe go swimming.'

'And we'll get to meet Slavic?' Nadia asked.

Vera blushed slightly. 'Yes, you'll get to meet Slavic. He will only be there for two weeks, as he'll have to come back in September for the rest of the harvest, but we will see him briefly.'

'And when will you get married?' Nadia was still bouncing.

'Who said we are getting married?' Vera tickled her sister.

'Artyom did,' Luba replied, without a smile. 'You won't live in the village when you get married, will you?'

'Nadia and Luba! You are getting ahead of yourselves. Slavic hasn't asked me to marry him. He is in the army for the next year, anyway. Who knows what the future holds? But wherever I live, whenever I get married, you two will always be welcome. I can promise you that! OK?'

The girls nodded – one joyfully, the other sadly.

'Talking of Slavic, I'm going to pop down and see if the mail has arrived. Will you two be OK here for a minute?' Vera asked, quickly checking there was nothing out of place in the room that could hurt the girls.

'Of course. We are big girls now.' Luba stood up straight.

Vera winked at her and grabbed her keys. Letting herself out of the room, she left the flat and skipped down the three flights of stairs. On the ground floor, near the front door, were the post-boxes for each flat. Although there were keys for each box, the children had long since got around the locks. Checking Baba Rosa's box first, it did not surprise her to see it empty. Baba Rosa had never mentioned family and never received any personal mail.

Opening their box, she was excited to see a couple of letters. One on standard brown paper she knew straight away was from Slavic. She pulled it out and examined the envelope. The stamp was perfectly straight, and above the first letter of his name was a tiny dot. He was healthy and doing well. Pulling the letter to her chest, she had a moment of gratitude, wishing she knew if she could thank God for the letter in the same way Babushka thanked God for every meal.

Reaching back into the box, there was another, thin letter. Looking at the envelope, she was surprised to see it was addressed to her mother. The handwriting was unfamiliar, and the envelope was of a high quality.

Vera looked in the top left-hand corner to check the sender and was surprised to see a male name. The address was in central Moscow. Vera racked her brain, trying to remember anything her mother had ever mentioned about friends or family in Moscow. The sound of a door opening above her, and quick footsteps on the stairs, broke her concentration. She looked up and was surprised to see her mother lightly skipping down the steps. She watched for a moment, marvelling at her mother's easy, fluid movements. She couldn't ever remember her mother moving with such carefree grace.

'Mama?'

Her mother's head whipped down, and she froze when she saw Vera standing in the foyer. For a moment, neither of them spoke. Vera had so many questions but knew that communal areas was never the place to voice them.

Her mother cleared her throat and lifted her head. 'I thought I'd check the mail. Is that for me?' She pointed to the crisp white envelope in Vera's hand. Vera nodded, holding it out as she slowly climbed the stairs. Her mother took it, checked the sender's address and giggled, skipping up the stairs, leaving Vera to follow her slowly.

Entering the room, Vera leaned back on the door and watched her mother return to her bed. She sat on the edge, opened the letter and immersed herself in the pages. The twins paid no attention to the titters and chuckles coming from their mother.

Nadia looked up at Vera. She must have noticed Vera's knitted brows and frown, because she got up and took Vera's hand. 'Mama has her happy letter,' she explained with an open smile.

Vera squatted next to her sister. 'Does Mama often get happy letters?'

'Oh yes!' Nadia smiles. 'Sometimes she gets a very happy letter and then she takes us to the park. But today is just a normal happy letter.'

Vera struggled to fight the discomfort in her stomach. Something was very wrong. Who was the man writing to Mama? Why hadn't the girls mentioned anything before? And what else was she hiding?

Chapter 26

Lincoln

'How did she get your number?' Mum asked, pulling on her coat and grabbing her car keys.

'I'd left my details with Darren, in case Linda wanted to talk to me, but I was still shocked when she called.' Fay stopped for a moment, remembering the uncomfortable phone call. 'She said she'd meet me, but she didn't know if she could help at all.'

'Well, I'm happy to drop you off, but I'm due at work, so you'll have to get home by bus.'

'I think I'll walk. It'll do me good and it's a nice day.'

'How was Grandad yesterday when you saw him?' Mum asked as they drove through town.

'He seemed really tired, so I just read a couple of his favourite psalms to him.' Fay bit her lip. 'It's so crazy how much he has aged since Granny Wendy's death. Two years ago, he would've been out all day in the garden, and still have energy for a walk after dinner. Now, he gets so tired and naps so much of the day. It's hard to get my head round.'

'It's so sad, isn't it? But that reminds me, have you thought any more about the volunteer reading programme?'

'Yes, I think I'd like to give it a go, although I'm not sure what to read.'

'We have a small library of things – short stories are really popular. We have some magazines, and a selection of old-fashioned writers people have donated, as well as some humorous ones.'

'OK, would you be able to bring a couple home so I could look through and find ones I think look good?'

'Sure, I'll do that today after my shift. I'll get you signed up. There'll be a couple of forms to fill in and a training session, but I think you'll really enjoy it.'

'Me too. Can you drop me here? I think I can see Linda through the window.'

Fay jumped out of the car and waved as her mum pulled away. Taking a deep breath, she walked into the café.

Linda was sitting at a table in the corner. She already had a cup of tea and nodded for Fay to sit down when she greeted her.

'So, tell me about your grandad,' she finally asked, looking at Fay through half-closed eyes.

Fay retold everything that had happened. The tea tin that she'd found in the cupboard that was so similar to one owned by her grandfather. Her grandfather speaking Russian and getting upset, him calling her Vera, and finally talking about a plan.

'A plan? What did he mean?' Linda leaned forward.

'He couldn't tell us any more.' Fay swallowed the lump in her throat, remembering how upset her grandfather had become. She took a sip of the cappuccino the waitress had just brought her. 'From what we understand, one of the girls from the Ballet told him she'd gone missing and another one – Grandad called her a nasty piece of work – said she'd killed herself.'

Linda lifted her eyebrows and tilted her head.

'Killed herself? That's a new one. I'd never heard that story, although there were rumours of a plan.'

'So, what do you know? What do you remember?' Fay took another sip and gave Linda her full attention.

'Obviously, I was very young at the time, and don't remember much at all. But Mum and I talked about it a lot after Dad's death. That's when I found out the details.'

Linda looked out the window.

'It was a big deal, having a Soviet Ballet come to Lincoln. Of course, we forget now how closed the Soviet Union was. They weren't allowed to stay overnight in the city. They were bussed away straight after the performance. They didn't go anywhere else or talk to anyone. Dad had to make sure all the security arrangements were in place. We really weren't told about any of them, but it turned out they were keeping their eye on Vera. She'd been flagged as a potential flight risk and had extra people watching her.'

'Why?'

'I'm not sure, something about coming from a suspicious family, but someone else said she'd lost someone close to her recently. No one seemed very willing to talk about it.'

'So, what happened?'

'From what I understand, she was in the chorus. They were needed in the first half, but then were not on stage for about an hour. During that hour, she left the dressing room to go to the bathroom, but instead went into the cupboard you were cleaning out, climbed up the shelves and out of the little window.'

'Wow, that's quite an achievement. The window is tiny, and fairly high up.'

'So high up, no one even knew it opened until she escaped through it. But you have to remember, she was a top athlete. She would have been very strong and nimble.'

'So, after she got out of the window, where did she go?'

'That's the real question. She must have escaped over the rooftops, I suspect, towards the Arboretum, although at that time you could have walked out of the city in any direction in less than an hour. By the time the alarm was raised, there was no chance of finding her.'

'I guess that didn't go down well with the Soviets.'

'Not at all! They were livid at the disappearance and even more angry that the *Echo* reported it the following day. They insisted that nothing else be reported. They didn't want the police involved or anything. We thought that was strange, but if they were spreading the rumour that she'd killed herself, obviously they wouldn't want her to be found alive and well. The Soviets argued it was Dad's incompetence that had led to her disappearance and insisted he be fired. He said that he hadn't been told enough. If he'd known she was unstable, he could have provided extra security.'

'Why did they bring her if they thought she might run away?'

'Apparently, she was the understudy for the prima ballerina, and was the only one who could dance in her place if she got sick.'

'So, she escaped. It was hushed up, with only that one article in the newspaper, and nothing else was ever heard about her again.' Fay ran through the details, as they knew them so far.

'I imagine she probably settled somewhere and lived a normal life. Maybe got married, had children and tried to forget about her life in the Soviet Union,' Linda said.

'And her family were told she'd killed herself, and so never tried to find her. What a sad story. Did your dad get into a lot of trouble?'

Linda sighed. 'Yes. He was fired and really rattled by the whole situation. I don't think he ever fully recovered.'

'I'm so sorry,' Fay whispered. 'It's just all such a mystery. I wish I knew more or could somehow put it together.'

'Sorry I can't be more help,' Linda replied.

'Oh no,' Fay looked up. 'You've been so helpful. I'm just so sorry your dad was so unfairly blamed.'

A village outside Leningrad

Stepping off the train at the familiar station, Vera filled her lungs with fresh air. She knew Babushka and Baba Tonya were expecting them, but she'd told them that she and the girls would walk to the village from the station. Taking a sister in each hand, she walked through the small ticket office. The stationmaster came out to greet her, a big smile on his face.

'So, these are the little beauties we have heard so much about!' He shook each girl's hand and bowed his head as though they were very important. Nadia giggled and Luba smiled. 'Hurry along now, I know two ladies who are eagerly waiting to see you.'

Vera led her sisters along the path, glad to be sharing this walk with them. She pointed out trees, different birds and animal tracks as they walked along. She told them about the people they would meet in the village and relived her rides and walks with Slavic.

As Babushka's hut came into view, Vera gave a cry of joy, seeing Babushka waiting at the gate, looking for them.

The two women ran to each other and hugged for a long time, laughing and exchanging words of love.

Finally, they broke apart, and Babushka turned to the twins. After glancing between the two for a moment, she knelt down. Looking at Luba, she said 'I see a child whose heart is so full of love – you must be Luba.' Luba nodded, her serious eyes twinkling with a deep joy Vera had never seen before.

'And you,' Babushka turned to Nadia after hugging Luba, 'see hope in everything around you – you must be Nadia.'

Babushka took the girls' hands and led them into the small house. Vera watched their curious eyes take in the old-fashioned kitchen.

'Where's Baba Tonya?' Vera asked quietly.

Babushka nodded towards the bedroom door. 'Go and see her. She's been waiting for you.' Vera raised an eyebrow. She'd never know Baba Tonya to sleep during the day. But Babushka just nodded and turned her attention to the twins.

Vera had only been in the bedroom a couple of times on her previous visit. She quietly opened the door and slipped into the peaceful room. Babushka's bed was under the window, and Baba Tonya's was pushed against the opposite wall. Vera approached the bed, treading lightly across the floor. Baba Tonya's face was pale, and her body seemed so much smaller laying in that bed than it had ever seemed when she was pottering around the kitchen. As Vera approached, Baba Tonya's eyes opened. Vera was surprised by the life and energy they held.

'You've arrived,' she whispered, struggling to pull her hand out from under the covers. 'I asked God to give us a little more time together before He called me home.'

'Babushka didn't tell me you were ill.' Vera recalled all the envelopes she'd received over the last few months, and how meticulously she'd checked for the dots in the address. Nothing had been amiss.

'There's nothing to tell.' Baba Tonya shook her head. 'I'm not ill. I'm preparing to go on the greatest adventure of my life, but I did so want to see you before I left.'

Vera frowned. 'I don't understand, Baba. Where are you going? You aren't strong enough for an adventure.'

Baba Tonya smiled and reached for Vera's hand. 'Do you remember when you first came to the village? You found a world you'd never thought possible. A world of animals and birds, seasons and beauty, a peace and understanding of God you'd been too busy to ever fully understand when you lived in the city.' Vera nodded. 'And you have spent all winter telling your sisters about it. But they didn't fully understand until they got here. It's the same with where I am going. I can't fully understand or explain, but I know it is more beautiful, more peaceful, more glorious than even our little village.'

Vera had a flash of understanding.

'Are you talking about... heaven?' she asked.

Baba Tonya closed her eyes, her mouth settled into a blissful smile. 'I'm talking about more than that. I'm talking about the presence of the One who I was created for. To be with Him, in *glory*.' She whispered the final word, as though she was talking about the most beautiful thing ever to be experienced.

Vera sat on the floor. She pressed her cheek onto the bed. Baba Tonya moved her hand to rest on Vera's head, and Vera breathed deeply, the peace in the room, filling her heart and mind. Closing her eyes, she fell asleep.

Chapter 27

A village outside Leningrad

When Vera woke, the sun was lower in the sky. It wasn't dark, but it wouldn't be fully dark for a few more weeks this far north. She checked on Baba Tonya, who was sleeping peacefully, although her breathing was very shallow. She got up and went in search of her family. In the kitchen she found Babushka quietly washing the pots. The girls were already asleep on the little fold-out sofa that Vera had slept on last time she came.

'Do you want to eat?' Babushka asked softly.

Vera nodded. 'What time is it?'

Babushka looked at the clock on the wall. 'Just gone nine o'clock.'

'Really? I've slept for hours.'

'You must've needed it. The girls came in and gave you and Baba Tonya a kiss, and they fell straight asleep.' She looked over at them. 'Do they always sleep like that?'

Vera smiled at the twins, fast asleep with their arms wrapped around each other.

'Always. They can't sleep without each other. I don't know how they do it.'

'Vera, Nadia, Luba - Vera, Nadezhda, Lyubov,' Babushka sighed. 'How I've longed to have you all together under my roof. I have something to show you.' She disappeared out of the room, coming back with her notebook, which held the words from the Book of Wisdom.

'"And now these three remain: faith, hope and love,"' she read. Faith – Vera, Hope – Nadezhda, Love – Lyubov. '"But the greatest of these is love." Not our love, my daughter – God's love. God's love for us, and through us. This is the greatest. That is what Baba Tonya has taught me. She has shown me the love of God every day, even in these final days. She never tires of sharing that love with others, even when I think we can't afford to give anymore, or when it gets her into trouble. "The greatest of these is love," she'd say to me. "Without that – everything else is worthless." She is an inspiration to me.'

Patting Vera's hand, Babushka reached up into a cupboard tucked into the chimney. She pulled out a little metal tin, the kind that once had tea in, but now probably held matches.

'This is for you.' Babushka handed Vera the tin. 'We both want you to have it.'

Vera looked inside and saw matches, as she'd expected. She looked at her grandmother and shrugged.

'Oh, my daughter. It isn't a normal tea tin. This tin holds life!'

Babushka reached and took it from her. She tipped the matches out on to the table. Looking at the sleeping girls, she beckoned Vera to follow her. They went outside, where Babushka violently knocked the tin against the side of the house. Looking inside, she smiled and led Vera back to the kitchen, setting it down on the table.

Vera looked inside the tin and was surprised to see that the bottom had lifted. Reaching in, Vera saw that only part of the bottom had dislodged and something lay underneath it.

'It has a false bottom?' she asked her grandmother in surprise.

'Let's just say – it has hidden depths; it's not as it seems.' Babushka squeezed her hand. 'None of us are. There are depths to all of us. The deep things that Baba Tonya has built her life on are eternal. She wants the same for you, and for them.' She nodded towards the twins.

Reaching inside the tin, Vera took out the false bottom, and carefully pulled out a small flat pouch, hand-sewn to fit exactly in the base of the tin. Babushka quickly stood up and went to lock the door. The key was rusty in the lock, due to lack of use, but Babushka persevered until it clicked in place. Whatever was in this pouch, Babushka was adamant it would stay secret.

Lincoln

The doorbell rang, and Fay glanced at the clock. Whoever was at their door at ten o'clock on a Sunday morning would just have to accept her in her pyjamas.

'Hi Fay, I've brought these for you and your mum.' Kate stood on the doorstep, holding a bunch of flowers. For a moment, Fay didn't know what to say, but noticing Kate's face get redder, she thanked her for the flowers and invited her in.

'Mum's out right now. Sorry I haven't been back to the Theatre all week. I hope you've been OK.' Fay realised she should've phoned Kate to tell her she wouldn't be there.

'I wasn't there either. I've decided to give it a miss for the rest of the summer. Mum suggested I get some of my old ballet costumes out and adapt them for my little sister. I think that might be more useful than hanging costumes. "Keeper of the Wardrobe" isn't a title I ever want to hear again.'

Fay nodded. 'It's a pity that Sabrina got sick. I think she had an amazing summer programme planned, and I was really looking forward to it, but without her, it just wasn't working.'

'No, I'm grateful that Darren still let us come down, and I've enjoyed sorting out the costumes that were there. It was obvious that no one had had any spare time to sort them out or fix them.' Kate bit her lip. 'Did he call you?'

'Darren? Yes. He phoned on Friday and asked if I was alright.'

'Me too. What did you tell him?'

'I was honest, and he was great. He apologised for not intervening and promised I could be part of their programme in the October half-term.'

'That's great. He offered my family and I tickets to the next performance they have,' Kate smiled. 'So, what are you going to do for the rest of the summer?'

'Mum's asked me to go into the hospital and read to some of the older patients who don't have any family to visit them. I'm going in for training on Tuesday.'

'Wow, you'll be great at that. I always get tongue-tied when I have to talk to strangers.'

'Do you? I love it.'

'I was hoping you'd say that.' Kate's mouth twisted into a hopeful smile. 'I've got a favour to ask. My sister goes to a dance school. It's quite serious, and she's there three days a week over the summer. They want to inspire the girls as well as teach them dance, so every week for an hour they have a special guest come in. It could be a choreographer, or a musician, or a street dancer. Anyway, they asked me if I'd go in and talk a little about ballet costumes. I know everything I want to say, but I'm not good at saying it. I wondered if you'd come with me.' It was the longest Fay had ever heard Kate talk. Fay watched her bite her lip.

'I'd love to help you,' Fay smiled, watching relief flood Kate's face.

'Really? That's great. It's on Wednesday afternoon. Could you maybe come round tomorrow, and we can chat about it?'

'I'd love to. I can't wait. I love public speaking.'

'Hi Grandad.'

'Beautiful Faith! How are you, my dearest one? You are the delight of my life.'

Fay was pleased to see the clarity in her grandad's face. She glanced around the room as she reached over and hugged him. There was no sign of the tins. Dad and Mum had been called away by the manager of the home.

'Your granny'll be in soon. I think she's just finishing up a batch of biscuits, but I needed to talk to you about something important before she comes in.'

Fay felt her heart drop. Her grandfather was obviously living in the past today.

'I need you to pray for someone. It's someone very precious to me. I keep waking up in the night needing to pray for her, and I think if more of us are praying for her, God won't need to keep waking me up about it.'

Fay smiled at her grandad's logic.

'I need you to pray for my sister, Vera.'

Fay schooled her features to remain calm.

'Is she older than you? Or younger?' she asked.

'She's three years older, but I haven't seen her since she was sixteen, so that's the age she still is to me.'

'What happened when she was sixteen?'

'It was a difficult time, and we had a plan to keep her safe, but it didn't work. We were told she died. But something in me refused to believe it, and I kept looking for her, but never found her. I began to think that maybe she had died, but sometimes I feel so strongly that I need to pray for her, that I think maybe she isn't dead after all.'

Fay tried to follow everything her grandfather was saying.

'The last few nights, I've been waking up, knowing I have to pray for her. And now this tin, Vera's tin, tells me she's alive.'

'Grandad, how does a tea tin tell you she's alive?'

He lifted his finger to his lips, showing her to be quiet, then leaned over to his bedside table. He opened the top drawer and pulled out two tins. Lifting them out carefully, he put them on the table next to Fay.

'This one's mine.' He pointed to one with faded yellow writing on, 'And this one is Vera's.' It was slightly taller and seemed to be blue underneath the rust. 'But they both hold a secret.' Grandad showed Fay the inside of his empty tin. Then, without warning, he banged it loudly on the table, making Fay jump. Taking Vera's tin, he did the same. When Fay looked inside them, she could see the bottoms had shifted. 'They both hold secrets. Initially, they both held this.' He reached inside his tin and pulled out a small handsewn bag, perfectly made to fit into the base.

'But Vera's is empty. She took it with her. She would never leave it.'

Fay looked inside Vera's tin. The space under the false bottom was empty. Fay looked at the pouch cradled in Grandad's hands.

'What is it?'

'This, my daughter, is life!'

Chapter 28

A village outside Leningrad

Vera held the pouch carefully, wondering what it contained that was so important. Babushka looked at the sleeping girls, and beckoned Vera through to the other room.

Glancing at sleeping Baba Tonya, Babushka sat down and patted the bed next to her. Vera joined her and carefully opened the bag. Inside were delicate, thin pages, printed on both sides with tiny writing. There were about twenty sheets, and the typeface seemed very old-fashioned.

'This is the Book of Wisdom,' Babushka whispered, gazing tenderly at the papers in Vera's hands.

'Babushka, these are pages from... from a Bible,' she gasped.

'They are words of life, my child.'

'But they're illegal,' Vera hissed, frantically looking around the room, in case anyone was hiding or listening. 'It's illegal for anyone but priests to read the Bible, and even then, only in special places. You are not only reading it; you *own* pages of it!'

Babushka took the delicate sheets from Vera and laid them on the bed. Taking both of Vera's hands in hers, she stared into her eyes.

'Vera, sometimes the rules of man are wrong. You have lived long enough to see that. People imprisoned under one leader are liberated under another. What is legal and illegal changes like the passing seasons. But the words of God are life. You have found God here in the village, surrounded by nature. You found something deeper and more meaningful than the life you led before, didn't you?'

Vera nodded, finding her eyes fill with tears. She glanced over at Baba Tonya, unable to express everything that had changed in her heart since her first visit.

'Now, you need to learn more so you can teach others. You need to learn the words of life for yourself, teach them to the children, as I taught them to you. Live them, even if they are unpopular, even if they are illegal.' Babushka smiled and squeezed Vera's hand. 'Because you have found that they are worth it, aren't they?'

Vera thought of the purpose she had found in her dancing, believing that she was created by God; the joy she'd found in the simple acts of preparing and cooking food, knowing that God's provision was so perfectly tuned to their needs; the patience she'd had with the children, knowing how God's patience is reflected in the slowly changing seasons. She nodded, a smile forming on her lips.

'But isn't it dangerous?' she asked.

A flicker passed over Babushka's face.

'More dangerous than you can imagine,' the old lady said.

Lincoln

'Vera was given her tin, by my grandmother, a woman I never met. But Papa gave me mine the last time I saw him.'

Fay had so many questions, but she knew that if she asked them all at once, Grandad could get confused. She had to listen to his story as he told it, or she'd probably never hear it at all. Grandad slowly opened the pouch and pulled out a small wad of thin papers, printed on both sides with tiny letters Fay couldn't read.

'Are they pages from the Bible?' she whispered, not even daring to reach out and touch the fragile sheets.

'The very words of life,' Grandad nodded, glancing at Fay with a smile. 'But these words were illegal in the Soviet Union. Just owning them was dangerous. And somehow rumours started, the way that rumours do, and a little truth was mixed in to make the rumours dangerous. We were on the wrong side of the wrong people, and we had to flee.'

A tear trickled down Grandad's face. Fay quickly knelt in front of him, took the tissue-like papers, placed them carefully on the bed, and held his hands.

'Dark times. They were dark times.' Tears continued to roll down Grandad's face, as he gazed into the distance. 'We all had to flee. We couldn't stay. Our beautiful family, so close, each other's best friends, we held each other one last time and said goodbye.'

Fay thought her heart would break. She couldn't imagine any danger that would make her consider leaving her family.

'And were they safe? Where are they now?'

Grandad looked at her for a moment, a wave of confusion crossing his face.

'I don't know,' he said simply, and Fay was unsure if that was the answer to her question or a confused response.

A village outside Leningrad

'There's something you aren't telling me, Babushka.' Vera knew the old lady well enough to feel the tension rolling off her.

Babushka nodded, placing the sheets of paper back inside their pouch and into the base of the tin. The false bottom went in with a click.

'There is a lot I'm not telling you. So much you don't need to know. But storm clouds are gathering, my darling, and all I can say is that you need to be prepared. This is the best preparation I can give you.' She pressed the tin into Vera's hands. 'Keep it with you. Learn these words, memorise them, like you did Baba Tonya's medicine instructions. Turn to them when all else fails, drink them in moments of despair.'

Vera's heart raced. 'Babushka, you are scaring me.'

'There is no need to be frightened. Your life is in God's hands. All of you children are. I don't know what is coming, but I know He will see you through.'

Vera didn't think she'd sleep at all that evening. She snuggled into the small bed with her sisters, wanting to think through everything Babushka had said. But the emotion of the day and the long journey meant she fell asleep as soon as her head touched the pillow.

Chapter 29

Lincoln

Fay closed the notebook and leaned back in her chair.

'If we aren't ready now, we never will be! What time do we have to leave?'

Kate looked at her phone.

'They want us to be there at three o'clock, so we've got time for a drink before we go.'

The girls walked into the kitchen. Kate grabbed some juice from the fridge and poured it into a couple of glasses.

'I never realised costuming was so technical. It's more than just clothes, isn't it?'

'Oh, so much more. There is so much to think about in the construction. It's so important to understand every movement the dancer will make in the garment, to make sure it flows in the right way and compliments the dance and doesn't distract the watcher.'

'So, you are pleased with how we are going to do this?'

'Yes, I think the activity will make the girls sit up and take note.'

'Have we got all the costumes you want to show them?'

'Yep. I'm ready. Let's go.'

When they arrived at the dance studio, they were shown into a room. A small group of seven to nine-year-olds were finishing their practising. Fay knew little about dance, but she was impressed by the way they moved to the music. One girl seemed to take it more seriously than the others, trying harder, reaching further. Fay wondered if that child had received additional coaching.

'OK, girls, come and sit down. We have two important guests for us today.'

The girls gathered round and sat on the floor. Fay was again drawn to the girl who took great care to sit down in a suitably 'ballerina' way.

'Hi everyone, I'm Fay and this is my friend Kate.' Fay felt a surge of confidence as she began speaking. 'We're here today to talk to you about costumes. Tell me, when you're thinking about costumes for your dances, what do you need to consider?'

Hand shot up all over the room, and Fay asked each girl to give their name before answering the question. She was impressed by their knowledge. They understood that the fabric had to able to allow the dancer to move and couldn't be too tight or too loose.

Kate took over with a slight wobble in her voice.

'I have two costumes here. I want you to tell me which one is going to look better on a dancer.'

She held up a beautiful, diamante-encrusted leotard with feathers and a headdress. The girls gasped when they saw it. The girl Fay noticed brought her hands to her face, as though overwhelmed with it. 'It's beautiful,' Fay heard her gasp.

'And here's the other costume,' Fay said, pulling out of the bag something that looked like a pile of rags. Everyone laughed. The girl leaned forward and said something to a couple of friends in front of her. They all giggled.

Fay pointed at her. 'What's your name? And what did you say?' She smiled encouragingly.

'I'm Amy-Hope,' the girl said. 'And I was just saying that looks like something my dad would make for me. He's not the best at sewing.'

The girls giggled again.

'OK, Amy-Hope, well, let's see what it looks like on? Would you mind wearing this costume?' Fay bundled it up and gently tossed it to Amy-Hope who pulled a slight face but caught the dress and skipped out of the room.

Kate pointed at her sister. 'Acacia, you can wear this one, since it was made for you anyway.' Kate handed the younger girl the ornate, structured costume. A teacher left the room to help her get into it.

'When the girls come back, we are going to look at the costumes on their bodies. Do they look better or worse than before? Then we'll watch them dance in the costumes. Which costume helps us see the dance better?' Fay looked up at the teachers. 'Do you have some music ready?'

One of the teachers nodded and hurried to line up a piece.

After a couple of minutes, the two girls came back in. Amy-Hope's costume hung off her like rags, but Acacia looked like a glistening snow-globe in her white, sparkly outfit.

'OK, let's remember to be kind, but which costume looks the most impressive?'

'That one,' said all the children, including Amy-Hope, pointing at Kate's sister.

'OK, first, we are going to watch her dance in her costume.'

The teacher played the music, and Acacia danced. It was obvious that the impressive costume was not designed for the ballet moves she was attempting. She danced well, but it was hard for her to make all the moves as freely as she wanted to in the restrictive clothing.

At the end of the piece, everyone applauded.

'What did you notice?' Fay asked.

'The costume sparkled in the light,' offered one girl.

'I think I was watching the sparkles more than I was watching the dance,' said another.

'And how was it to dance in?' Fay asked.

'Well, the costume was designed for a carnival, where I mainly have to walk. It wasn't really comfortable to dance in.'

'OK. And now let's watch Amy-Hope dance the same piece, in the costume her dad made.' Fay winked at her.

The teacher played the same piece of music, and Amy-Hope danced. The costume flowed with her like a shadow, accentuating every movement as though it had its own complementary role in the dance.

At the end, everyone was silent for a moment, then burst into applause. Amy-Hope's face was flushed, and her eyes were shining.

'How did that feel?' Fay asked.

'That felt like magic,' Amy-Hope shook her head slightly, as if trying to explain what she'd just felt. 'It was like I was dancing with someone else. The way it moved around me – it was amazing.'

'And the rest of you, what did you think?'

'It made me want to cry,' one girl said.

'It was just so beautiful. I felt like I was watching the dance for the first time,' added another girl.

Fay nodded. 'That tells me two really important things – lessons that we can all learn. The first is that the costume must be designed for the dance. The sparkly costume is perfect for carnival but doesn't work for ballet. The second point is that sometimes something that seems ugly can be very beautiful in the right place at the right time. Never dismiss a costume because it looks ugly. It may be perfectly designed for the dance.'

The children applauded and Fay turned to see Kate smiling.

'That was more amazing than I could've imagined,' Kate whispered, squeezing Fay's arm. 'You were great.'

One teacher stepped forward and waited until she had the girls' attention.

'That was inspiring. Thank you, Kate and Fay. You have given us an important life lesson today, as well as an excellent introduction to costume. Now, children, who would you like to hear from next week?'

Amy-Hope's hand went straight up. 'Miss, I've just found out that the old lady next door to me used to dance for the Russian Ballet.'

Fay felt like her stomach drop.

'She's been helping me with my posture, giving me lessons over the back fence.' Everyone giggled. 'Maybe I could ask her if she wants to come in and teach us all or tell us about her time as a ballerina.'

'That would be interesting to hear. I don't think I've ever met anyone who danced for the Russian Ballet personally. Yes, would you mind inviting her, Amy? Hopefully she'll be able to come next week. OK, children, that's it for today. I can see your parents gathering outside.'

The room erupted in noise. Parents came in and the children came up to Fay and Kate to thank them for their talk. Fay kept a watchful eye out for Amy-Hope, who'd disappeared to get changed. She wanted to ask her more questions.

After a couple of minutes, she saw her come back, with the costume draped carefully over her arm. She was holding hands with a giant, bearded man, who was listening intently as she skipped and chattered away next to him.

Amy-Hope brought the costume to Fay. 'Thank you so much. I loved dancing in it.'

Fay took a deep breath. 'I wanted to ask about your neighbour. Do you know which Ballet she used to dance for?'

Amy-Hope turned to her dad, who shrugged, but turned to stare at Fay. Fay laughed lightly. 'It's just I think I had a family member who danced in St Petersburg years ago, when it was Leningrad. And I just wondered if maybe they knew each other. It's a small world. What's her name?'

'Mrs Peters,' Amy-Hope answered before her father interrupted.

'Well, thank you very much, Amy-Hope really enjoyed everything you had to say. I'm sure I'll be hearing about it for days. But we must go now.' Turning to his daughter, he asked, 'Do you have everything?'

Amy-Hope ran off to pick up her bag and jacket. She waved cheerfully as they went out of the door, and her father followed, glancing back at Fay with a frown.

Fay struggled to breathe. Peters? Was it a coincidence? But Amy-Hope had said 'Mrs Peters' – had she got married? Was Vera living next door to Amy-Hope and her dad, or was this just a strange coincidence?

A village outside Leningrad

Vera tossed and turned in her little bed. Right now, Slavic would be getting on the train to come here. Tomorrow, she'd see him again for the first time in eight months. They hadn't been able to openly share their feelings in letters, but enough letters had passed between them for it to be understood.

She rolled over and looked at the children sleeping next to her. Nadia and Luba were thriving. They were up early, eating well, learning about the fruit and vegetables growing in the garden. They played with the other children in the village and helped care for Baba Tonya by singing to her and sometimes feeding her. Vera was surprised to hear them singing. They would make up little songs and sing together. She'd never heard them sing before, mainly because they had to stay quiet in the flat. Vera recognised the change in them as similar to her own the previous year. She wondered how these two little ones would go back to the confinement of the flat after the freedom of the village.

They had been delighted with Babushka's words from the Book of Wisdom, although Vera was more concerned now she knew they came from an illegal book. Nadia especially loved the words. She insisted Vera help her learn each verse by heart and even asked Babushka to teach her how to read and write them. Luba, although quieter and more contemplative than her sister, was also relaxing a little.

Vera was glad the children had the chance to meet Baba Tonya, even though it might only be for a short while. Vera dreaded losing her, yet at the same time, she was filled with a sense of peace and thankfulness whenever she thought about it. She'd talked to Babushka about these conflicting emotions a couple of times. Babushka had smiled a rainbow smile, a smile accompanied by tears, and Vera knew she understood.

But tomorrow, Vera would get to introduce the children to Slavic. She was excited to talk about their future and make plans together.

Chapter 30

Lincoln

'Don't you think that's strange?' Fay looked at both of her parents. 'A Russian dancer called Mrs Peters?'

'What's this we're plotting? Are you going to become a Russian spy?' Tom walked into the room, winking at his sister, as he went into the kitchen and put the kettle on.

Fay ignored him. 'What do you think, Dad?'

Dad blew out his breath. 'I honestly don't know! It could be, but it might not. Neither Peters nor Petrov are unusual names, and maybe she is married. It could be miles away from what we're thinking.'

'But what are the chances?' Fay felt her face going red, as she tried to convey the sense of connection she'd felt when Amy-Hope started talking about Mrs Peters. 'A Soviet-trained ballerina, escaping in Lincoln, presumed dead, then years later, someone with an anglicised version of her name shows up.'

'Russian names aren't so unusual here.' Tom leaned against the door frame. 'Wasn't there a big Prisoner of War camp nearby in the Second World War?'

'There were several,' Dad said, 'and many Soviets were captured. After the war, they were released and lots of them headed to Lincoln, settled down and created communities, rather than head back to the Soviet Union.'

'So, could your "Mrs Peters" be one of those?'

'I don't know.' Fay sighed. 'But another thing, Amy-Hope's dad seemed quite suspicious. He didn't want me asking questions. I don't know. I just think there is something going on. And look at it this way, we have been praying for things to come to light, then I just happen to be at the dance school and Amy-Hope just happens to mention her neighbour. Surely, it's more than a coincidence.'

'Well,' said Tom, pouring hot water into the teapot, 'for someone who is so adamantly opposed to God, you sure have a lot of faith in the power of prayer.' He winked at her.

A village outside Leningrad

'Are you meeting Slavic at the station, or is he coming here?' Babushka asked, sipping her tea and looking out over the garden. Vera was enjoying the summer rhythm of the village, where most of life was lived outside.

'We hadn't arranged anything, but I thought I'd go to meet him. Do you think that would be OK?' She paced back and forward, too excited to eat or sit.

'I assume he would've caught the overnight train to Leningrad, then taken the first train out here. He should arrive within the next hour. Do you want to go now? I'll get the girls up and ready for when you come back.'

'Really? Thank you!' Vera leaned over and kissed the old lady.

'But take something to eat – you'll never manage it to the station and back on an empty stomach. He'll be glad to see you, but he won't want to carry you home!'

Vera ran into the kitchen, cut herself a slice of bread, and waved it in farewell as she hurried down the road towards the station.

Vera was quite surprised the stationmaster wasn't in the ticket office when she arrived. Instead, a young boy, who Vera thought might be his son or even his grandson, sat behind the counter.

'When's the train arriving from Leningrad?' asked Vera.

The young boy looked at her for a long time, and Vera wasn't sure if he'd heard her question. Just as she was about to ask again, he looked at the clock.

'In twenty minutes,' he muttered.

'Where's the stationmaster?' she asked, hoping the older man's cheery conversation would distract her until the train came in.

'Telegram. Bad news,' the boy said, pursing his lips as though he'd already said more than he should have.

Vera's heart went out to the stationmaster. What a day to get bad news. The sun was warm and bright. The birds were singing, and the air was fresh.

For the next twenty minutes, Vera split her time between sitting on the bench, walking the length of the platform, and trying to identify the different birdsong. Every time she looked over at the large station clock, the hands seemed to have hardly moved.

At last, Vera heard a different sound in the air. The train was finally coming. A couple more people joined her on the platform, some preparing to sell food and drink to the passengers, others about to join the train themselves. Vera was surprised to see the sullen boy selling tickets. Whatever news the stationmaster had received must have been dreadful to take him away from his duties.

As the train pulled into the station, Vera hopped up and down, looking from one end of the train to the other, wondering which carriage Slavic would travel in. How should she greet him? Should she shake his hand? Would it be acceptable to share a kiss on the cheek?

The train seemed to take an age to come to a stop, and as Vera watched all the carriages pass, she saw very few people waiting to alight. Finally, the doors opened. Vera watched the passengers, but none of them wore an army uniform, and none of them had Slavic's familiar frame. She looked harder, wondering if she hadn't recognised him because of the change that had taken place in the army, but none of the passengers were even their age.

As the train pulled away, the platform cleared of people and Vera was left standing alone. Maybe he'd been held up and got on the next train.

She wandered back through to the ticket office.

'When is the next train from Leningrad?' she asked.

In a repeat performance, which would have been comic if it hadn't been so frustrating, the boy stared at her for almost a full minute, before leaning forward, looking at the clock, and saying, 'In an hour.'

Vera wondered how she'd wait another hour. Maybe she should've brought a book to read.

'Is there any mail for the village?' she asked, wondering if maybe Slavic's plans had changed, and he'd written to tell her the revised dates.

'What village?' the boy asked after his customary stare.

Vera tried not to roll her eyes and named the village.

A flash of shock and something Vera didn't recognise crossed the boy's face, before he schooled his features back into the bored look, which he had obviously perfected in the classroom.

'Nope,' he responded, quicker than usual.

'Don't you need to check? Maybe something arrived for us yesterday.'

'Nope.' He stared at Vera, who sighed and walked back out to the platform.

After another ten minutes of sitting on the bench or pacing up and down, she heard an unfamiliar squeak. Glancing down the road towards the village, she saw the stationmaster approaching on his bicycle. Vera frowned, wondering why he was returning to his post after receiving bad news. As he got closer, she saw his face was paler than usual and his eyes were downcast, lacking their usual twinkle.

Stepping out to greet him, and eager to pass on her condolences, she registered his surprise as he looked up and saw her standing there.

'Vera, my child, what are you doing here?'

His face seemed to grow paler. He glanced around.

'Are you here alone?' he asked.

Vera nodded. Something about his response was unsettling.

'I heard you had some bad news. I wanted to pass on my condolences.' Vera placed her hand over her heart and dipped her head slightly.

The stationmaster propped his bike against the wall and approached her. As he drew nearer, something about the sadness in his eyes and the pity in the tilt of his head made Vera back away. He reached for her hands and gently squeezed them.

'You need to go home,' he whispered softly, nodding back towards the village, as though she needed confirmation that he meant there, and not her city home.

'I'm waiting for... Slavic.' The words come out in a whisper, and Vera caught the older man's wince as she mentioned the younger man's name.

He cleared his throat, but his voice was still husky when he spoke again.

'You need to go home. I'm sorry.' He gently pushed her towards the road, nodding kindly when she looked back at him.

Why was he sorry? Why couldn't she wait for Slavic? What was the bad news he'd heard earlier that day?

Vera felt like she was walking in a tunnel. She could no longer hear the birdsong; she could only hear the beating of her heart. She couldn't feel the warmth of the sun; she only felt the constriction of her skirt against her legs, slowing her down as she hurried towards the village.

What had seemed like a long walk to the station on her way to greet Slavic now seemed ten times longer. She'd never imagined walking back without him, and a sense of foreboding picked at the edges of her mind. She tried to remind herself of the verse from the Book of Wisdom that she and Nadia had learned the day before, something about love driving out fear, but she couldn't remember it and her mind couldn't seem to find it.

Vera stopped for a moment. Where was she going? Why was she returning to the village without Slavic? Surely, it'd be better if she waited for him at the station and they came back together? Whatever the bad news was, they could handle it together. Her heart ached at the thought of him making this journey alone, without her, heading back to whatever bad news the telegram had delivered. Maybe she should go back to the station and wait for him. The stationmaster obviously didn't understand how close they were, and couldn't know how much he'd need her support, or how much she needed him.

Looking around, she noticed she was about halfway back to the village. For a full minute she stood, not knowing whether to go forward or backwards; scared that whichever decision she made would be the wrong one and would lead to a lengthening of this torturous not-knowing.

'God, please help. I don't know what to do.' Vera realised that was the first time she'd spoken out loud to God. Could that be classed as a prayer? 'I don't know whether to go on to the village or back to the station,' she whispered. A longing for the familiarity of Babushka's kitchen overwhelmed her for a moment. She needed to go home. As she took a step towards the village, thoughts of Slavic filled her mind. Her desire to be close to him was driving her back to the station.

'God, please help,' she repeated.

'Vera! Oh Vera!'

Vera's head jerked up, hearing her little sister's cry.

'Nadia, what are you doing here?' she said, sweeping the whirlwind of a child up into her arms, but the child didn't reply. She just clung on tightly.

Olya followed her up the path from the village, holding Luba by the hand.

'Olya?' Vera's voice held a thousand questions, but Olya refused to meet her gaze. She looked down at Luba and gave an empty smile.

'We thought we'd come and meet you, didn't we?'

Luba nodded; her face downcast.

They all turned and walked towards the village, Nadia still clinging on to Vera's neck. Vera was grateful for the warmth of her sister's body, even though the child seemed to grow heavier the further they walked. No one asked where Slavic was. Surely, they would've been expecting to see him with her? Isn't that why they came out? To meet Slavic? So why did no one ask where he was? Why couldn't Olya look her in the eye?

Vera felt fear grab at her heart. She tried to voice the thoughts prowling through her head but could not articulate them.

Who was the stationmaster's telegram for? She'd assumed it was personal, but replaying his reaction to her, and now Olya's silence, she began to wonder if it hadn't been for someone else.

Finally, she could take it no more. She lowered Nadia to the ground, noticing the tear tracks down the little girl's face.

'Olya?' Vera forced her voice out of her throat. 'What...?'

Olya turned, placed her hand on Vera's arm, and slowly raised her eyes. Vera saw infinite pain and the realisation of all her deepest fears.

'Slavic?' she asked in a whisper.

Olya nodded slowly, and Vera felt all her strength leave her. She was unsure of what happened next, aware only of Olya's strong arms around her and a searing pain through her stomach and chest. Olya must have sent the children back to the village, because Vera watched them run away, and it was as though her happiness and her dreams were running away from her and she could not call them back.

In her pain, all she wanted was Slavic. His friendship, his strength, his steady faith, to help her deal with all of this, but like a wave washing over her, she remembered he wasn't there, and that was the very cause of her pain.

Each breath was like breathing in hot burning coals, and she couldn't hear anything but a ringing in her ears.

Slowly, she noticed other voices around her, strong arms lifting her up. The familiar voice of her grandmother, encouraging her forward. They helped her back to the village. She desperately wanted to go back to Babushka's house, to hide away and weep, but she had no voice, and it would appear, no choice. She was led by the hand to Slavic's grandmother's house.

As she entered, the silence in the room felt deafening. She approached Slavic's grandmother, leaned down and kissed her cheek. The old woman looked straight ahead as though she was made of marble, but Vera had tasted her tears. She was shown to a seat across the room, where she sank down into the quiet. The room was full of people, and Vera felt comforted by the company of those who loved Slavic too, but she also felt stifled by their presence.

She looked across the room to Slavic's grandmother, a woman she had also called Babushka out of respect. The two women locked eyes. For both of them, the most important man in their world had been taken away. One held only memories, the other held only dreams, but both women were now cut adrift and did not know how to live without him. One had no more need to, and the other had no choice but to.

Slavic's grandmother suddenly arose, causing everyone else in the room to rise too. She shuffled towards the door, stopping anyone from following her with an upheld hand. She turned, looked at Vera, and beckoned her to follow.

The two women stepped out into the sunshine. For Vera, noticing the sun for the first time since leaving the train station, it seemed incongruent that the sun should still shine when her world had just ended.

Slavic's grandmother closed her eyes and held her face up to the sun. She reminded Vera of a sunflower, turning its head to follow the path of its namesake.

'You must leave. He planned for you to leave. It is too dangerous for you to stay.'

Vera shook her head. She had expected words of kindness, sharing of memories, stories of Slavic's childhood, but not this. Her heart had been shattered in a million pieces, her mind too numb to process the questions of how and why that pierced the fog. And now she was being pushed in another direction, being forced to picture the future he had planned for them, but without him by her side.

Slavic's babushka nodded. 'It's too much for you now, but you must know this. He knew you needed to leave. He was preparing for it.'

'Leave where?' Vera looked around at the little village she had grown to love.

The old lady waited until Vera's gaze returned to her face.

'You need to leave Russia.'

Chapter 31

A village outside Leningrad

The day passed with a string of people coming and going. A quiet core of women sat in Slavic's grandmother's house, with others coming in, sitting for a while, then leaving, with a quiet word to Slavic's babushka and a glance towards Vera.

As evening approached, Vera registered the sound of a bicycle coming down the track and the gate opening. She stood up, hoping the stationmaster had more news for them. When she got outside, he was already in deep conversation with her own babushka. As Vera approached, the two fell silent.

'I want to know,' Vera said, pushing the words out through dried chapped lips. Babushka nodded, and the stationmaster talked. As soon as he opened his mouth, Vera realised she didn't want to know, wished she could run away, cover her ears, anything to escape the sounds that told the story. But shock froze her body, and she stayed and listened to the information the stationmaster had gleaned.

'There was an explosion at the army base. The warehouse containing the munitions blew up. We don't know how. Everyone on site was killed instantly. Although it wasn't Slavic's team that was on duty in the warehouse, he'd offered to do that shift to cover for a friend who was sick. There is no way they can return the body to us. Everything was destroyed.'

Vera watched the tears run down her babushka's face, and shivered, feeling cold in every part of her body.

'I need to take her home,' Babushka said to the stationmaster, glancing at Vera. 'Can you stay with her for a moment?'

The stationmaster nodded, and Babushka returned to the hut, probably relaying the news to those waiting inside. Vera began to shake and barely registered the stationmaster's hand on her shoulder. Slavic's grandmother came out of the hut and watched as Babushka led Vera away. As they passed Olya's house, Olya came out with the twins. Nadia climbed on the gate and launched herself into Vera's arms, ignoring her grandmother's chiding. Vera caught the child instinctively, and Nadia clung on to her. Vera's arms tightened around the little girl, and the warmth of the child slowly warmed her. The beating of the child's heart encouraged hers to keep beating. And her little whispers of love in Vera's ear soothed the memory of the stationmaster's words, giving Vera the strength to make it home.

Upon reaching her house, Babushka tended to Baba Tonya before making some tea, while the girls quietly got dressed for bed. Vera drank the tea without tasting it.

'Babushka?' Nadia's voice rang through the gathering fog in Vera's mind. 'Do you remember the words from the Book of Wisdom today?'

Babushka screwed up her forehead, and stared at the wall, as though trying to remember.

'"My flesh and my heart may fail, but God is the strength of my heart and my portion for ever."' Nadia recited. 'Do you think that wisdom was put there especially for Vera today?'

Babushka's eyes filled with tears. 'I think so,' she said, leaning over and kissing the child's head. They helped the children into bed, Vera automatically replaying the movements she had made every night since the girls were born, her babushka helping when needed. She whispered the love-filled words that she always said, kissed their heads, and then lay down next to them. Sleep overtook her without allowing her to process everything that had happened that day.

The next morning, the light hurt Vera's eyes when she tried to open them. She shifted slightly and groaned.

'Here,' Babushka said, putting a glass of water in her hand.

'What time is it?' croaked Vera, taking a sip. 'And what did you put in my tea last night?'

Babushka gave a nervous cough. 'Let's just say that there is a reason Baba Tonya has always kept me well away from her potions and mixtures. I'm not as gifted as she is.'

Vera sat up and looked around. The bed was empty and there were empty bowls on the table.

'Where are the girls?'

'They are out in the garden with the chickens. Vera, today will be a hard day. Are you ready?'

A physical pain shot through Vera's chest, and it took a moment for her mind to recall the events of yesterday. Confusion filled her mind as losing Slavic had to be processed all over again.

Babushka sat on the edge of the bed.

'You do not need to have all the answers today, my child. Today is not a day to plan your future. Today is a day to say goodbye. That's all you must do. Tomorrow we can look at what is next and what the future looks like. Today, you just need to breathe.'

Vera looked up at Babushka. 'I don't think I can even do that,' she said weakly.

Babushka's smile disappeared, replaced by a steely edge Vera had only ever glimpsed briefly.

'My daughter, everyone in this village has lost someone: fathers, brothers, husbands and children,' Babushka choked on the last few words. 'Here, we greet the loss with a raised head. We accept it with God's strength, knowing that He is by our sides. You can weep here later, but today, you do Slavic proud and give him a send-off that honours him, not one that centres on your sadness. You are not the only one with a broken heart today.'

Vera felt strangely comforted and strengthened by Babushka's scolding. She nodded, determined to be the strong woman Slavic was coming home to.

A familiar footstep on the porch caused Babushka and Vera to turn to the door.

'Mishka!' Babushka was swept up into Papa's arms and her father's huge frame seemed to fill the little house.

Vera struggled out of bed and was waiting for her father's embrace when he put his mother down.

'I'm glad you're here,' she said, as he held her.

'Be strong,' he whispered, drawing back and looking her in the eye. She nodded.

Lincoln

'The End.' Fay lowered the magazine and sighed contentedly. There was something so fulfilling about a beautifully written short story. She looked up, only to find that the woman she'd been reading to now had her eyes closed and her mouth wide open. A snore emerged, by way of thanks, and Fay chuckled to herself.

'She hasn't slept for days,' came a voice from the bed behind her. 'You should come and read to her more often. Can I book you for three o'clock in the morning?'

'That might cost you.' Fay turned to the sprightly woman in the next bed.

'Whatever you charge, I'd pay it, rather than being woken up by her asking if my Yorkshire pudding recipe could beat hers. The rubbish that goes through her mind in the early hours! I might just try to get some shut-eye while she's asleep, but I think I'd rather stay awake and revel in the peace.'

Fay smiled and moved nearer to her bed. 'So, have you been here long?'

'Only a week. What about you? And since we're asking cheesy questions – do you come here often?'

Fay laughed out loud, then hushed herself, checking the woman behind was still sleeping. 'It's my first day. I'm here to read with people who don't have family visiting them.'

'Well, you'd better stop talking to me then,' the old lady said, her eyes twinkling 'I've got thirteen grandchildren, and they're queuing up to visit me.' She laughed, pointing to the many handmade cards stuck on the wall behind her bed. 'With tomorrow being Saturday, they'll be here in force. I came here to get away from them all. Here they can only get to me for a couple of hours a day! I'm only joking – they make my life worth living.'

She pointed to a bed by the window. It seemed bereft of personal touches and the occupant laid low, looking out the window and ignoring the goings-on in the rest of the ward.

'I've noticed the woman over there hasn't had anyone visit yet. It could still be early days. She's new in, but when all the other families come, she doesn't even look up. It's as though she isn't expecting anyone.'

'OK, thanks, I'll go over and say hi.'

'I'll call you next time I want her putting to sleep.' The lady nodded at the woman in the neighbouring bed, and Fay had to stifle a giggle.

'Hello, my name's Fay. I'm here with the volunteer reading programme. I was wondering if you would like me to read with you,' Fay asked, as she approached the bed by the window.

The woman in the bed looked over at Fay, then back out of the window.

After a moment of uncomfortable silence, Fay coughed slightly, but on getting no response, she walked away, determined to try another time.

Chapter 32

A village outside Leningrad

Papa and two older boys from the village carried an empty wooden coffin to the cemetery. Since a body would not be returned, this was the only chance for the village to make their farewells. Seeing the people gathered, Vera was struck by the lack of men. Babushka's words came back to her, that everyone in the village had lost someone, and the stark reality shook her. She raised her head higher, determined not to let this band of strong women down.

Slavic's grandmother walked alone behind the coffin. After a couple of steps, she stopped and looked around. Seeing Vera a few steps behind, she beckoned her over, took her arm and the two women continued together, heads held high, hearts broken.

The official who had travelled from the nearest town, said a few words at the graveside, before returning to his car, parked on the edge of the village.

In the silence that followed, Papa stepped forward to the head of the grave and began to speak.

'Yet I am always with you;
you hold me by my right hand.
You guide me with your counsel,
and afterwards you will take me into glory'

There were a few murmurs of agreement from the crowd, and Slavic's grandmother repeated the last line under her breath, joining with Papa as he continued:

'Whom have I in heaven but you?
And earth has nothing I desire besides you.
My flesh and my heart may fail;
But God is the strength of my heart
and my portion forever.'

It took Vera a moment to realise that he was speaking the same words that Babushka had spoken the day before. Slavic's grandmother squeezed Vera's hand, as though wanting to impress those words into her heart. Papa continued, and a few other voices joined him, whispering under their breath:

'Those who are far from you will perish;
you destroy all who are unfaithful to you.
But as for me, it is good to be near God.

I have made the Sovereign Lord my refuge;
I will tell of all your deeds.'

Papa looked around at the gathered people.

'Slavic put his trust in God, and we know he has been received now into glory. And we will see him again on that final day. I know he would want me to remind you of the words our Lord spoke before his death. "Peace I leave with you, my peace I give to you. I do not give to you as the world gives. Do not let your hearts be troubled and do not be afraid."'

'Amen,' Slavic's babushka whispered, patting Vera's hand, before releasing it to greet Papa. Papa approached, took the old woman's hands, and kissed them. They shared a moment of silence together, and gradually everyone around the graveside moved away. Papa took the old lady's arm and reached over for Vera's hand, leading the women away from the grave. But as they walked, Vera knew she didn't have the same confidence that the rest of the village seemed to share.

Lincoln

'Hello again, we met yesterday,' Fay smiled as she approached the bed in the corner. 'I've been reading to others in the ward, and I wondered if I could read to you.'

The woman in the bed continued to look out of the window. If Fay hadn't noticed her flinch when she first spoke, she'd assume the woman was deaf.

Determined to persevere, Fay sat down in the chair next to the bed, pulling it round slightly, so she could see out of the window, too. After taking a moment to admire the view, she tried again.

'My name is Faith Peterson.' For a moment, Fay was surprised that she had used her birth name. She hadn't used it for years, but it had just felt right. She looked back at the bed and was surprised to see the woman staring at her intensely.

'Faith Peterson?' The woman asked, her eyes wide.

'Yes, my mum is a nurse here. I'm with the volunteer reading programme.'

'What's your father's name?'

Fay could hear a strong accent in the woman's voice. She'd raised herself up slightly on the bed and was reaching for the call buttons. Confused at the question and the increasing panic in the woman's eyes, Fay answered, 'It's Michael.'

The woman shrieked, leapt backwards, and pressed the button.

'Nurse, nurse!' she shouted. 'Help, nurse.'

Fay stood up and quickly backed away.

A nurse came running over. 'Now, now, what's wrong?'

'They've found me. They're going to kill me. Get her out of here.' The woman's hand shook as she pointed at Fay.

Upset and confused, Fay rushed out of the ward. She paced up and down in the corridor, not sure what she had said that so upset the woman.

After a couple of minutes, the nurse came out.

'Hi Fay, are you OK?'

'I think so. I didn't mean to upset her.'

'Don't worry about Mrs Peters. She's on medication after her surgery and is very confused.'

'Mrs Peters?' Fay repeated, finding it hard to catch her breath. Could this be the same Mrs Peters that Amy-Hope mentioned? 'I didn't mean to frighten her. Is she going to be OK?'

'She had a nasty fall, and no one found her for a few days. She was quite dehydrated, but she's doing better now.'

'A few days? Why so long? Doesn't she have any family?'

'Not that I'm aware of. The neighbours have recently moved in, and they found her. There doesn't seem to be any other family. Anyway, maybe you could finish up now, and come back another day. Hopefully she'll be calmer.'

Fay nodded and glanced back into the ward. The curtains were drawn around the bed.

'Get yourself a cup of tea before you go home, OK? You look pale,' the nurse said, before heading back inside the ward.

Fay was left alone in the corridor. Had she just met her great-aunt? No wonder the woman was frightened, meeting someone with an English version of her own name. Petrova, Vera Mikhailovna meet Faith Peterson, daughter of Michael.

Chapter 33

A village outside Leningrad

Vera sat on the floor next to Baba Tonya's bed. The peace that filled the room was the only comfort Vera could find. Baba Tonya seemed to drift easily between sleep and being awake. Her lips moved in silent prayer in her wakeful moments, and would often pause while sleep overtook her, and continue again as though nothing had happened, when consciousness beckoned. Vera knew Baba Tonya was praying for her and felt strengthened by her prayers.

Kissing Baba Tonya's forehead, Vera rose and went in search of her father. Checking the garden and still seeing no sign of him, she wondered if he'd gone back to the station without saying goodbye. Vera found herself drawn in the direction of the cemetery. Her feet seemed to go there all by themselves. She wasn't sure why, or what she was hoping to find, but she was surprised to see her father finishing filling in the grave. In the city, it was taken for granted that these things are sorted out somehow, but in a village with very few men, the job wasn't so easy.

She stood for a while, watching Papa work. Finally, he stopped and stretched out his back. Looking around, he noticed her standing by the gate, and nodded for her to join him on a rough bench nearby.

For a long time, they sat together in silence.

'Do you really believe those words? That Slavic is "in glory"?' Vera finally asked.

'Yes, I do. I believe it with my whole heart. I'm sorry if I haven't been better at teaching you children these things.'

Vera shook her head. 'They are dangerous words, Papa. It's not easy to trust children with these things. Nadia is intent on learning Babushka's words of wisdom, but I'm worried they'll get her into trouble.'

'No, daughter. They will always lead her out of trouble. They are the greatest gift we can give the little ones.'

'But it's not safe, Papa. You know it's illegal to own or speak those words.' Vera's frustration came out in tears, and once they had started to fall, they wouldn't stop.

'"The Lord is with me; I will not be afraid. What can mere mortals do to me?"' Papa's voice was gentle as he quoted another phrase that Vera had heard Babushka say.

'What can mere mortals do to me?' Her anger took her by surprise. 'They can kill you. That's what they can do to you! Haven't you seen enough? You know what man can do. It happened in your own family, to your own

259

grandfather. We have a reason to fear. It's foolish to pretend we haven't.'

'I choose to believe the words of the Bible. They are words of life. You found God here in the village, now you need to learn to trust Him.'

'Even when He can take everything away?' She pointed towards the freshly filled-in grave.

'That is why it's called faith. That's why you are called Faith. We don't know, we don't understand, but we choose to believe.'

'I don't know if I can, Papa.' She leaned on his shoulder and began to sob.

'I pray you will be able to, my daughter.' He kissed her head, and they stayed there for a while.

Father and daughter walked back from the cemetery together. Returning to Babushka's house, they sat with her and the girls, sharing a cup of tea and some of the fruit the girls had picked that day. The twins were excited to tell Papa everything that they had experienced in the village, although Luba kept her hand firmly in Vera's, as though sharing her pain, even as she related the fun of the summer.

Vera asked about home, and was relieved to hear the boys were well, although father was quite vague when she asked about her mother. Vera shook off the niggling feeling that he wasn't telling them everything, and they arranged that they would return home in a week's time.

Vera would have four weeks of practise before going on the international tour, and Papa and Artyom were working closely with the Ballet to make sure all her paperwork was up to date.

Papa glanced at the clock hanging on the wall. He sighed and looked tenderly at his daughters.

'I need to go,' he said, 'but I must discuss some things with your grandmother first. Give me hugs, daughters, and I'll see you again at the end of the month.' After energetic hugs from the twins and a long silent embrace with Vera, Papa left the room, following his mother out into the garden.

After five minutes, Babushka returned, hurrying straight into her room, before coming back in her gardening clothes, and suggesting that they all spend some time in the fresh air working in the garden.

'Today?' asked Vera, thinking that she could be excused on the day she buried the man of her dreams.

'Today.' Babushka was resolute. 'Today of all days, you need to be reminded of the God who created us all and holds us all together. And there are some tomatoes on the vine that need to be brought in today, so get changed and meet us out there.'

Lincoln

Grandad's face lit up as Fay walked into the lounge.

'Have you come to visit me?' he asked, looking around the room, as though checking whether there was anyone they'd prefer to talk to.

'Of course we have, Grandad.' She leaned over and kissed his cheek.

'Wendy's just in the kitchen. We'll have a cup of tea soon.'

Fay's heart sank.

'Hi Arthur,' Mum smiled as she entered the room, putting something in her bag.

Grandad looked at Mum for a minute, confusion written across his face. Not missing a beat, Mum reached out her hand. 'My name's Lisa,' she said.

'Lisa,' Grandad took her hand and smiled warmly. 'What a lovely name. Do have a seat. My wife is just getting us some tea.'

'Should I help her?' Mum asked.

Grandad looked around, clearly lost.

'Well, yes, if you know where you're going.'

'I'll find it.' Mum winked at Fay as she left the room.

'So, how's school?' asked Grandad, settling himself back into his chair.

'It's fine. We're on summer holidays now.'

'Holidays? Well, that's a fine thing. So how are you keeping busy?'

'I was part of a summer programme at the Theatre for a while, but that didn't really work out, so now I'm volunteering at the hospital, reading to people who don't have visitors.'

'Oh, that's nice.' Grandad rubbed his hands together and looked around the room, as though looking for another topic of conversation.

'Sorry, there isn't going to be a Sunday service today,' Fay said. 'Dad is away preaching at another church. But maybe I could read to you instead. I read a story the other day which I think you'd like. It's about a boy who liked trains.'

'Oh, that sounds interesting. Yes, please.'

Fay pulled a magazine out of her bag, and quickly finding the place, began to read. She noticed that other residents in the lounge also leaned forward, and she raised her voice slightly so that everyone could hear.

At the end of the story, there was a small ripple of applause, and Grandad sat back with a satisfied smile. 'Well, that was lovely,' he said.

Mum came in with a tray of tea.

'Is Wendy cooking up a storm?'

'Yes, she is,' Mum winked at Fay. 'What's your favourite thing she cooks?'

'Oh, I love everything Wendy makes. It's all so tasty. But I remember one time she made some oat biscuits. She was so disappointed. She didn't put enough sugar in, and then over-cooked them. She blamed it on the pregnancy and was about to throw them out. But you know what?' Grandad gave a little chuckle. 'They were the best thing I'd ever tasted. Reminded me of such a special day. I asked her to make them like that every time, but she never did.'

'What was the special ocassion?' Mum gently prodded. Fay shot her a scowl, but she ignored it and kept talking, gently and quietly. 'Oat biscuits? That must've been a good day.'

'It was,' Grandad smiled, leaning back in his chair. 'Vera and the girls were coming back from the village. We wanted to have a little party.'

'Of course you did. Had they been there long?'

'Just a month, but a lot had happened. We knew it'd be the last party we'd have together, but of course, they didn't know it then. Usually Vera cooked, but my cooking wasn't up to hers, and Mother, well, she'd already gone.'

'Gone... died?' Mum asked gently.

'Oh no, she left us.'

Fay gasped. 'She left you? She left her children?'

'It's hard to imagine, isn't it?' Grandad reached out and took her hand. 'She'd been ill. They'd have a fancy name for it now, but she never got out of bed, never went anywhere.'

'Was she disabled?' Mum passed Grandad a cup of tea.

'Oh no, her legs worked when she wanted them to. She just never wanted to. And then she started getting these letters. She tried to hide them from us, but you can't hide much in a one-room apartment. We never knew who she was writing to, but I have to say it was a relief when we came home from work to find her and her things gone.'

'Why was it a relief, Grandad?'

'It's hard to put into words. It was like a cloud had lifted. We didn't have to whisper all the time. There wasn't the constant tension in the room. Of course, once she left, we knew it would only be a matter of time before she told someone what she knew. We knew we'd have to get away.' Grandad sighed, shaking his head. 'I've never understood how a mother could leave her children without so much as a goodbye. But those were the times we lived in, and we all did what we had to, to survive.'

Fay sat stunned for a few minutes. Grandad sipped his tea, as though he'd just talked about a television programme, rather than his own family. *Her* family. She glanced at Mum, who took a deep breath.

'So, Arthur, does Wendy make good cakes?' Mum's question drew Grandad back from the dark memories of his childhood.

'Oh, her chocolate cake is to die for. You'll never taste anything so good. Lovely and light, and the cream she makes with it. Oh, I used to sneak downstairs and help myself to a bit while she was sleeping. I'm sure she knew. She'd always say "Oh, it looks like the mice had a party last night, I'm glad they enjoyed such a large slice of cake!"'

Grandad chuckled at the memory and then yawned.

'Looks like we've worn you out,' Mum said. 'We'll head off now.'

'Do come again. I've enjoyed our little chat. I'll ask Wendy to make you that chocolate cake next time you come. You'll love it.'

'I'm sure we will, Arthur.' Mum kissed him goodbye. Fay gave him a quick hug and waved goodbye as she left, troubled by everything she'd heard.

Chapter 34

A village outside Leningrad

The evenings were drawing in, although it was still warm and bright until late into the evening. The night before they were due to leave, Babushka beckoned Vera into her bedroom as soon as the twins were asleep.

'They've grown so much this last month,' Babushka said, as she and Vera sat on the edge of her bed.

'I've never seen them as happy as they have been this summer. Thank you for loving them so much. They've just blossomed.'

Babushka looked down at her fingers, then over at Baba Tonya's sleeping form.

'They aren't happy in the city?' she asked.

'Well, there isn't as much room for them in the *kommunalka*, and because Mama sleeps so much, they have to stay quiet. I've so enjoyed seeing them play and hearing them laugh. There isn't much of that at home.'

'I wish they could stay longer,' Babushka glanced at Vera.

'Oh, wouldn't that be wonderful?' Vera sighed. 'They could help you with the garden and caring for Baba Tonya. They would grow up healthy and strong. I wouldn't have to worry about Nadia repeating any of the words of wisdom in awkward places.'

Vera paused for a moment, thinking about how much more life the children would have if they were raised outside of the suspicion and shadows of the city.

'But Mama would never agree with that,' she finally sighed. 'We were all so surprised when she agreed to let them come this summer. I think she needs to feel like she is in control and letting them come here was the first time I've ever seen her give up control so easily.'

'And you, my daughter,' Babushka reached for her hand. 'Your world has turned upside down these last few days. What are your plans now?'

Vera squeezed her hand.

'I don't have any. I will dance, go on tour, but then? I really don't know. I can't seem to think ahead of the next month. I can't see my future in Leningrad, nor do I see myself returning here. I just don't know. But I'm OK not knowing, right now.'

'God will show you at the right time,' the old woman said, patting her hand.

'Maybe.'

'I want you to take the tea tin back to Leningrad. Keep it with you always. Study and learn the words of life. They will keep you. Wherever you go in the world, look for people of faith who also know these words and live by them. They will be life to you.'

Vera glanced at her grandmother. 'You make it sound like I'm going on a huge, long adventure to faraway places.'

'Isn't that what an international tour is?'

'Yes, but I'm coming back again. I'll only be gone for a couple of months.'

Babushka leaned back on the bed and turned to look out of the window, watching the sunset. Vera knew there was so much she wasn't telling her, but she also knew that she didn't necessarily want to know.

Vera got up early the next morning and sat by Baba Tonya's bedside for a while. The old lady looked at her, her eyes sparkling with a life which seemed so much greater than her frail body.

'It's nearly time for you to go,' Baba's voice was thin, but determined.

'Yes,' Vera said. 'Our train leaves in a couple of hours.'

Baba Tonya shook her head slightly, the effort of the movement causing her pain.

'No, you must go further. You must leave this life of fear and embrace the life you were created to live.'

Vera frowned.

'What do you mean, Baba Tonya?' she asked. But the old lady closed her eyes, and the gentle rise and fall of her chest told Vera that she was sleeping again. Vera replayed Baba Tonya's words in her mind, but still couldn't understand them.

Quietly leaving the room, she hurried through the village to say goodbye to Slavic's grandmother before they left for the train.

'I was hoping you'd come, my daughter,' she said, greeting Vera. 'There is so much I need to tell you, and you need to hear me.'

Vera finally felt brave enough to listen. Since the old lady's declaration on the day of Slavic's death, she'd been wary of spending any time alone with her. She hadn't wanted to know what Slavic's plans were for them as a couple, for their family. But her grandmother's conversation last night and Baba Tonya's words this morning had planted the seeds of a life outside of the Soviet Union. Was this what Slavic had planned for her? She couldn't leave the village without finding out more.

'Slavic knew you couldn't stay here,' his babushka explained. 'The reputation of this village, of your family, it would ruin any chances for you to progress in the Ballet, regardless of your talent. He wanted you to have a life away from fear, away from suspicion. It had taken him a long time to get to that decision. At first, he wanted you to stay in the village here with him, but as he prayed for you, he felt God telling him He had a life for you outside of Russia.'

Vera shook her head. 'I'm still new to this, Babushka. I am struggling with the idea that God talked to Slavic about us and our life. Especially that He would say something so specific, so unusual.'

Slavic's babushka laughed. 'My child, only a God of my own making, would tell me things that didn't surprise me. He knew it was God *because* it was so different from anything he could imagine.'

Vera had never considered that.

'All I'm saying is that if God has a plan for you outside the Soviet Union, He will bring it to pass, even though Slavic is no longer here. If you get the opportunity to leave, you must. You'll know the right time, but you will need to be brave. Can you do that?'

The old lady gripped Vera's hands, squeezing so hard that Vera struggled not to wince.

'I will, I promise,' she said.

Vera kissed the old lady's cheek and left the house, turning to wave to her as she stood in the doorway.

As she passed Olya's house, Olya came out and joined her. Vera was grateful for her friendly chatter. She wasn't ready to think through the implications of what Slavic's babushka had said.

As she gathered up her belongings and checked the twins hadn't forgotten anything, she wondered if she'd ever come back to this village and whether she'd ever see this little house again.

Lincoln

Fay's heart was beating quickly as she headed to the ward. After Mrs Peters' reaction to her last week, she was nervous about going back.

Mum had assured her that Mrs Peters had settled down quickly and encouraged Fay to return.

Pausing outside the ward to gather her courage, Fay was surprised to hear her name.

'Look, Dad. It's Fay from dance class. Hi Fay, what are you doing here? I don't think anyone here needs a dance costume.'

Fay laughed. 'Hi Amy-Hope! I think you're right, but sometimes I read to the people here who haven't got any family.'

'Mrs Peters doesn't have any family, and she's here. Have you read for her?'

Fay was very aware of Amy-Hope's dad observing her, and hoped her face remained calm, although she could feel her neck getting hot. What were the chances of Amy-Hope's Mrs Peters ending up on her ward?

'I tried to,' she said, looking at the dad and offering her explanation. 'But she got very upset. Do you remember I said I think I have a family member who danced for the Kirov Ballet? Well, I was named after that person, and I wonder if my name brought back difficult memories for her.'

'That would explain it. She said something yesterday about a girl with a name that upset her. I wouldn't want to see her that upset again.' The man's eyes narrowed.

'Neither would I,' Fay agreed. 'But maybe she has information that could help me, or maybe I know things that could help her. If she is who I think she is, we might even be related.'

'Wow!' Amy-Hope jumped up and down, 'That would be so amazing. She doesn't talk about her family. And I know she misses them.'

Fay found her eyes filling with tears. The thought that Vera and her brother could have been living so close to each other for so long, without knowing it, was too painful to think about.

'But how can we do that without upsetting her?' Amy's dad looked serious. 'I understand you want answers, but I'm not prepared to see her upset.'

'Let me think about it. Can you meet me here tomorrow, and maybe I'll have a plan?'

The man nodded. Looking down at his daughter, he squeezed her hand.

'Ready?' he asked. She grinned at him, and they stepped into the ward with a friendly greeting.

Fay stood back and watched Mrs Peters' reaction. She seemed genuinely pleased to see Amy-Hope and her dad. She obviously felt safe with them. As her face broke into a smile, Fay gasped, realising that the woman in the bed had the same smile as her grandfather.

Chapter 35

Leningrad

Vera led two weary girls off the train and through the ticket office to the outside of the station. She'd noticed a change in them as the train had travelled through the outskirts of Leningrad. Their smiles and easy conversation evaporated as a cloud of despondency came over them. She couldn't blame them. The thought of returning to the *kommunalka* to play quietly while Mama slept would be enough to sap the life out of anyone. She was grateful she could escape to the Ballet, but the little girls were trapped there until next year when they turned seven and were finally old enough to go to school.

She wondered if anyone would be there to meet them and took a moment to look around. The station was busy, and the girls seemed overwhelmed by the sheer number of moving people. As they walked towards the metro, Vera saw a familiar figure leaning up against the wall.

'Vlad!' she called out, giving her brother a quick hug. He held her for a moment, before gently pushing her away, as any self-respecting ten-year-old would do. He nodded gruffly to the girls, took Vera's rucksack off her back, and picked up her heavy bag. Free of her burdens, Vera took both girls' hands and followed her brother down the steps to the metro. Vlad did not seem eager to talk on the journey home, and Vera allowed the suspicious silence of the city to seep into her soul. She watched the same response in her sisters. It was almost like watching the lights go out in their eyes. It was heart-breaking to see. Vera didn't remember her return being this difficult last time.

When they got back to the flat, Vlad let them in through the big door, then unlocked the door to their room. Vera was surprised. Usually, it was never locked because her mother was always there. As they walked in, Vera noticed that the bed that her mother occupied was stripped bare and had been returned to a sofa position.

'Where's Mama?' she asked, after Vlad had shut the door. The two girls stood, looking at the sofa as though they had never seen it before. Vera realised they probably never had, not in that position at least.

Vlad shrugged. 'I don't know. She left. Papa and Artyom will tell you more. I need to get back to work. Are you OK to cook dinner?' He raised his eyes, hopefully.

Vera was confused. Where had their mother gone, and when would she be back? But Vlad ignored the questions in her gaze and waited for her to answer him.

Vera tried to smile back. 'I'll figure something out. Take care at work, OK?'

She wasn't happy that he was working at only ten years of age, although Artyom hadn't been much older when he'd started. Papa felt it would be beneficial for Vlad, arguing that it didn't do him any good sitting around the flat all summer. At least at work, Artyom could keep an eye on him and help keep him out of trouble.

She looked around the flat, feeling totally lost. She had never imagined she'd be returning to this flat, having not seen Slavic. She imagined that she'd come back to tell her mother that she was engaged. Now there was no engagement, and she wasn't sure when she'd be able to tell her mother.

'Let's get something to drink, then head out to the river for a walk before I start dinner,' Vera suggested and was rewarded with heartfelt smiles from her younger sisters.

Lincoln

'What if we were to take Grandad to see her?' Fay looked at her parents.

Mum shook her head. 'He equates hospitals with losing Granny Wendy. We couldn't put him through that.'

'What if we were to ask her outright if her name is Vera?' Dad suggested.

Again, Mum shook her head. 'She seems to think that the KGB are after her, following her. If we ask her to confirm an identity she left behind years ago, she'll think the KGB have found her.'

Fay bit her lip, trying to think of an idea that would work. 'Is there any way we could get her to come to Grandad's care home? Have her meet him there? Or just be there, and see if he recognises her?'

'I know,' Dad got up and left the room, coming back, a minute later, with some flyers.

'The manager of the care home said that since we were doing weekly services now, she wanted friends and family of residents to be able to come too. She printed off some flyers. Why don't you invite Amy-Hope and her dad to bring Mrs Peters to a service there? That way, if she is Vera, she and Grandad will have the chance to recognise each other.'

Chapter 36

Leningrad

Vera's head whipped round as the kitchen door opened.

'Welcome home, sister!'

'Artyom!' Vera flew into her brother's arms. For a long minute, the siblings held each other. The frozen edges around Vera's heart threatened to thaw in her brother's embrace, so she pushed him away and turned back to the stove.

'Vera...' Artyom waited for her to face him. Slowly she turned, not wanting to see the pity and grief held there. 'I'm sorry about Slavic.' Vera shook her head. 'I know how much you cared for him.'

Vera closed her eyes. For a moment, the peace she'd sensed in Baba Tonya's room seemed to surround her, before disappearing like a mist. She tried to hold onto it, remember it, but it faded away as quickly as it had appeared.

'Vera!' She turned back to her brother. 'You need to listen to me.' The severity of her brother's tone sent a chill through her. His eyes held a steely resolve she hadn't seen before.

'What is it? What's happened?'

'Mother has left us,' he said gravely.

'I noticed she'd gone out. I was surprised. When are we expecting her back?'

'No, sister, she's gone. She left the day after you took the girls to the village.'

Vera heard the words but could not process what he meant. She stared at her brother as her fingers and toes began to go numb.

Artyom led her over to a wooden stool and had her sit down. He poured some water and handed it to her. Vera focused on the seat underneath her and the chipped cup in her hand as she heard her brother tell a story which was so fantastical it didn't seem to relate to her life.

'Mother had been receiving letters from a man in Moscow for some time. They'd been writing to each other, and she agreed to leave with him. The day after you went to the village, Baba Rosa saw Mother leave with a suitcase, and get into a car which was waiting outside.'

'But why? I don't understand. Did she leave a note?'

'No, nothing. Papa said that she'd spoken to him about leaving a while ago but hadn't mentioned anything since then. Honestly, Vera.' He squatted down in front of her. 'I think it's for the best. Now we are free to leave, and we don't need to worry about Mother getting in trouble.'

Vera pushed Artyom away, and stood up, returning to stir the soup on the stove. 'Leave? What are you talking about? Why is everyone talking about leaving? It makes no sense, Artyom. Why would we leave?'

'Don't you see? Can't you understand how difficult things are here? They whisper about us.'

Vera spun around. 'No, Artyom. I can't see that,' she hissed. 'I don't want to see that. All I want to do is dance. Why does life have to be more complicated than that? Everywhere you see conspiracy and shadows. I choose to listen to the birdsong and enjoy the sunsets. I don't want to live with the secrets. I'm not strong like you.' She slowly lowered the wooden spoon that she'd been holding.

'OK,' Artyom pulled her into a quick hug. 'We don't have to talk about this now. But we do need to tell the girls about Mama.'

Vera nodded, and taking the food off the stove, followed her brother into the family's room.

'Nadia, Luba, we need to talk to you,' Vera coughed to clear the lump in her throat.

'Is this about Mama? We already know.' Nadia took Vera's hand and led her over to their sofa-bed. For a moment, Vera wondered who the older sibling was.

'Mama told us before. But it was a secret,' Luba said, joining Vera on the sofa. 'She told us not to tell you.'

'What did she say?' Artyom asked. Vera could tell he was forcing his voice to be patient.

Nadia and Luba exchanged a look which seemed to contain a conversation. Luba nodded slightly and Nadia explained.

'She said that she needed to go away. Another family needed her. And we should be happy for her because she was going to the happy-letters man.'

Vera heard Artyom mutter under his breath. She glared at him before turning back to the twins.

'She was going with the man who wrote her those letters? Did you ever meet him?'

Again, Nadia and Luba exchanged a look.

'He came here sometimes, and he and Mama went out for a walk.' Luba's voice shook a little. 'I don't think I am happy that she's gone,' she whispered, looking over at the empty sofa.

Vera gathered her up into a hug. There had been too much sadness and too many missed goodbyes. Vera's mind could not take it in. But she knew her arms would offer comfort to the children, even if her heart had nothing left to give.

The atmosphere in the *kommunalka* was strained. Vera put it down to her mother's leaving. Except for Baba Rosa, everyone ignored her; leaving the kitchen when she entered, turning the other way when they met in the corridor. Papa and Artyom were also very secretive, gathering papers, bringing in small packages and squirrelling them away. Vera would often wake to find them sitting in the dark, whispering frantically between themselves.

Baba Rosa now became a regular fixture. She looked after the girls while Vera was out at the Ballet, cooked for the family and even taught the twins how to read and crochet. They thrived under her care, and she seemed to get younger simply by spending time with them. Knowing they were safe made it much easier for Vera to go out every day.

Yet each day seemed to drag. Whereas before, she'd hurried home to see if there was a letter for her, now the post-box remained empty. In the spring, she'd mentally noted the colour of the sky at sunset, the words of a new song, the feeling of a dance, so she could pour it out in her letters to Slavic. In the autumn, her notes were unsent, added to her other unsent letters in the tea tin under her bed. She felt as though life had lost its meaning and colour. But she found again and again, the words of wisdom came back to her, often unbidden:

Earth has nothing I desire beside you...
God is the strength of my heart
and my portion for ever.

'What does that even mean?' Vera asked herself in quiet moments. She wanted it to be true, but she really wasn't sure.

The schedule at the ballet was intense in anticipation of the tour. They often had to dance for many hours a day, and, twice a week, Vera had to dance the main role, to ensure that she would be an effective understudy. She knew that Irina resented the position that Vera had been given, and Vera had to constantly watch her back, knowing how capable Irina was of hurting her.

The night before the trip, Vera wondered how she'd get to sleep. She dreaded leaving her family. Her father came home earlier than usual, and they had one final meal together as a family. Baba Rosa excusing herself, saying this last goodbye was a special one just for them.

Vera must have fallen asleep because it was still dark when she was shaken awake.

'Papa?' she whispered, taking a moment to focus on the figure kneeling by the bed.

She sat up, reaching for her warm shawl. Papa returned to the table, where he and Artyom sat, their faces dimly lit by a small candle stub. Checking the twins were sleeping soundly, she joined them at the table.

'We have to flee,' Papa mouthed slowly.

Vera furrowed her brow, not understanding what he meant.

'Our family is in trouble, and we all need to leave. We've been making the preparations. We will wait until you are abroad, and we will all go.'

'Go where?' Vera whispered.

'Artyom will go west and try to get to Germany. I will take the girls to the village, to Babushka, then Vlad and I will head south and try to find work, maybe in Ukraine. When it's safe, I'll come back and get the girls.'

'And me?'

'You must try to escape on the tour.'

Vera's mouth fell open. 'I can't do that. It'll bring disgrace to the Ballet. They'll find you and punish you if I run away.'

Artyom reached for her hand across the table and squeezed it, as though trying to give her strength.

'The Ballet will come up with a story to save face,' her brother said. 'And by the time they come for us, we won't be here. But you need to use this opportunity to get away.'

'Away to where? I can only speak Russian. I know nothing about the world outside.'

'God will guide you, my daughter,' Papa said. 'He will lead you to the right places and the right people.'

Vera opened her mouth to speak but closed it again as her father continued.

'You'll know the right place. Somewhere small and provincial, somewhere where you'll find people of faith who will care for you.'

'When will I come back?'

Papa shook his head. 'You can never come back.'

'Will we ever be together again?' Vera squeezed Artyom's hand with both of hers.

'If not here, we'll meet again in glory.' Papa held her gaze.

Vera never knew she could hate a phrase with such intensity. 'What if it's not real, Papa? What if there is no "glory"?'

'But daughter, what if there is?' He opened his arms, and she went to him, crawling onto his lap like Nadia would do. She held him and sobbed, feeling his tears land on her hair. Artyom moved next to them, leaning onto her shoulder. Vera felt her heart was breaking all over again. She looked across at the sleeping heads of her twin sisters, clasped together in their sleep, and deep, heart-wrenching groans shook her whole body. How could she leave them? They had just lost their mother. How could she leave them, too? This was too difficult.

Lincoln

Fay reached into her bag and pulled out a book, acutely aware of the flyer there. Somehow, she needed to give the flyer to Amy-Hope and her dad without Mrs Peters knowing it was from her. She'd never agree to attend the service if she thought it had anything to do with her. She'd just think it was a trap.

Fay knew that if Amy-Hope saw her, she'd come running over and say hi. Whispering a quick prayer, she opened the book and began quietly reading, noticing that the woman in the next bed was also leaning over to hear.

About twenty minutes into visiting time, she saw Amy-Hope's dad come in alone. He glanced at her as he went past, but his face registered no recognition. He headed straight for the bed by the window and talked quietly to Mrs Peters.

Fay mentally calculated how much more she had to read to finish the story and found herself reading a little faster. After finishing the story and leaving both women sleeping, Fay slipped out into the hall to wait. She was standing there for ages, wondering if the clock on the wall had broken. Finally, Amy-Hope's dad came out. He nodded at Fay, and pointed down the corridor, where there was a small seating area.

'I'm not happy with you upsetting Mrs Peters,' he said, as they sat down. 'I don't want to see her hurt.'

'Neither do I,' Fay replied. 'But, you see, my grandad is from Russia, although he never spoke about it at all. He's begun to suffer with dementia since my Granny Wendy died, and sometimes when he's confused, he talks about his family. We think he is related to a dancer who went missing from a Soviet Ballet company while they were visiting Lincoln in the 1960s. She was called Vera Petrova, and I'm named in her honour – Faith Peterson.'

The large man nodded slowly. 'Why now? Why has this suddenly all come to light now?' he said, stroking his beard, his eyebrows knitted together.

'I found ballet shoes and a tin that we think belonged to Vera in a cupboard at the Theatre. Dad recognised the tin because Grandad had a similar one.'

He continued looking at her, and she felt herself go red.

'There's something you aren't telling me.'

Fay sighed. 'I don't want you to think I'm weird.'

He raised his eyebrow in a way that suggested he already did.

'We've been praying for Grandad, for Vera, for them to meet up if she's still alive and if it's the best thing for them.'

'Why would I think that's weird?' The man's face was unreadable.

'Well, prayer. It's weird, isn't it?'

'Not to me,' said the man.

'Oh.' Fay really wasn't sure what to say. Then she remembered the flyer in her bag. Reaching down, she pulled it out and put it on the table.

'My grandad lives here,' she pointed to the name of the care home, 'and my dad's a pastor.'

The man looked up at Fay again.

'We've started having a Sunday service for the residents. It seems to help them, and they enjoy singing the old songs. The manager wants it to be open for family and friends to come. I wondered if maybe you and Amy-

Hope would want to come with Mrs Peters. If she is my grandad's sister, they'll maybe recognise each other, but if they aren't,' Fay shrugged, 'at least she might enjoy the songs.'

'Let me talk to Amy-Hope, and Mrs Peters, when she is well again. I'm not promising anything, but we'll see.' With that, Amy-Hope's dad pushed his chair back and stood up. Without looking back, he strode down the corridor.

Chapter 37

Leningrad

The next morning, Vera tried to feign excitement. But looking into the innocent faces of her baby sisters, she found her heart was breaking. At the train station, Vera held each of the twins tightly, whispering her love into their ears. Vlad held her for a moment but couldn't look into her eyes. Did he also know this would be a last goodbye?

Artyom stepped forward and held her in a tight bear hug. 'I'll come for you,' he whispered. 'Wherever you are, I'll find you. I promise.'

Vera didn't have enough strength or faith to hold onto his words, but looking into his eyes, as they pulled apart, she knew he meant it with every fibre of his being.

Turning to her papa, she clung on to the bearded giant that had always been the centre of her world.

'Papa, was it a mistake to send me to the village?' she whispered into his shoulder, as they held each other.

'I don't regret it for a moment, daughter.' Papa pulled away and gazed into her eyes for a long minute. 'Don't forget the life you found there.'

Vera wiped away a tear, nodded, drew a deep breath, and glanced around at the family one last time. Her heart still raw from losing Slavic, she wondered if she'd be able to breathe without them, too.

Slowly, feeling as though her body were made of stone, she went to join the rest of the ballet troupe waiting on the platform.

They climbed into their carriage; an entire wagon reserved for the Ballet. Vera sat with Masha and Katya, but soon zoned out their giggles and excitement. Instead, as they travelled, the sound of the rails seemed to bring back to her mind the verses Nadia had learned in the village:

Whom have I in heaven but you?
And earth has nothing I desire besides you.
My flesh and my heart may fail,
but God is the strength of my heart
and my portion for ever.

Is that true? Is it possible to live believing that truth? Baba Tonya did, and Babushka. Papa did and Slavic had. Could she? The reality of one line hit her starkly:

And earth has nothing I desire besides you.

This was now her reality. Even as the train was carrying her away, her family was preparing to leave. Within days, they would be scattered, and she would have no way of contacting them. Vera couldn't put into words the why, but with the whispers that had always filled their flat, her mother's suspicions and emotional withdrawal, all her life had been surrounded by secrets she couldn't quite put her finger on, and those secrets had now split her family apart. She felt as though she'd always known this day would come.

Looking out the window, Vera tried to stop thinking about her family, but a tear fell down her face. Her two friends reacted with kindness. Katya got up to find the conductor and ask for tea, while Masha held Vera's hand across the table. The sweet tea gave Vera the strength to keep up her facade. She smiled and joked, hiding her raw, lonely heart behind a familiar mask.

The train journey was inconsequential, but the night's sleep was interrupted by border guards coming through to check the paperwork. Irina and a couple of others joined them when it was time to sleep in the six-berth carriage but left again in the morning. After two and a half days of travel, they arrived in East Germany and were taken from the train to a hotel.

Vera hadn't been in their room long when there was a knock. Masha opened the door, and the acting director of the ballet, responsible for the troupe on their journey, stood outside with another man in a dark coat.

'Petrova, Vera Mikhailovna. Come with us.'

Vera glanced at her friends, their eyes wide. She silently followed the men.

They led her down a corridor and down a flight of stairs, into a small windowless meeting room. She sat down in the chair they pointed to, and they sat across the table.

'Where are your family?' The man in the coat, with cold grey eyes, didn't introduce himself.

Vera was genuinely shocked. She had neither expected to be asked, nor expected the family to leave Leningrad so quickly.

'I'm sorry, what?'

'Your father, brothers and sisters. Where are they?'

'I, er, I don't know. At home?'

'They haven't been home since seeing you off at the station yesterday.'

'Are you sure?' Vera sucked in her breath, wishing she could retract the question as soon as it came out.

'Of course we are sure.' The man smirked, and Vera felt her body go cold. Were her family being watched? Had the dangers been even more real than she had been told?

'What do you know of Petrov, Vladimir Artyomovich?'

Vera frowned. She knew that was her grandad's name, but nothing more than that. Although Babushka had told her briefly about her great-grandad, Vera realised neither she nor her papa ever mentioned her own grandfather.

'I know nothing,' she said honestly.

'And that didn't strike you as strange?'

'Not until now. I always thought there were things we weren't to know and weren't to ask about. Family always seemed part of that.' Vera tried to be as honest in her answers, although hearing them spoken out loud, she realised how foolish she sounded.

However, her answer seemed to satisfy her questioner, as though she had confirmed his thoughts of her as a simple child.

He nodded and dismissed her. 'You may go.'

Vera remained in her seat. 'But what about my family? Where are they? Are they safe? I don't understand.' Vera's voice was raised, and she felt her face grow hot.

The man looked her in the eye. Vera shivered at the coldness. 'As you said, Vera Mikhailovna, there are things you aren't to know and aren't to ask about. I'm sure if we have any news about your family, you will be told. Your director here informs me you are an integral part of the ballet, otherwise we would not have sanctioned your participation. But once you return from the tour, we will talk further.'

Icy fingers of fear seemed to grab Vera's numb heart, making it hard for her to draw breath. She nodded slightly and hurried out of the room. In the corridor stood a uniformed man who silently followed her to her room. Masha and Katya's conversation stopped when she entered. She couldn't look at them, but went and lay down on her bed, turning to face the wall. She was too numb to cry. Her hand reached inside the bag and felt the cool of the tea tin. Somehow, it gave her peace.

Her family was being watched. They had all fled. And now she had to escape as well. Her father's words came back to her: 'You'll know the right place. Somewhere small and provincial, somewhere where you can find people of faith who will care for you.' How would she know the right place? How could she live without her family? What was there to live for?

Lincoln

The next time Fay went to the hospital, Mrs Peters was no longer on the ward.

'It's all right, love. You don't need to worry. She's gone home now.' The friendly grandma, with her growing collection of home-made cards, commented, seeing Fay walk in and glance at the bed near the window. 'That lovely young man came to take her home yesterday. You know, the one with the little girl? I could tell they weren't family; you look more like her than they did. Turns out they're just her next-door neighbours. Nice when folk get friendly with the neighbours, isn't it? Anyway, you don't need to worry about her shouting at you anymore.'

'It wasn't her fault. I think I frightened her.'

'Well, I don't know why. It's not like you're a scary person, is it?'

'It depends on who you ask,' Fay laughed, pulling out a magazine she'd found with a couple of interesting stories in. 'Do we want a romantic story or a bit of a mystery?'

'I'll take romance any day. The story-book kind is all I'm ever going to get now!' The old lady laughed.

Chapter 38

On Tour

The tour was going well, and the director of the group was happy. So far, Vera had only needed to fill in for the Prima Ballerina three times, but each time the reviews had been excellent, and he was pleased with her. However, no one else was. The 'minders' who had taken residence outside her room were constant reminders that she was being watched; she was a person of suspicion. Masha and Katya kept their distance, and Vera couldn't blame them. They did not wish to have their own futures jeopardised by her friendship.

There were moments when the physical strain of travelling and dancing, and the emotional strain of the last few months, losing the people most precious to her, threatened to overwhelm her. Vera was always the first to go to sleep and the last to wake up, preferring the comfort of sleep to the turmoil of her own mind. Those around her viewed her with suspicion. Her own heart was aching and raw from the loss of Slavic, her mother, and then the rest of her family. It became overwhelming. The only thing that gave her the strength to get through each day was the memory of her father's words at Slavic's graveside, 'Whom have I in heaven but you?' These words echoed through her mind as she dropped off to sleep and whispered to her as she awoke. They were her only hope in those dark days.

Most days they were travelling, usually by train. They would arrive in a city mid-afternoon, go straight to the theatre, practise, perform and then be back on the overnight train for the next city. Occasionally, they didn't need to travel so far and would stay overnight in a hotel. The constant travel and daily performances dragged on everyone, and days off were few and far between. So far, all the cities had been large, and Vera began to wonder if she'd ever find somewhere provincial. One theatre looked much like another, one hotel like all the others, and Vera soon even lost track of which country she was in.

The train clattered and shook. Of all the trains they had been on, this had to be the worst. Vera felt as though her bones would be rattled out of her joints. They seemed to pass through miles upon miles of countryside.

'Where on earth are we going?' she overheard someone say. 'It seems to be the middle of nowhere.'

Hearing those words, Vera's heart began to beat quicker.

'The director is so angry. Apparently, there was an error in the translation, and this place was put on the list. They couldn't change the plans without looking bad, so here we are. Fortunately, they don't have a hotel large enough for us, so we will be taken out of here straight after the performance.'

Vera looked out of the window. In every direction, all she could see was countryside.

'God, is this the right place? Please give me a sign,' she whispered.

The train rounded a bend, shaking everyone in their seats. Out of her window, Vera saw a hill rise ahead of her. On top of the hill was the most spectacular church she had ever seen. It wasn't like the domed churches of Leningrad. This had three tall towers looming over the city beneath it. 'People of faith.' Vera had her sign. This was the place where she needed to escape.

Lincoln

It was the second Sunday since Fay had given the invitation to Amy-Hope's dad. No one had been surprised when they hadn't shown up the first week. Mrs Peters had only been home a couple of days, and Mum doubted she'd want to go anywhere new.

Dad was quiet as he drove towards the care home.

'Are you OK?' Mum asked, placing her hand on his knee. He returned a half-smile.

'I'm just having an argument with God.'

Mum laughed. 'Good luck with that. What's it about?'

'I'd prepared a great talk for today, encouraging, uplifting, slightly funny. One of my greatest works.'

'In your own humble opinion.' Mum nudged him.

'Exactly. But God is telling me that all He wants me to do is read part of a psalm.'

Mum shrugged. 'What's wrong with that?'

'Well, it's about death and growing old. Not very encouraging, is it?'

'Maybe it's exactly what someone needs to hear.'

'But I think my sermon would be more entertaining, especially if there are friends and family there.'

Mum tried to hide a grin. 'And who do you think people would rather hear from, God or Michael Peterson?'

Fay tried to swallow a giggle and ended up coughing.

Dad grinned at her in the rear-view mirror. 'What do you think?'

'Personally, I'd rather hear what God wants to say.'

'OK, I'm overruled. Here we are.' They pulled into the car park behind an unfamiliar car. Fay suddenly felt dizzy as she watched Amy-Hope jump out of the car in front of them.

Chapter 39

On Tour

'This is your dressing room, and along there are the toilets.' At least, that's what Vera assumed the young man had said. It was the same in every place. No one spoke Russian, and they spoke nothing else. Instructions were limited and predictable.

Katya and Masha went off to explore the theatre, as they had done at every stop, leaving Vera alone in the small room. She sat down and tried to think through her plan. Reaching into her bag, she felt for the tea tin. She'd need to find somewhere to hide it. Once she disappeared, they would thoroughly search her things. She needed to put anything that would implicate her into the tin, and hide it somewhere in the theatre, but not in this room. Somewhere where it wouldn't be found until after the ballet troupe had left. She unpicked the lining of the rucksack and removed the letters she'd written to her family and to Slavic, but never sent. She wished there was somewhere she could burn them to get rid of them, but there wasn't. Opening the tin, she removed all the sanitary products she'd been keeping there and replaced them with the notes that would further implicate herself and her family if ever they were found. Seeing a programme for that night's performance, she put that inside the tin too, hiding her letters underneath it. Burying the tin in the bottom of her bag, she pushed her bag into the corner with Masha and Katya's and started working on her makeup. She'd be dancing in the chorus tonight, which meant there were nearly forty minutes from being on stage in the first half, before she'd be needed again in the second. Would that be enough time to hide the tin and get away? And how would she do it? The minders were constantly outside her door.

A feeling of peace swept over her, and the verses she'd learned when she first went to the village came back to her mind:

When I consider your heavens,
the work of your fingers,
the moon and stars
which you have set in place.
what is mankind that you are mindful of them,
human beings that you care for them?

This would work. She wasn't sure how, but it would work.

Coming off the stage at the intermission, the chorus ballerinas hurried back to their dressing rooms.

They all quickly removed their tutus and wrapped up in housecoats to keep warm. Vera reached for her bag and rummaged inside until she found her tin. Using it for sanitary products meant that none of the girls questioned when she left the room holding it, assuming she was going to the toilet. As had become usual, the girls paid little attention to Vera.

Leaving the room, Vera was surprised to see that the minders who usually accompanied her everywhere were not there. She wondered where they had gone. It was the first time she hadn't been followed since the start of the tour.

She passed a door that was slightly open. Glancing in, she could see it was a cupboard that obviously hadn't been sorted out in a while. Boxes had fallen off the shelves on to the floor and had pushed the door open. She looked around, saw she was alone in the corridor and disappeared into the cupboard. Pulling the boxes in behind her, she shut the door. The cupboard was dimly lit from a window above the top shelf and was in such disarray that Vera knew it was the perfect place to hide the tea tin. It wouldn't be found here for years, if ever. Putting it down, something in her heart tugged. Picking it up again, and opening it, she flicked through the letters she'd sewn into the rucksack, remembering those first few days in the village and the way her life opened to an awareness of God for the first time.

Looking in the bottom of the tin, she saw that the false bottom was lifted slightly. She had thought she would have to leave behind the words of life, since the action required to lift the false bottom was too noisy, but it was already lifted. She pulled out of the handsewn pouch, slid it underneath her clothing, and quickly replaced the contents of the tin.

She looked around and decided to hide it on one of the top shelves. She quickly unlaced her shoes and used the shelves as a ladder to climb up to the top. Hiding the tin on the top shelf, she was about to climb down when something made her look again at the window. It had a small latch on it. Maybe it opened. Looking through it, she could see the roof of another part of the building. If she could get out, could she escape over the rooftops? Climbing back down, she picked up her ballet shoes. She saw a small pile of practise shoes and raked through until she found a pair that would fit her. They would be easier to run in than her performance shoes, but she held her pale pink shoes next to her face for a moment, remembering the kindness and sacrifice of her papa. A voice in the corridor startled her. She had to move. Grabbing her ballet shoes, she quickly climbed the shelves, leaving the shoes on the top shelf with the tin.

The voices outside the door got louder. She could now make out the voices of a couple of her minders, arguing about whose turn it was to watch her. She pulled her legs up, so she was laying across the top of the shelf. Were they looking for her, or just arguing? The window was about an arms-length from her head, but she didn't dare move while she could still hear the men arguing just outside the cupboard door. The argument changed to which room was the girls' changing room. The cupboard door opened slightly. Vera could hardly dare to breathe.

'No, this is just a cupboard. Let's try the next door.' They moved down the corridor but didn't close the door behind them. If she made a sound, she'd be heard. She inched towards the window, trying not to knock anything off the top shelf. What if it was stuck shut? What if it made a noise?

Reaching out to touch the window, she held open the latch and pushed. The window opened silently. She breathed out a prayer of thanks. She quickly pulled herself out of the window and out on to the roof top, closing it quietly behind her.

Looking at the hotchpotch of rooflines stretching up the hill ahead of her, she knew she would need all her agility, to navigate them. But where should she go? Above her, spread out on the top of the hill, was the large church she had seen from the train. Her father had told her to look for people of faith. Surely, she'd find them in a church. She began her most dangerous dance, across the rooftops of Lincoln.

Chapter 40

Lincoln

Fay ducked down in the car.

'What are you doing?' asked Dad.

'If that lady sees me, she'll never go inside. That's Mrs Peters.'

Dad watched as Amy-Hope's dad helped Mrs Peters into a wheelchair. Amy-Hope held the old lady's handbag.

'She looks like Dad,' he mumbled, watching as they went inside. 'Let's go in.'

'Can we pray quickly?' asked Fay, causing her parents to look at her. 'What?' she asked, seeing the surprise on their faces. 'It's a big day.' Ignoring her parents, Fay bowed her head.

'God, we bring Grandad and Mrs Peters to you. If she is his Vera, please can they recognise each other? But if she isn't, please can she just have a nice day out, and not be freaked out when she sees me? Amen.'

'Amen,' came voices from the front seat.

Fay stood in the corridor and peeped into the lounge. She saw Amy-Hope and her dad pulling up chairs on either side of Mrs Peters. She couldn't see her grandad and told her parents she'd get him from his room. The lounge was quite full, and Fay hoped he wasn't having a bad day.

Knocking quietly and pushing open his door, she saw her grandad sitting, holding the two tea tins in his hands.

'Grandad?'

He lifted his head, and she saw the tears in his eyes.

Hurrying to his side, she sat next to him and waited for him to talk.

'My Vera.' He gently stroked the tin. 'I asked God last night if I could see her one last time. Is that wrong? Can I ask that?'

Fay's stomach clenched. Knowing that the answer to her grandad's prayers could well be sitting in the lounge. What if it wasn't Vera? What if it was, but they didn't recognise each other?

She heard the strains of a hymn down the corridor.

'Shall we go to the Sunday service, Grandad?'

Grandad gave the tins one last look and then sighed. Turning to her, he nodded. She gently took the tins, moved them to a shelf, as Grandad stood.

He seemed distracted on the walk to the lounge. Fay linked her arm through his.

The song finished as they reached the end of the corridor, and Fay heard Dad stand up and introduce himself.

'Hello, my name is Pastor Peterson. I'm just going to read a psalm today.'

Grandad hesitated at the doorway, holding back and shaking his head. He lowered his head reverently as Dad began reading.

'Yet I am always with you;
you hold me by my right hand.
You guide me with your counsel,
And afterwards you will take me into glory,

A small cry interrupted him. Fay leaned forward and glanced into the room. Mrs Peters was staring at Dad with wide eyes, her hand in front of her mouth. Dad continued reading.

'Whom have I in heaven but you?
And earth has nothing I desire besides you.
My flesh and my heart may fail;
But God is the strength of my heart
and my portion forever.'

Tears rolled down Mrs Peters' cheeks. Amy-Hope leaned onto her shoulder and rubbed her arm.

Dad cleared his throat. 'Usually I say a few words, but God just told me to read that out. I have nothing else to say.' He stood still for a moment, and Fay could tell he felt awkward.

Grandad lifted his head and continued into the lounge, searching for a seat. As he looked around the room, his eyes were drawn to Mrs Peters, who was now fumbling in her bag for a tissue. As she lifted her head, she saw him at the door.

Fay saw a look of confusion, then a flash of recognition, then a thousand questions pass over Grandad's face. Glancing back to Mrs Peters, she saw that she had locked eyes with Grandad and the same emotions flicked across her face. The old lady dropped her bag on the floor and struggled to get to her feet.

Immediately, Grandad let go of Fay's arm and stepped towards Mrs Peters.

'Vera?' he whispered. 'My Vera?'

'Artyom?' she gulped, choking on a sob.

Grandad crossed the floor between them in a moment, and they fell into each other arms, sobbing and laughing.

Fay glanced over to her parents and noticed that Mum had left the piano stool and stood with her arm around Dad, who had tears falling down his face. She felt a tug on her arm, and turned to see Amy-Hope, frowning.

'Who is that man?' She glanced at Grandad.

'That's her brother, my grandad,' Fay whispered. Amy-Hope nodded and returned to her dad, leaning over to whisper the news. A shadow lifted from her dad's face, to be replaced by a genuine smile.

Lincoln

Someone pushed a cup of tea into Vera's hands, then took it out again as it nearly shook out of the saucer.

'Are you OK, Mrs Peters?' Amy-Hope whispered, standing by her elbow.

'I've never been better.' She managed a weak smile, knowing that she had a long story to tell her young friend when she was a little older. Beckoning her closer, she whispered in her ear, 'I don't feel afraid anymore!' Amy bounced up and down and clapped her hands quietly.

Vera looked back at her younger brother. His eyes were fastened on her, ignoring all the fuss and flutter of people around them.

'*Ti* zheev! – You're alive,' she whispered, slipping into the Russian of her childhood.

'You too. We were told you were dead.' Artyom spoke English with a slight Lincolnshire accent. She shook her head, trying to associate this English-speaking old man with the teenager she'd left in Leningrad.

'I didn't believe them,' he continued. 'I came here looking for you.'

They stared at each other, both so full of questions. But this was a moment of joy. The questions could wait.

'My family, I forget myself. You must meet my family.' Artyom reached for the young girl next to him.

'This is my granddaughter, Faith.'

Vera's eyes filled with tears.

'You named her after me?' Vera took Faith's hand while still looking at her brother.

'Of course! Who else would I name her after?' Artyom looked from Faith to Vera, and his eyes sparkled. Vera smiled at the young woman, who seemed vaguely familiar.

'Have we met?' she asked, tilting her head on one side.

'I think you met her at the hospital. You were quite upset at the time,' Amy-Hope's dad said, softly.

'Then, I am sorry.' Vera looked at Faith. 'Dave said I was rude to you. I wanted to apologise when he told me.'

'That's OK. I didn't mean to frighten you.'

Vera leaned forward. 'I don't remember much about those days in hospital. But I am sorry.' The young girl relaxed and returned an open, genuine smile.

'I'm Michael, Arthur's son.' The pastor stepped forward and introduced himself. 'And this is my wife, Lisa.'

Vera smiled at the couple, then turned to her little brother. 'Arthur? Nice name.'

He grinned back, like a young child. 'And what do they call you?'

'My name is Mrs Anna Peters.' She held out her hand as though they were meeting for the first time.

'Mrs?' Lisa asked, sitting down next to Faith. 'Are you married?'

A wave of sadness took Vera's breath away. 'No. I have a young man waiting for me "in glory".' She nodded at Pastor Peterson, acknowledging his earlier words. 'But we never married.'

'My Wendy is waiting for me too,' Artyom's voice cracked, and his eyes grew red and watery.

'So, you two are brother and sister,' interjected Amy-Hope's dad. 'Do you have any other family?'

This was the question Vera had been dreading the most; the one she needed to ask but couldn't bear to have answered. She closed her eyes, holding onto the last few seconds of joy, basking in the reunion, before she steeled her nerves to hear whatever update her brother had on the rest of her family.

Opening her eyes, she looked at her brother. A shadow flickered across his face. He looked around, drawing quick breaths and clenching and unclenching his hands. The young girl next to him sensed his agitation and gently hummed an old hymn. As he turned and focused on her, a look of peace settled over him. Vera noticed the others discreetly left the room, giving them some privacy. She dreaded the news her brother had for her.

Lincoln

Fay could see that Vera was waiting for a response from Grandad. Of course, she wouldn't know about Grandad's dementia. Fay was wondering how to tell her when Grandad's voice interrupted her thoughts.

'We had a plan. You and I would head west. Slavic would join us as soon as he could.'

Vera gasped. 'You planned this with Slavic?'

'Of course we did. We had it all planned, but when he died...' Grandad shook his head. 'Why do I still have difficulty accepting that he's gone?'

'Me too,' whispered Vera. 'That's why I never married. I always felt like he was still out there somewhere.'

Grandad reached over and grabbed her hand, letting large tears fall from his face.

'I looked for him. I went to the barracks. I asked questions, but no one knew anything. No one had survived the explosion, and although it hadn't been Slavic's shift, he had taken the place of a friend who was sick. He was such a good man.'

Vera shook her head, not allowing her mind to settle on thoughts of Slavic. 'What did you do after that?'

'I worked in a couple of big cities, but after a while,' he paused, as though groping for memories, 'I don't know how long, I went to the village to find the girls. They weren't there. Babushka had died, and Papa and Vlad had been and collected the girls. They refused to tell anyone in the village where they were going, so that if ever they were asked, they'd be able to answer truthfully. At that point, I decided to find you, and headed west.'

'So, Papa went back for the girls? I feel better thinking that they are together. I pray for them. That helps when missing them hurts so much.' Vera's voice wobbled.

'I do too. I've been praying for you, and for them. Sometimes I get confused and find myself praying for Slavic, too. I hope God forgives my foolishness.'

Fay swallowed a lump in her throat. For so long, she'd rationalised her parents' prayers as a sign of their weakness. Now, as she looked at her grandad and his sister, she saw their prayers had been a source of strength as they had endured such deep pain.

'Why did you have to leave Russia?' Fay's gaze flitted between the older people.

'Because of our faith and our father's faith,' Vera answered.

'And our grandfather's,' Grandad added in a whisper. Vera turned sharply and looked at him. 'Our grandfather?'

'Papa's papa. Didn't he ever tell you?'

Vera shook her head. 'No.' Her lips mouthed the words, but no sound came out.

Grandad nodded slowly. 'One day, I'll tell you, if I can remember it all. It's hazy.'

After a moment's silence, Fay looked at Vera. 'You came to the service today. Do you usually attend church?'

'I need to start. I only just returned to my faith, thanks to Amy-Hope and her family. They are helping me. I lived in fear for a long time; fear of being caught as a defector, fear of loving and losing that love. But they have helped me and taught me how to believe again. They are the closest thing I have to family.'

'Until now,' Grandad said, squeezing her hand.

'Until now.'

Chapter 41

Lincoln

'Can I go to see Grandad today?' Fay asked for the third time that week. 'Please don't tell me I can't go because Auntie Vera is going to see him. I know he'd want to see me, too.'

'OK, why don't you and your brother go together?' Dad suggested, looking up from his book. 'It'll be the last chance you'll get before Tom goes back to uni.'

'Will Great Aunt Vera be there?' Tom asked, taking a bite of toast as he walked in from the kitchen. 'I so enjoyed meeting her last week.'

'I think so. From what I understand, she's been going to see Grandad every day. Sometimes they sit and talk, sometimes they listen to music together. I think it's really helping him.'

'Are you ready to go now?' Fay asked, grabbing her coat.

'Someone's impatient,' Tom laughed. 'OK, come on.'

'It's strange knowing I'm going back to university with a new family member I'd never heard of before,' Tom said as they walked through the city towards the care home.

'I can't help thinking about how close they must have been growing up, for him to come after her like that,' Fay sighed.

'And yet they never found each other. Can you imagine how much Granny Wendy would've loved Auntie Vera?'

'And how much she would've fed her! She and Grandad talked about someone called Slavic,' Fay remembered, 'but I got the feeling maybe he'd died or something. It feels rude to ask. Do you remember how Grandad used to tell us off for asking questions when we were little?'

'He did, didn't he? And Dad never knew the answers to all our questions, either. Maybe we are finally getting the answers after all. Better late than never.'

'Maybe.' Fay sighed. 'But I can't help feeling a little sad about all those wasted years.'

'Look,' Tom nudged her as they neared the care home and pointed through the window. Inside were two elderly people, sitting at a small table, lost in deep conversation, looking at two tea tins. 'I'd say there is nothing at all to be sad about. Let's join them.'

Epilogue

'That's everything!' Tom shut the boot and turned to face Fay. 'What a summer, eh? I'm gonna miss you!'

Fay hugged him. 'Who knows, this time next year I might join you!'

'I think Dad will need a bigger car!' Tom laughed, glancing at the weighed-down Citroen. 'Are you really thinking of applying to York?'

'It's on the list. Pray I make the right choice.'

'Now, that's a phrase I never thought you'd say.'

Tom turned to Mum and wrapped her in a big hug. Fay felt a lump in her throat.

After the obligatory promises to call and come home at Christmas, Dad and Tom drove off, and Mum and Fay returned to the house.

'What have you got planned for today?' Mum asked, gathering her bag and coat for work.

'I was thinking of dropping these ballet shoes over to Auntie Vera. I think she'd be surprised to see them. Oh, one minute.' Fay looked at her phone to see an unknown number. 'Hello?'

'Fay, is that you? It's Linda, from the theatre.'

'Hi Linda.'

'Remember we talked about Vera? I was wondering if you'd found out any more information.'

'Well...' Fay hesitated. She wasn't sure how much her great-aunt would appreciate the information about her getting out.

'Because Darren's just called me. He was going through some old paperwork, and he found a letter addressed to Vera.'

'What?' Fay grabbed Mum's hand to stop her from leaving. 'I'm putting you on speaker. My mum's here.'

'Yes, he said he found a letter in the files. He rang me because he didn't know who it was for. It's an unopened, hand-written letter, addressed to "Petrova, Vera Mikhailovna."'

'And who is it from?'

'I don't know. There is an address in the top right-hand corner, but it's in Russian.'

'Could I come and pick it up?' Fay gasped, glancing at her mum with wide eyes.

'Of course, but there's something else you should know. The postmark is nearly 20 years old.'

To be continued...

If you enjoyed this book...

... and want to know what happened after Vera climbed out of the theatre window, you will enjoy the next book in the Petrov Family Series, *The Letters She Never Sent. (Read on for the first chapter!)*

If you loved this story, please leave a review and tell all your friends about it, as this helps other people know it is a great book and worth their time.

To find out about other books I've written, check out my website, **www.joyvee.org** and sign up for the newsletter to stay up to date with new books bubbling away in my mind!

The Letters She Never Sent

Prologue

Lincoln, 21st September 1963

The cold took her breath away as she climbed out the window. She looked around; rooftops of various ages provided a patchwork of opportunity and danger. But a tumble from this height would still be less painful than the alternative. She had to get away. She moved carefully, keeping the cathedral in front of her. After climbing and scrabbling for about ten minutes, she saw some rooftops a few feet beneath her and lowered herself on to them. From this height, she could drop to the ground.

Grateful that the city was poorly lit, she continued to climb, trying to stay off the main streets. She tiptoed through gardens and little alleyways, zigzagging up the steep hill. After another ten minutes, the ground levelled off, and she entered a wide square. To her left was the dark walls of an old castle and to her right, the shadowy, black hulk of the cathedral. Slipping through a large stone arch, she hunkered down in a darkened doorway. Now what?

'Lord, have mercy,' she whispered, repeated the well-known refrain of the priests.

'Oh, here you are. I've been waiting for you.'

Her heart stopped beating as she heard a voice speak in a language she understood. She slowly turned.

Saturday 27th July 2019

Dear Diary,

Mum suggested I keep a diary because I keep forgetting everything that I do when I am home with Dad. I don't really forget, I just can't be bothered to tell her everything, and some things she won't want to hear, like when Dad and I had a burping competition – and I won!

So, I'll keep this diary when I am here and try to write in it every day, then choose bits to read to Mum.

Dad told me that some famous people in history wrote diaries too. Can you imagine? How good would it be if lots of people read my diary? The first thing they'd want to know is… Who am I?

My name is Amy-Hope. I love my name, but sometimes people get lazy and just call me Amy. Amy is OK, it's not a bad name, but Amy-Hope is so much more, well, hopeful. Teachers are the worst. They'll start the day with Amy-

Hope, but before break, they'll have switched to Amy, and it's all downhill from there.

Mum always says there are two sides to every story, so I have to put myself in the teacher's position. When I do that, I can see there are so many children with creative names in their classes, I figure they are just trying to get a bit of it right. (There is a boy in our class, whose name has a clicking sound in it. We all spent half a day trying to learn how to say it properly. It's one of my favourite names ever.) So, I guess I should be pleased that all my friends and family call me Amy-Hope, not Amy. It's not that difficult. But it does show that they are truly my friend when they use all of my name.

It's the start of summer and I'm really excited. Dad has enrolled me in a special dance school over the holidays. It's three full days a week. Can you imagine? Three days just to dance! We will be learning different kinds of dances, and at the end of the summer, we're putting on a small performance for the parents. Mum has already booked the day off work, and I really want to do a solo. I'm going to work so hard and be the best dancer there. I've even decided not to argue if the teachers call me 'Amy'.

So, I'll be dancing on Tuesdays, Wednesdays and Thursdays. Then I'll spend Monday with Dad and Friday with Mum, like I usually do. The only upsetting bit is that I can't take my dog-brother, Cosmo, with me to dance class. He misses me when I go to school, and I'm sure he was looking forward to spending all summer with me. Now I'll be out most of the time and I know he's going to be sad. But I'll make sure I show him all my dances when I get home.

Cosmo follows me everywhere, like a shadow. Like me, he has a bed at home with Mum and a bed at home with Dad. This is still new. Before we all lived together, but now Mum and Dad have different houses. So, now I have a home with Dad and a home with Mum. I swap over every weekend – one weekend with Mum, the next one with Dad. It means I have two bedrooms so I suppose I should be grateful. But Cosmo is still getting used to it. It's sometimes a bit confusing. I can tell when he's upset about it because he doesn't want to eat. Then I'll sit with him, and we'll talk things through and sometimes I'll feed him little bits from my hand. He likes that.

Tomorrow is Sunday, and after church I'm going to practise dancing, so I'm all ready for the dance school. If I can get a solo in the show, I'll be so happy. I love the thought of people watching me when I dance.

I'll write more tomorrow.

Love from

Amy-Hope

Dearest Artyom!

Sometimes I think I am a crazy old woman, like the one who lived in the downstairs flat. Do you remember? She always talked to herself when she swept the floors. I think I have become her. I write letters I will never send, to a brother I have not seen in over fifty-five years, in a language he does not speak. I am crazy!

My new neighbours are not as bad as I feared. They moved in a week ago. I was happy living next to an empty house for the last three years. When it went up for sale, I worried a little. (Please ignore the last few letters, where I imagined the worst – thankfully, none of those things happened.)

It is a young man and a little girl. But no mother that I can see. You and I know what that feels like, don't we? To have an absent mother.

I remember when they came to view the house. She is a happy little thing, always dancing. Does that remind you of anyone? She saw me through the window when they were in the garden and waved at me. I tried to smile back but it made my face hurt. Can you imagine, Artyom? My face hurt because I tried to smile! Have I been sad for so long? I sat in front of the mirror for a long time, trying to practise smiling. It wasn't a pretty sight. I don't think I will try that again.

Anyway, somehow, that little family felt peaceful. When I saw them together, a big man with a bushy beard and a little girl dancing around him, it reminded me of Papa with us girls. It almost took my breath away.

To be honest, for two weeks after they looked around, I hoped they would not buy the house. I didn't want such a reminder of family constantly near me. But I kept thinking of them, and I was relieved when it was them who moved in.

I will tell you more next time.

Your loving sister.

The Letters She Never Sent,

by Joy Vee

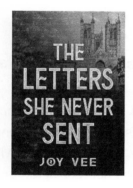

Amy-Hope keeps a diary.
Anna writes letters.
Can this unlikely friendship
give one a voice
and help the other
escape the past?

Available wherever books are sold.

Paperback: 978-1-915034-20-5
E-Book: 978-1-915034-21-2

Author's Note

A Very Potted History of Russia and the Soviet Union

Part of this story is set in Leningrad in Russia in the early 1960s. This city was originally called St Petersburg and used to be the capital of Russia. After the Bolshevik Revolution of 1917, the city was renamed Leningrad and anyone with a connection to the Tsars and the previous ruling powers were punished. The name 'St Petersburg' was restored after the fall of the Soviet Union in the 1990s.

The Soviet Union (officially called the Union of Soviet Socialist Republics or USSR) was a collection of countries, such as Russia, Belarus and Ukraine, formed in 1922. It extended to China in the East, including countries such as Kazakhstan and Azerbaijan, and into Europe in the West, eventually having a ruling influence in Poland, Hungary and East Germany. A central committee headed the Union, often referred to as 'The Party'.

The Soviet Union was very closed, with restricted access in and out. They believed in a form of communism which made religion and belief in God illegal. (Although the Orthodox Church could operate, many suspected it was just a political puppet.)

Two major events before this story had a deep impact on our characters' lives. The first is the Siege of Leningrad, which took place during the Second World War, from 1941 to 1944. The Nazis surrounded the city, cutting off food, water and energy. Over 1.5 million people died in the city. There was a resistance movement that smuggled in food, but these people were later viewed with suspicion as traitors and Nazi collaborators. The Siege left a deep scar on the souls of the people of St Petersburg. When I lived there in 2004, it still haunted the lives of the residents.

The second major event was the reign of Stalin, from 1929 to 1953. Stalin used 'gulags' or labour camps to punish everyone who disagreed with him. As his reign progressed, people lived in fear of 'The Knock' – the Secret Police (KGB) knocking on the door to arrest someone. People were rewarded for informing on neighbours or family members who didn't adhere to the party line. Anyone could be sent to the gulags for any reason, including religion, political leaning, contact with the west, disagreements with those in authority, etc. After Stalin's death, many people were released from these gulags and allowed to return home, although countless numbers died in the camps.

This story is set ten years after Stalin's death, but the shadow of suspicion still lingered and affected the lives of those we read about.

Russian Names

Russian names consist of three parts: A surname, a first name and a patronymic (which is a male or female version of their father's name). When introducing themselves, they would always do it in that order. Our main character is Petrova, Vera Mikhailovna. Her family calls her Vera. There is no equivalent in Russian for 'Miss Petrova'. To show respect to someone older, instead of calling someone Mr or Mrs and their surname, you would use their first name and their patronymic. So, Vera refers to her dance teacher as Nadezhda Vladimirovna. Although that sounds like a mouthful to us, it's perfectly natural in Russian.

Every Russian name has variations which people use for fondness, like we might use Mike instead of Michael. I have only used these a couple of times, as they can get confusing. Also, in the Russian language, people use the words 'son' and 'daughter' when speaking to young people, and titles like 'Auntie' or 'Baba' – Granny, when talking to an older person. This is a sign of respect. These names and terms of endearment are used much more in the Russian language than we would find comfortable in English.

Pronunciation Guide

Baba / Babushka [BA-ba / BA-bush-ka] (not ba-BUSH-ka, as you might think) – Granny.

Artyom [art-YOM] – Vera's brother.

Vlad [v-LAD] – Vera's brother (short for Vladimir).

Nadia [NAR-de-ya] – Vera's sister (short for Nadezhda).

Luba [LOO-ba] – Vera's sister (short for Lyubov).

Anna Igorevna [ANN-a ee-GOR-ev-na] – A ballet dancer,

Dejournaiya [de-JOUR-nigh-ya] (JOUR – like the French for 'day' or SURE in pleasure.) – a pensioner who fulfils the role of caretaker/security in public offices.

Nadezhda Vladimirovna [na-DEZH-da vlad-ee-MEER-ov-na] (ZH is like French 'JE' – if you don't speak French – use a short 'sh' sound – you won't be too far wrong!) – Vera's dance teacher.

Ivanova, Irina Andreyevna [ee-van-OH-va, irr-EE-na an-DREY-ov-na] – Vera's colleague in the ballet.

Petrova, Vera Mikhailovna [pe-TROV-a, VE-ra mi-KHAI-lov-na] (KHAI is pronounced like 'high' but with a hard KH at the beginning – like the sound at the end of the Scottish word Lo<u>ch</u>.) – Our heroine.

Ekaterina / Katya [ye-kat-e-REE-na / KAT-ya] – Vera's friend

Maria / Masha [ma-REE-ya / MA-sha] – Vera's friend

Kommunalka [kom-oo-NAL-ka] – a communal flat, usually four to six families having their own rooms, but sharing a kitchen and bathroom. (The plural is *kommunalki.)*

Smetana [sme-TA-nah] – thick soured cream.

Mishka / Mikhail [MEE-sh-ka / mi-KHAI-eel] – The Russian form of Michael. Mishka is the form used for little children or close friends.

Slavic [SLA-vic] – Vera's friend (short for Yaroslav)

Olya [OL-ya] – Slavic's grandmother's neighbour (short for Olga)

Pra-dedushka [PRA-d-YE-dush-ka] – great-grandfather

Kasha [KA-sha] – a grain dish that can be used as an accompaniment or eaten as porridge.

Tvorog [tva-ROG] – a dairy dish. Used to be called *whey* – like cottage cheese.

Bible Verses

In this story, there were several passages from the Bible. I have written them out here for you.

When I consider your heavens,
the work of your fingers,
the moon and the stars,
which you have set in place,
what is mankind that you are mindful of them,
human beings that you care for them? *Psalm 8:3-4*

And now these three remain: faith, hope and love. But the greatest of these is love. *1 Corinthians 13:13*

There is no fear in love. But perfect love drives out fear, because fear has to do with punishment. The one who fears is not made perfect in love. *1 John 4:18*

Yet I am always with you;
you hold me by my right hand.

You guide me with your counsel,
and afterwards you will take me into glory.
Psalm 73:23-24

Whom have I in heaven but You?
And earth has nothing I desire besides you.
My flesh and my heart may fail,
But God is the strength of my heart
and my portion for ever. *Psalm 73:25-26*

Those who are far from you will perish;
you destroy all who are unfaithful to you.
But, as for me, it is good to be near God.
I have made the Sovereign Lord my refuge;
I will tell of all your deeds. *Psalm 73:27-28*

Peace I leave with you; my peace I give you. I do not give to you as the world gives. Do not let your hearts be troubled and do not be afraid.
John 14:27

The Lord is with me; I will not be afraid.
What can mere mortals do to me? *Psalm 118:6*

Acknowledgements

Thank you to Jesus – without whom there would be no story!

Thank you to my daughter, Anna. You have pushed me to write the best story I've written so far. Thank you for being there to bounce ideas off, and for all your valuable input. You make my world bright!

Thank you to my beta readers who commented and made this book better! I don't want to miss anyone out – if I do, I'm sorry. Karen Ingerslev, Natalie Coles, Miriam Mathie, Gail Dunn, Sheila Keel, Special thanks to Sheila Jacobs, Emma Kilkelly and Ruth Johnson.

To my family near and far, Andriy, Michael and Anna, Mum and Dad, the Nordens, the Keels, the Rogers, the Meighs, the Velykorodnyys. Thank you for believing in me and being excited about every step. To the Bells, thank you for opening your heart and your dinner table to us!

Finally, to everyone who has written a review, bought a book for a young friend or family member, or let me know how much you've enjoyed my writing – thank you beyond words. Every review is a precious gift, and every email saying how much you enjoy the books, is like a bouquet of flowers. Thank you.

About the Author

Joy Vee has moved over 25 times in her life, including seven years living in Ukraine and just under a year in Russia. She loves meeting new people and hearing their stories. If you have ever met Joy, you might end up in one of her stories!

She started writing a couple of years ago. She wanted her nephews and nieces to know that the greatest adventure in life was living with Jesus. Then people began asking if she'd write a book for adults, and this is it!

Joy continues to be passionate about seeing children equipped with the skills they need to serve God in today's world – a world with many problems and not many easy answers. Her stories reflect that and tackle difficult issues, but in an easy-to-read way.

Joy is always looking out for people who love her books and want to talk more about them. Especially children who love them. If you want Joy to speak to your school or

Sunday School Class, she'd love to try to make that happen. You can email her at joyvelykorodnyy@gmail.com.

You can find out more about Joy's stories, as well as up to date resources she is producing, on her website:

www.joyvee.org.

Sign up for the newsletter, to be kept up to date with new projects.

Lightning Source UK Ltd.
Milton Keynes UK
UKHW010951110422
401398UK00001B/103